Dave Hill is a freelance journalist working primarily on the *Independent*. His previous books are *Prince: A Pop Life* and *Designer Boys and Material Girls*.

D0785117

'Out of His Skin'
The John Barnes Phenomenon
DAVE HILL

faber and faber
LONDON · BOSTON

First published in 1989
by Faber and Faber Limited
3 Queen Square London WCIN 3AU

Photoset by Parker Typesetting Service Leicester
Printed in Great Britain by
Richard Clay Ltd Bungay Suffolk
All rights reserved

British Library Cataloguing in Publication data is available

ISBN 0–571–14256–7
ISBN 0–571–15472–7 (Pbk)

For Denis Hill, my dad

For Liverpool 8. Thanks for having me.

Contents

List of Illustrations

Acknowledgements

Thanks to all those whose comments and observations are included in this book.

Also, to:

Joey Joel, Tom Jones and all the rising stars of the South End
Clive Tyldesley at Radio City
Alan Bleasdale . . . for hospitality
Brinsley Forde . . . for conversation
The Football Supporters' Association
John Williams at the Sir Norman Chester Centre for Football Research
John Walsh
Andy Bull and Tom Sutcliffe at the *Independent*
Michael Steele
The library staff at the *Liverpool Echo* and *Daily Post*
Duncan McKenzie and Alan Whittle
Patrick Barclay, Phil Shaw and the rest of the *Independent* football staff
Ken Jones
Will Sulkin at Faber for sticking his neck out
Bob Thomas Sports Photography
Almithak FC, its players and supporters
Sara Fisher of A. M. Heath . . . the ultimate agent
Nicki and Laura . . . love you both
Luther Vandross . . . essential listening
William Lloyd George Reid
Ferdi Dennis
Adrian Goldberg and *Off The Ball*
When Saturday Comes
Dave Clay and the Liverpool Community Relations Council

David Lipsey, for *New Society* commission, autumn 1987
New Statesman And Society for European Championship commission
Professor Ken Roberts at Liverpool University
Liverpool Anti-Racist Arts and Community Association
Harold Hughes
Graham Smith
Alison and Sorrel Osborne
Danny Thomas

Extra special thanks to Ted Thorogood, my intrepid matchday companion.

Finally, thanks to the many and varied Liverpudlians I spoke to, at length or in passing, in pubs and hotel lounges. Some are quoted in what follows, others are not. Some are named, others prefer anonymity. Either way, any qualities this book may have could not exist without them.

Preface

When the story broke that John Barnes might be joining Liverpool Football Club, I immediately found myself more interested in football than I had been for years. It was not simply that I knew Barnes was a very exciting player. Nor was it because Liverpool had always been my favourite team. It was, rather, that I knew the progress of this new combination would tell us a great deal about the man, about the club, about the city of Liverpool and the English national game. I did not expect all the results to be pretty. Contrary to cliché, modern day sport has more to do with maintaining barriers than bridging them. Barnes, I thought, was going to have a job on his hands.

My ambivalent feelings towards the game go back a long way. As a ten-year-old I was obsessed with football. In the classic schoolboy tradition I was out there in the playground or on the field out the back, kicking a ball whenever the chance presented itself. I dribbled stones down the country lane that led to my junior school, leaving strings of imaginary full-backs in the dust. I played in school teams, cub scout teams, teams from the local council estate, area representative sides and was even invited to train at nearby Bristol City one night a week after school.

But as I entered my teens, I somehow grew tired of it all. Contemporaries began bandying commentators' jargon and perfecting their professional fouls. The players I watched on TV or from the terraces seemed to spend their whole time squaring up and squabbling. As my interests began shifting towards music and existential angst, the palaver that went with even schoolboy soccer began to seem like a waste of time. Somehow, though, I never stopped reading newspapers from the back page. And I never stopped listening out for the Liverpool result on a Saturday afternoon. When Barnes came on the scene, I sensed a story in which many of the things I cared about most would come crashing together in the immediate events of one man's career.

What happened to John Barnes in the 1987–88 season was, I believe, both dramatic and significant. It brought back to the surface of our culture things that many vested interests would prefer to remain submerged. One is that English football has been allowed to become an arena where the vilest instincts of the nation are let off the leash. Racism is just the most virulent of a dozen foul varieties that flourish virtually without censure on Saturday afternoons. It does not have to be that way. I believe the failure of the football establishment to address these kinds of issues is the key to the morbid condition of the domestic game today both on the field and off it. Barnes's progress on Merseyside has thrown them all into sharper relief.

This book is not, then, a biography or a profile of a star. Rather it is an interpretation of the impact of one man upon a key institution of a city that stands alone as the capital of English football. It is, too, about the game of football itself and why it matters. Also, it is a story of glory and ignominy, power and poverty, subtlety and brutality, idealism and insularity. It is told through the experiences of, and the reactions to, John Barnes. The story is bigger than the individual, but without that individual, the story would be harder to tell.

Barnes himself declined to co-operate with the project. Well, to be precise, his agent, Mr Athole Still, told me: 'We are not going to help you with what you're doing in any way at all.' Which seemed fairly conclusive. It is a pity in a way. But the effect of Mr Still's rebuttal – which I had taken for granted anyway – was to release the project from the shackles Barnes's co-operation would have imposed. Much of his success as a player at Liverpool has been due to his talent for making friends with the people of Liverpool. Being associated with a book like this would not, I fear, be consistent with his diplomatic goals and I have no wish to hinder his pursuit of them, any more than, as a white man, I intend to pass judgement on it. Those assessments are for others to make, and it is the perceptions of others that matter as much as Barnes's perception of himself. I believe that what he has achieved, though, has required nerve, charm and no little courage in the face of considerable odds.

This book is an attempt to assess those achievements and analyse what they might mean, with particular reference to his first, unforgettable season, and to both past and subsequent events.

I began work on this book in the summer of 1988. I was making my final amendments when they cleared the Hillsborough pitch at six minutes past three on 15 April 1989. I did not get much more done that weekend. The facts of the catastrophe unfolded, the news bulletins became filled with trembling Liverpool accents, their anguish mixed with rage. Deep passion has never been lacking in the people of that city. Their courage and humanity in the heat of the crisis were uniquely poignant.

In the days that followed I looked again at what I'd written. By then the voices on the radio were telling us what went wrong. Politicians were manoeuvring. Policemen were wriggling. Football's bureaucrats were bumbling. The debate swiftly subsided into trivia – a few plastic seats and it would all be OK. Even before the dead were buried, the bulk of the British press were busy assigning blame in accordance with their established prejudices.

Meanwhile, in Liverpool, hundreds of thousands of people turned the Anfield football stadium into a shrine. A whole city seemed to close ranks against the surrounding squalor in a way no other city could. I considered the words I had already set down and decided a few additional sentences, simply marking the event, would be enough. The rest I have left as it was before the Hillsborough nightmare because it still expresses my view of Liverpool as I experienced it and as I was welcomed by it. It is not always beautiful, though much of it is. All I can say is I came in search of the truth. That, I hope, is a measure of my respect.

London, 22 April 1989

PART ONE
As Good as Gold

I
'One Man, Two Man, Three Man'

The Jamaican hotel taxi man was not the tearaway checker cab pile-up merchant of modern legend. He was a dapper, middle-aged gent with a soft, brown cap and a soft, brown voice driving a long, clean saloon. He spoke to me as if to an honoured emissary from what his generation of Jamaicans would have grown up thinking of as the 'mother country'. It was a perception rooted in another time: 'I got a daughter in England, you know. It sounds like a nice place. She's doin' very well.'

Our destination was the Up Park military camp on the fringes of Kingston. I had an appointment, at 1100 hours sharp, with Colonel Kenneth Barnes, second-in-command of the Jamaican Army, the man who led the united West Indian forces in the relief of Grenada and a society figure of considerable standing. He also has a child in England, a son. At the time of our meeting, he too was doing very well. It was the beginning of March 1988, and Liverpool Football Club was not just at the top of the English Football League (that is to say, with due economic deference, the Barclays League, Division One); they had already reduced all-comers to also-rans with a footballing charm-offensive as seductive as any in the last twenty years. At that point in the 40-game League season, Liverpool's record was: played 27, won 21; drawn 6, lost none. They led the 21-team table by a margin of 14 points, scoring 65 goals in the process and conceding only 12. Distinguished football writers were already engaged in historical conjecture. Was this the greatest English club side of all time? It was not merely the statistics which informed these debates, but the aesthetics. The team's supremacy had been attained through a painless mating of rigorous team work and individual self-expression which at moments had touched the sublime. And the player most associated with this immaculate footballing conception was Colonel Barnes's boy, John.

It required little intuition to surmise that sporting passions run deep in the Barnes family. The Colonel cuts a strikingly handsome figure, long, lean and athletic, in the heroic mould. Ushered into his office by a cowering armed sentry, I found him sitting behind a vista of desk top, reclining but alert in his chair, listening to a radio commentary from nearby Sabina Park where Jamaica were playing Barbados in a one-day cricket international. Politely, and manfully concealing his regret, he switched it off so that my recording of our conversation would not be obscured. But the greatest demand made on the Colonel's military self-control came not with this wrench from the unfolding of the cricketing drama, but when asked to consider the recent exploits of his son. It was as much as he could do to contain the urge to purr. 'What he's doing now . . . I feel so proud. As far as I'm concerned he's making us as proud, or prouder, than anything I can think of.'

John Barnes has inherited much of his sporting prowess from his father. The Colonel represented his country at football several times, as centre-back and captain and later as team manager. Today he sits on a committee of the Jamaican Football Federation and watches videos of his son in action wearing the all-red strip of the English game's mightiest power. Ken Barnes saw his son's potential at an early age and encouraged it, not that much additional stimulus was required. Barnes Junior, an energetic youngster, excelled at both football and cricket while a student at what the Colonel describes as 'an ordinary primary school'. He agrees, though, that his son's social environment – and that of his two elder daughters – would not have been that of the typical Jamaican youth. 'We live in the camp, and when we moved here he must have been about two or three. So he grew up here. I suppose growing up in an army camp is very different to the average Jamaican child. I think maybe he grew up more *disciplined* than the average child.'

The Colonel touches here upon a favourite theme. He is, after all, a top-drawer military man and you don't rise to those heights in anybody's army if you don't learn how to do – and be – what you are told. Clearly, it was a parental priority for him and his wife Jean to make sure their boy was properly broken in. 'He got the eleven-plus,' the Colonel resumed, 'then he went to one of the good secondary schools in Kingston, St George's College, which is a Roman Catholic school.' Neither Colonel Barnes nor his wife are practising Catholics now, but both received a Catholic education. The Colonel detailed its benefits with the hint of a chuckle in his voice. 'That one certainly had a reputation for *good discipline*. They were very aware of its importance for young boys . . . and he needed it! So we thought, "Yeah, have him go to a school where the priests cane him every weekend. That'll be good for him!"' The young John's exposure to papist severity lasted only one term before being interrupted by what transpired to be a turning-point in his life. His father was posted to London to fill a diplomatic role as military attaché at the Jamaican High Commission and the family were to go with him. Without this twist of fate it is unlikely that John Barnes would have had a career in professional football at all.

The West Indies, of course, are known and feared on the international sporting scene for their cricket. The post-war years have seen the cream of cricketing talent from this enormously disparate group of islands welded together into a force which now belies the once popular stereotype of high calypsonian colour, but brittle competitive will. Jamaica has provided its share of batting and bowling stars to this seemingly unstoppable force: Michael Holding, Patrick Patterson, Jeffrey Dujon, Courtney Walsh. It is a surprise then, to learn that in Jamaica, despite the international status of Caribbean cricket, football stands unchallenged as the people's favourite game.

'Football is the grass roots sport,' explains George Ruddock, editor of the London *Gleaner*, the main carrier of Jamaican news in the UK. 'Everybody identifies with football, especially the youngsters, and as a spectator sport, football really plays its part.' The reasons why there has never been a unified West Indies soccer team run on similar lines to its cricket are many and complex. There have been various attempts to achieve it, and there is a Caribbean Football Union. But Caribbean cricket evolved within the paternal parameters of Empire, a metaphor for dominant English values abroad and organized as such. Cricket helped bind the colonial territories together. Football, though, did not enjoy the same prestige among the British imperial classes, and, more recently, with neither the expertise nor the resources available, there has never been the momentum for the creation of a West Indies representative football team. This historical tendency was confirmed by the nature of world football's main international event. The World Cup is for teams representing individual nation states, not collectivities. Yet just because Caribbean football is ill-equipped to compete with the highly professionalized soccer nations of Europe and South America this does not mean that its role in Jamaican society is any less significant, or the passions it arouses less profound – simply, that they cater to different desires.

Perhaps because the game offers next to no wage-earning potential in adult life, the most intense football encounters take place among schoolboys. From senior or high school age upwards, teams in the metropolitan (Kingston) area and the rural districts take part in contests for, respectively, the Manning Cup and the da Costa Cup. These competitions run concurrently from September to December and, at the end of the season, the two winning sides play each other for the Oliver Shield. It is these teenage events which draw the biggest crowds. The national stadium has a capacity of 35,000, and the annual Manning Cup Final sees the arena filled close to capacity.

It is on such occasions that the pervasive spirit of the domestic game becomes apparent. It is an attitude which George Ruddock, significantly, describes largely in terms of the expectations of the crowd: 'Jamaican players tend to be dribblers because they like to play towards the gallery. They like it when they beat one man, beat two man, and the crowd goes wild. The difference is that they don't do it here in England. You beat two players and you might not get any response from the crowd. But if you were sitting there in the national stadium, and you see a guy take on a defence and he beats two, three men, then he loses the ball, don't think the crowd is gonna boo him. The fact that he has dismissed three players in one move has got them going.' In Britain, top-flight professional football is about winning – or, perhaps more to the point, not losing. In Jamaica, it is about something considerably closer to what the former Tottenham Hotspur wing-half Danny Blanchflower had in mind when, taking issue with the pragmatic sensibility of the post-war English game, he said that, first and foremost, football was not about winning and losing – it was about glory .

For most Jamaican footballers, events like the Manning Cup Final are the most glorious they will ever know. It is possible to go on from school to continue in serious competitive football and make it pay, but not very much, and only for a few. There is one island-wide competition, the National League, where some of the players are paid and some are not. But even those who do pick up a cheque for their endeavours on the field cannot make a living from it. In short, the only way a Jamaican man can support himself through playing football is by taking his aspirations abroad.

The few Caribbean tribunes to the global élite have not enjoyed great success. Perhaps the most famous home-grown Jamaican footballer was Alan 'Skill' Cole, a star of the domestic game in the mid seventies. Cole is remembered by Colonel Barnes and others as a charming and talented man, and also as a rebel. A Rastafarian, Cole was a close friend and sometimes business partner of the late Bob Marley, the great exponent of reggae music. Marley himself was a very useful footballer. The impromptu scratch games he and his entourage liked to play contributed to his legend, and in turn lent the game an almost mystical significance in Rastafarian circles. The cancer which brought about Marley's premature death is sometimes alleged to have been related to a toe injury contracted during a kick-about at his studio in Kingston's Hope Road. 'Skill' Cole attracted the attention of a Brazilian club: but after two seasons, he and his South American employers fell out. Stories filtered back to Jamaica that the Brazilian coaches thought their dreadlocked employee was 'too lazy', and that his Rastafarian taste for smoking ganja had done nothing for his image in the profession.

Cole might respond that, as a representative of a militant Jamaican folk culture, his philosophy of life was never meant to satisfy the Babylonian prerogatives of the corporate game. But his failure to last the professional course comes as no surprise to Colonel Barnes. For him, a man like Cole would have been woefully lacking in the very personal qualities he had been so anxious to instil in his son. The Colonel reflected upon these matters as we took lunch on the elegant terrace of the Barnes's Up

Park Camp home. Jean Barnes, a programme presenter on Jamaica television and a history researcher in the Ministry of Culture, joined us for a generous meal of chicken and local vegetables, prepared and served by the household cook. Conversation touched lightly on the international fame of Jamaica's reggae stars, a phenomenon Colonel and Mrs Barnes acknowledge for its cultural significance, but whose values are clearly at odds with their own. The Colonel had already dwelt upon the tendency of the reggae men to be, in his understanding of the term, 'unreliable'. Skill Cole was discussed, not coldly, but in the blandly regretful tones which officers of the law reserve for perpetual criminal recidivists. What could you expect from a guy like that? We sat only a taxi ride from the ravaged ghettos of Trenchtown, but, as the cook cleared the tables and silently served us our dessert, that impoverished other Jamaica of gun play, ganja, and the radical pulse of the bass guitar seemed a universe away. As far, almost, as the crumbling council estates and boarded-up shop fronts of Anfield, Liverpool 4.

Earlier in the English season, John Barnes had run out for Liverpool for his first match in a red shirt against their local rivals, Everton, blue-shirted representatives of a competing soccer citadel, just a 15-minute walk away. Barnes's impact on the Merseyside football scene had already been significant, not simply because his performances to that point had made the £900,000 paid to Watford Football Club for his services look like a knock-down price, but also because he was a black man entering what had effectively been a white man's domain. In the past, only two black footballers had represented the first teams of either of the two big Liverpool sides, both of them natives of the city. For Everton, a winger, Cliff Marshall who came up through the local leagues, took the field a handful of times in the mid-seventies. A year or two later, Howard Gayle, another winger, had worked his way into the Liverpool first team squad, making five appearances in the 1980–81 season, including a notable one in a European Cup semi-final second leg against Bayern Munich. Neither player was able to fully establish himself at the highest grade. Marshall has since left the game, and now runs a pool hall in the south Liverpool district of Liverpool 8 where the majority of the city's black citizens live. After a spell on loan to Fulham, Gayle went on to play for a succession of clubs – Newcastle United, Sunderland, Birmingham City, Stoke City – finally ending up at Blackburn Rovers where, as he entered his thirties, he helped transform that famous old club into one of the late eighties' stronger Second Division sides. Apart from those two, both of Merseyside's First Division giants had been composed entirely of white men, despite Liverpool 8 being home to the oldest indigenous black community in Britain, despite the fact that black Liverpudlians have been active and successful for decades in the city's amateur leagues and despite the fact that black footballers had become a routine feature of League teams of all standards and in all other parts of the country. From time to time people wondered why.

John Barnes entered his first-ever Merseyside derby as a hero to the fans wearing red, but a target for those in blue. For him, even more than the others players, it would not be just a football match but a trip into a war zone. Encounters between Liverpool and Everton Football Clubs are momentous occasions. Vicarage tea parties take place on grass, and so do Merseyside derbies, but there the comparison ends. Their first and obvious characteristic is the extraordinary intensity of each team's desire to vanquish the other. As soon as the whistle blows, the midfield area of the pitch makes the Battle of the Somme look like a free week at Pontins. For an hour and a half, twenty-two men cut, thrust, kick seven shades out of each other and sometimes, just sometimes, contrive a shot at goal. The competitive fury of the players is echoed and encouraged by the fans. The partisanship of the city's footballing public is legend, and should any purple neutral dare to raise an appeasing voice, may he forever rest in peace. As a hell-bent celebration of how the game can be played, it is a mighty long way from the showmen of Jamaica.

And yet there is another side to this intercommunal ferocity, an aspect which manifests itself in the way that blue hats are often accommodated within the waving sea of red behind the goal at Anfield's Spion Kop terrace, or in the stories you hear on Merseyside of how those holding tickets for the 'wrong' part of either ground can reach agreement with a rival fan in the same predicament: you stand next to a turnstile and shout 'swap!' Anywhere else in the country you would be guaranteed to end up as a scarlet smear on the asphalt. It might easily happen in Liverpool too, but the existence of stories to the contrary speaks volumes. The Merseyside football derbies are occasions when tens of thousands of Liverpool's population celebrate a *shared* pride in their city, and a cauldron of blood, guts and football becomes the arena for its expression. Verbal abuse and a little taste of GBH is the Liverpool soccer-watching public's way of showing everyone else in the country just how great the rest of us ought to think they are.

But if football has provided a vivid focus for many thousands of Liverpudlians' sense of a distinctive cultural pride, that has not meant all Liverpudians – it has meant *white* Liverpudlians. Black Liverpool's representation has always been thin on the terraces, the composition of the crowds implicitly confirming that of the two home line-ups. And everything about the success of a Liverpool side – its power, its vigour, its durability, the primacy it gave to teamwork over individual indulgence – represented a triumph for pragmatic rationality and true Mersey grit, qualities which white Liverpool celebrated at football on a Saturday afternoon. Liverpool FC, in short, stood for the practical application of a philosophical 'whiteness' and it had set the football team apart. The folk culture that celebrated that supremacy evolved in tandem. White players, white fans, and so-called 'white' values prevailed season after season. No wonder the black footballing community of Liverpool 8 lived in another world to that of Liverpool FC.

Into this Caucasian hotbed stepped the twenty-three-year-old only son of Jamaican Colonel Ken Barnes to become an instant star, tormenting opposing defences with an exhibition of exquisite footballing ability which emphasized above all others the type of exuberant derring-do which had, with notable exceptions, been absent from the succession of victorious sides representing Liverpool FC over the previous quarter of a century. The crowd, enraptured, sang his name. And the boos and taunts and chanted abuse with which Liverpool supporters had previously besieged so many black footballers wearing another team's shirt ceased virtually overnight. It was as if the bigots of Anfield had been smitten with contrition and the forces of reason had prevailed.

But when the reds met the blues from across Stanley Park one autumn Wednesday night, Everton's supporters made up for their rivals' abstinence. The reception they meted out to the Colonel's son was, without doubt, the most voluble expression of terrace racism on a British football ground in years. An entire dimension of Merseyside soccer chauvinism became explicit, glorying in what for years had been goadingly implied in the treatment handed out to others at both Anfield and Goodison Park: 'Everton are white! Everton are white!'

In his office at the Up Park Camp, Colonel Barnes reflected upon his son's introduction to the unacceptable face of the Merseyside football ferment. Not a man much given to displays of indignation, he offered a rationalized response. 'You know, even I fell into the trap of referring to "the Everton fans". But of course, it was not strictly so, because one of the things I've always said to Johnny, and to other black youngsters when I was in England, is that for every white person who might boo, or who might be antagonistic towards you, there will be a hundred who want to pat you on the back and say, "Well done!" I don't think there is any black sportsman in England who can put his hand on his heart and say this is not so. There may have been white critics, or white National Front types. But for every one of those, I am certain, there are a hundred who say, "well done, we are with you, congratulations."'

There was about Colonel Barnes little of the excessive pomp and ceremony that might be expected from an equivalent in the British armed forces. His manner was crisp, especially in the presence of subordinates. But as a host he was never less than eminently amiable. Even so, his perspective on the issue of racial prejudice reflects the firm-jawed conservatism that might be expected of a military man. 'I think it's very wrong when I see black people going around with a chip on their shoulder, saying "society's against us" or "the selectors are against us." To my mind it's just not true. Twelve or fifteen years ago there were very few black players. Now every team seems to have one. Arsenal have got about four. So to

my mind ... I don't believe in magic. I don't believe that people's
racial bigotry is going to disappear because Martin Luther King
marches on Washington. I don't believe in that kind of thing. I think
it takes time, and what changes it is when your own team has a black
player or two and the guy does well.' He repeated the point for
emphasis: 'That is what changes people's ideas – when the black
players seem to be doing well.'

John Barnes was doing very well as an unlikely new star in the
most vibrant and independent of England's provincial cities, a place
of legend, a place apart. This upper class, Jamaican-born Londoner
who could dismiss one man, two men, three men and *still* have the
ball, had ventured into a key cultural territory in the defiant,
working-class, splendidly insubordinate northern metropolis of
British urban life and been taken to thousands of its people's hearts.
Here he was, the black player doing well, and seeming to bear out
everything his father believed. Never mind those Everton fans. In
Colonel Barnes's view, all his son had to do in the face of hostility
was shrug his shoulders and *perform*. 'At Liverpool, if he didn't
make the grade, it would be because of lack of ability. It wouldn't be
because he was put under pressure from racist types ... He can
deal with that, I'm sure.'

2

'Always Respect from John'

Colonel Barnes came to London to take up his position as Jamaican military attaché in the early mid-winter months of 1976. It was a time of heightening social trauma and imminent political change. A beleaguered Labour government was in power and wrestling with the onset of a severe economic depression. For Britain's indigenous black population it was a period where individual instances of progress had to be weighed against frustrations which, before long, would find expression in a major uprising against the Metropolitan Police at the Notting Hill Carnival that summer. It was not the last incident of its kind to occur in the course of the next dozen years.

The racial intolerance which prompted these revolts was nowhere more loudly expressed than at England's football grounds. The sons of the West Indian families who had responded to government overtures and settled in Britain in the 1950s were now reaching adulthood and beginning to make an impact on the nation's professional sport. In the Football League, Brian Clough had blooded a young full back, Viv Anderson, into his Nottingham Forest side. Within two years, Anderson would become the first black player to be selected for the full England team. At Cambridge United, Brendon Batson, now Deputy Chief Executive of the Professional Footballers' Association, was refining his skills under the management of Ron Atkinson, who would later take him with him to West Bromwich Albion and nurture a revival in that club's fortunes based largely on not only the playing skills, but also the publicity value of Batson and two other gifted black players, Cyrille Regis and Laurie Cunningham – the so-called 'Three Degrees'. At Watford, the Jamaican-born, British-raised Luther Blissett would soon make a scoring début for the Third Division side that Graham Taylor later led to the First with Blissett among his key men.

Black footballers were becoming a conspicuous part of the fabric

of English sporting life. But the English football culture did not
greet them with unanimous delight. The National Front, a neo-
Nazi political party favouring the 'repatriation' of all Britain's non-
white residents, was enjoying limited, but significant, success at the
ballot box. It was in West Bromwich, home of Batson, Regis and
Cunningham, that in May 1973, Martin Webster, who later became
the Front's leader, saved his deposit at a by–election. It was the
beginning of an erratic, but noteworthy period of electoral results
which only went into protracted decline with the General Election
victory of Margaret Thatcher in 1979 when much of the National
Front's vote defected to her new-style Conservatism. Of those
sympathetic to the Front's policies, the ones who marched through
the streets of racially cosmopolitan inner-city areas behind the
Union Jack, the biggest proportion were drawn from the traditional
post-war base of fascist support in Europe, the white working class
– the very section of society that still provides most of the money
taken at football club turnstiles up and down the land.

It was not, then, so very surprising that some of the most clear-
cut celebrations of white hostility to blacks should occur at the
places where the British national game was played, much of it either
fomented or exploited by the National Front. The visibility and
vulnerability of black men on the field of play encouraged the
National Front's concentration on football terraces as prime sites
for their grass roots recruitment drive. Racial abuse from the terraces was swiftly recognized by black footballers as a fact of their
sporting lives, and in the heat of the fray there was only one way to
deal with it: 'You have to grin and bear it,' says Brendon Batson. 'If
you let it upset you, your game would go to pieces, and I'll tell you
straight, those people would follow you around. So really, you just
can't win.' It was a scenario which came to be recognized, with
varying degrees of dismay, by every black Englishman craving a
career in the game. They were sitting targets for concentrated doses
of the kind of malice which most had probably been familiar with all
their lives.

But in this John Barnes was again an exception. Aged twelve, he
arrived with his mother and two sisters one month after his father
and soon settled into the kind of life befitting the son of a visiting

dignitary. Having checked in to the smart Selfridge Hotel just off
Oxford Street, the Colonel set about finding a more suitable family
abode and schools for his children. First, he rented a flat in Paddington, 'but just temporarily. It was an upstairs flat, and Johnny
kicking his football around would have obviously not made us very
popular with the other tenants. It was very difficult to keep him still.'
Soon after, the Barneses found a more permanent dwelling, a house
in the affluent north London district of Hampstead, but not before
the Colonel had succeeded in enrolling his son in one of the more
prestigious inner-city state schools of the time, Marylebone
Grammar.

It was a careful choice, reflecting the general conservatism of the
Colonel's views on life and his desire to see his offspring get on in
the world. 'We had been advised before we went to avoid com-
prehensives. And, of course, we would never have just sent our
child to the nearest school. We would go and find one with a good
reputation, and we would do everything we could to get the child
into that school. So we tried to find a grammar school. And it was
fortunate for Johnny that this grammar school was right next door to
where we were living for that couple of months. But when we
moved up to Hampstead he stayed there. It was an old-fashioned
type boys' grammar school, where they wore uniform and all that.
Very nice. And rugby. He played rugby for them.'

Though fresh from the Jamaican top drawer and entering into a
whole new world, the adolescent Barnes Junior did not seem to his
father to find it difficult fitting in to the world of a traditional
English grammar school. Rugby was something new, but his father,
with a predictable goal in mind, had cajoled him into participating
in competitive swimming back in Kingston. 'He wasn't very good,
but he did it. If at the age of eight, nine, ten you're involved in this
swimming programme which is 365 days a year, just up and down a
pool, it is not much fun, but in the end you're a good swimmer. He
hated it. But I think boys at any age are accepted at school if you can
play games. So he was a new boy, he didn't know anyone, and they
said, "Can you swim?" and he said, "Yeah". And he would have
been better at it than a lot of the boys there. So I think this helped
him to be accepted and popular.' It would also have helped that

Marylebone Grammar already had a lot of black boys there, mainly
the sons of British professionals and others who, like Colonel
Barnes, were foreign VIPs on extended working visits. Marylebone
Grammar was no deprived educational concrete jungle: 'Of course,
I was a little worried about him at first. But within a few weeks I saw
boys coming home with him after school, black and white, you
know.'

John Barnes's school priorities soon become obvious, at least to
his father. Sport was what he loved. Academic stuff was what he put
up with. 'You had to push him to do his homework,' recalls the
Colonel, laughing. 'Not easy. My wife was the good one for that.
I'm not the disciplinarian at home with my children. She was the
one who tried to push him to do his school work. It was a fight all
the way!' Barnes eventually went on to the lower sixth form at
Haverstock Comprehensive School when Marylebone – after a
celebrated court case – was closed down, a last bastion of the
grammar school era. 'He got a few O Levels,' shrugs the Colonel,
'but he was not a great scholar. I think if he was interested in
academic work, he would probably have done well. He's not a fool,
you know. It's just that he really didn't have any interest at all.'

The Colonel was conscious that the only thing his son was
lacking at Marylebone was the opportunity to play football. But he
soon put that right. Also in the Paddington area, not far from the
flat, the school and the Jamaican High Commission, was a teenage
sporting institution with particularly strong traditions in boxing and
football, called Stowe Boys' Club. It is still thriving today, located
on the Harrow Road, which, fittingly enough, is the main west-
bound carriageway leading to Wembley Stadium. 'He played football there in his spare time. They had matches in Regent's Park and
all that kind of thing. It was a good club. Well run. They looked
after the youngsters well.'

Stowe Boys' Club was not an institution designed to serve the
sporting sons of gentlemen. Its main constituency was the rank-
and-file inhabitants of Paddington, a predominantly working-class
area with a large, poor, non-white population and more than its
share of tower-block kids. Never mind that six or seven Stowe boys
out of ten would also have been black, and mostly of Caribbean

extraction. For Barnes, this was to be another exercise in adapting to a new social world.

At Stowe, John Barnes was supervised by two men in particular. One was Joe Lowney, a project leader at the Boys' Club to this day, and the man with whom Colonel Barnes first made contact. The other was Ray Sullivan, then the team coach with the Middlesex League side Sudbury Court, and also, as now, a part-time coach at Stowe. The youngsters were grouped according to age, and Sullivan was put in charge of John Barnes's year. From the beginning it was clear to Sullivan that this new lad from Jamaica was a talented athlete. But that was not his only virtue. 'We played him at centre-half,' Sullivan recalls, 'basically because he was one of the few kids who was disciplined enough to try and stay in the position where he was asked to play.' Sullivan ascribes this quality directly to an upbringing which, it was immediately apparent, was quite different from that of Barnes's Stowe peers. 'John was totally different to the other lads because of his background. If you looked at the other kids, I should say that 60 or 70 per cent of them were from single-parent families. And it's a pretty tough old area around Stowe. But the difference with John was very marked. You could talk to him quite intelligently, and he listened. You always got respect from John. You didn't really have to prove a point with him as you did with the other kids.

'Some of the others were real stroppy artists at times. I can remember one of the earlier nights when I was there, and one of John's great mates, who was a real tough kid, a real hard black boy. He was giving me a lot of aggro at one stage, and I've never stood for anything like that. In the end I just said, "Right, you're the coach, *you* run the session." And of course, he just dried up within thirty seconds. I never had a problem with him after that. But you never had that problem at all with John.'

Not surprisingly, Sullivan attributes this respectful attitude to authority to the influence of the Colonel and Jean Barnes, and it certainly had its benefits on the field of play: 'Football-wise the discipline thing is a really important factor. You didn't have to teach John so much about his responsibilities within the team. If you said, "Well, we want this sort of job done in tomorrow's game", and why, that would be fine. That was his dad's home coaching coming out. I can remember a few years on, we had John turning out for a Sunday-morning park team I played in, and the Colonel would come along to every game. I'd have six of these young black kids playing for us. My black pearls. We'd all be sitting around having a drink after, and John's dad suddenly started talking about zonal defence systems and all this. And a couple of the lads just looked up at him and thought, "What's he on about?" But it was obvious that a lot of his thoughts on the game had got through to John. That was one of the things that struck me about John very quickly. He was *aware* of what it was all about, and he did whatever was needed in any situation, whereas a lot of kids at his age, around thirteen, would, all right, take the ball off a guy, then he'd want to beat him two or three times, or go off on a mazey run, beat four and lose it to the fifth one. You never had that problem with John either.'

There was another dimension to Barnes's attitude that set him apart. It still does, even at the very top of the professional game. Again, it is a virtue which the Colonel would probably consider commendably old-fashioned, and again it harks back to a decidedly English gentlemanly code of values which have become virtually redundant in big-time soccer – John Barnes is a genuine sports-man. In other words, he does not cheat.

'We are very big on all that at the Boys' Club,' says Ray Sullivan. 'John and all the kids in that particular year were very good in that respect. I can see the difference, seven or eight years on. The kids now are growing up with the big macho thing: you've got to smack a guy in the face if he pulls your shirt or something. With John, it makes me laugh today when people say, "Oh, he took a dive for that penalty", or something. If John gets fouled, he gets fouled. He hasn't got that so-called professional attitude that if you get the slightest touch, you go down.'

John Barnes's sporting outlook is very much to his credit. It is also a testament to his upbringing: good home, good discipline, good respect for what closely resembles a classic English public-school approach to The Game. It is not to detract from that outlook to speculate that it is likely to have been a good deal easier for him to approach competitive sport in that way than it would have been for his Stowe contemporaries. Football was not his only possible passport to material comfort and social standing. For John Barnes life would, if push came to shove, have offered ample opportunities outside professional soccer. But for the 'stroppy artists' he mixed with at Stowe, life was already a very different ball game. Respect does not come so easily when you have to start at the bottom of the heap.

Ray Sullivan noted too the equable approach that has continued to serve Barnes well, even if it has not always suited the men who tried to manage him: 'It wasn't his burning ambition to be a pro footballer. He never gave you that impression, unlike a lot of kids of twelve or thirteen who've been through the professional training syndrome. You know, twice a week at a pro club, and that's all they can set their sights on. Their education just takes a back seat, because all they were geared up to was football. I wouldn't say it wouldn't have mattered to John if he hadn't made it. But I believe he always thought he could do something anyway. He was a fairly laid-back young guy.'

According to Ray Sullivan, it was a characteristic which would not have been greatly put to the test in the environment at Stowe, certainly not by racial antagonism. 'We've never had a racial problem at Stowe, and I've had nearly ten years there. I've never known an incident, a fight or anything, that's happened over race.' Sullivan elaborates: 'He's got strength of character, which is something people don't always give him credit for. He can adapt to new surroundings quite easily. I suppose with his father perhaps being used to bringing home influential people or whatever, it's not so much of a culture shock, if you like, being dumped into a different environment. He's always struck me as being very relaxed, wherever he was.' And of course, John Barnes's footballing ability demanded peer-group respect. There were, Sullivan recalls, a couple of other lads who stood out in that year, but young Barnes was the best. 'Basically, he had so much talent you could play him anywhere. He had a good physique and he was naturally good at ball games. His [football] technique was outstanding. You could play a ball to John and his control was brilliant. Fitting that into the sort of framework in which he was playing, you certainly had to believe that he was going to be reasonably good.'

It was a combination – spontaneous talent, well schooled and harnessed to a sympathetic team structure – which came to such opulent fruition in Barnes's first season at Liverpool. Ray Sullivan firmly believes that the leeway he was given to express himself at Stowe helped his development as a teenager and enabled him to retain certain special characteristics of his game. 'It's difficult to say how far I thought he could have gone at that stage, because he wasn't playing football other than for Stowe. All the other kids were playing for West London Schoolboys and what have you. And everyone [on the scouting circuit] was missing him. That was one of the contributory factors in his success. I'm sure if one of the bigger clubs had got hold of John as a schoolboy, they might well have knocked a lot of the natural flair out of him.'

John Barnes continued to play for Stowe Boys' Club until 1980 when he was sixteen. During his four years there, he would have been well aware of Britain's new wave of black footballers continuing to impress themselves upon the soccer scene. Even in Jamaica he had seen Viv Anderson legging it up the touchline for Forest. Then Anderson was followed into Ron Greenwood's England sides by Cunningham and Regis. In the south particularly, more and more young black players were establishing themselves in First Division sides. Different though he was, Barnes understood the significance of those advances. He knew he was a black person in a society that thought of itself as white. Quoted in Anderson's 1988 biography, he paid tribute to the symbolic value of the Forest full-back's break into the national side: 'It was a big achievement and should be recognized as such ... for a seventeen-year-old coloured kid over here it must have been very important because it showed that it could be done.' And in 1983 he had reportedly declared: 'There is a new era, especially for coloured players. We are all conscious of that. We have been given the chance and we must prove that we are good enough to take it. It is a marvellous incentive for coloured people in this country.'

Perhaps it says something about the man that he has frequently preferred, in his relatively few public utterances, to use the term 'coloured' to describe himself, rather than the more assertive 'black'. It is a language of moderation coupled with a stress on individual achievement which reflects the comfortably conservative impression he gave to those who knew him as a youth. But his remarks surely indicated too a consciousness, however benign, of what it might mean to be a black man in England, however well bred. Indeed, if he had any illusions, the football world would have soon seen them off.

As the profile of black footballers rose, so did terrace opposition to them. In the spring of 1978 the National Front launched a recruitment and propaganda campaign outside several London clubs, the most prominent being Chelsea, West Ham, Millwall and Arsenal. By 1980, the party's youth paper, *Bulldog*, ran a regular football column 'On the Football Front' encouraging fans to support their racist aims. It was only a matter of time before supporters of the National Front and various equally violent, right-wing splinter groups organized themselves as core activists in the hooligan campaigns of English football fans abroad. The English football authorities seemed unable to regard the role of white supremist philosophies in fan disorders as anything other than incidental. Indeed, a representative of the Football League reportedly dismissed it as 'just the latest fashion'.

'Laid-back' though he seemed to those around him, the young Barnes would have known better than to dismiss the activities of the National Front so lightly. His father can vouch for that: 'As a teenager he was a great man for discos. He would go to them down town somewhere and he would always run home up the hill. So at two in the morning we'd hear these footsteps. His mother always would. She'd keep awake. I always thought, "A couple of miles running uphill won't do him any harm." But I remember once, something that he said and it stuck in my mind. He said he was always conscious of the National Front thugs and so on. And he tried to get home quickly. Because you never can tell.'

3
'Just a Nice Lad'

On 13 September 1980, John Barnes made his competitive début for the Middlesex League side Sudbury Court. His performance in a 3–all draw was a revelation to team manager Des Lawlor, who had seen him play for the first time in a pre-season friendly a week or two before. Ray Sullivan had brought the lad over from Stowe, and Lawlor gave him a twenty-minute run-out at the end. He remembers his initial reaction with amusement. 'Actually, when he first came to Sudbury, I thought he was a really lucky little sod. He was sort of riding tackles. He's just pushing the ball past people, hurdling with a sort of lunge, and carrying on. I thought, "Well, he's had a purple patch, but he won't do that next week." And the following week we played him, and he did . . . and he just carried on doing it.'

The transition from Stowe Boys' to Sudbury Court was another leap into a new world for John Barnes. This was men's football. Here was a tender teenager stepping into a team of adults in their twenties, performing at a level where, although all the players were amateurs, the will to win was strong. It was goodbye to the Queensberry Rules, and hello to the rough-and-tumble of the big boys' game. It was also an introduction to a new social environment of dressing-room chat, bar-room bravado and the deadly serious business of being one of the lads. Ray Sullivan appreciated the potential culture shock. He also watched with relief as the young John Barnes seemed to take it in his stride.

'It's terrible the first time you come into the dressing-room with a strange team, no matter what level you're playing at. You've got to be a really ebullient, out-going personality if you're going to stamp your mark on it straight away. Very, very difficult. And John was quiet. He only knew me at Sudbury in the early days. But the lads would talk to him and make a bit of a fuss of him, and he settled into it. Within a couple of games he was as good as gold.'

Not only was Barnes young and new and well bred, he was the only black member of the Sudbury team. But his acceptance seems to have been swift and, so far as those around him could tell, painless. It would have helped that Sudbury Court had had black players before and that one of them had gone on to enjoy national fame. He was Brian Stein, the expatriate South African who has enjoyed a distinguished career with Luton Town and who won an England cap in 1984. Stein had been Sudbury's Player of the Year in the 1976–77 season, scoring an astonishing 55 goals that season. (Another notable black Sudbury Court old boy did not make his name in football, but in that other English national game fallen on hard times – cricket. Phillip DeFreitas, the England all-rounder, was a regular with Sudbury Court's first team a few seasons after Barnes's departure.) Barnes, in turn, was swiftly recognized as a spectacularly gifted player, which always helps. In addition he was a novelty, a kid from a different home life altogether, yet whose most obvious personal quality was his self-effacement. The Sudbury players took him to their hearts.

'Our team looked after him,' says Lawlor. 'He was a nice lad, wasn't he? They used to, like, mickey-take, but not about race or anything. John always seemed happy at the end of the game. It didn't matter how well he'd played, if you gave him a hamburger and a coke he was all right.' Ray Sullivan agrees: 'His idea of a big night out was going to McDonald's. Some of the guys he was playing with would steam into ten or twelve pints after the game and have a bloody good night. John would sit there, quite happily, having a coke, and he'd still enjoy himself. There was one time when we were playing away somewhere, and he was in a car with three of our really wide boys, who used to put themselves about each night. I was in the car behind. And two of them suddenly mooned in the back seat of this car. I thought, "Jesus . . ." But John was sitting there in absolute stitches. To see his expression when they did it was great. I think he settled in very quickly. He was obviously apprehensive at the start. But I think Sudbury Court was the ideal stepping stone for John, because not only did it introduce him to men's football, it brought him into a team atmosphere where he could fit in very quickly, which for a young lad is really important.'

Barnes immediately established himself in the Sudbury team, playing on the right hand side of midfield. He was picked regularly through the autumn months to the end of 1980 and on into the New Year, missing only two games. These fell on either side of Christmas which the family celebrated in Jamaica. He scored his first goal in his second game, a 5–3 away win against Hillingdon, but missed out on an 8–nil obliteration of Ruislip. In fact, Barnes did not notch another until the last day of January in a 2-all draw with Bedfont and it was not really until March 1981, in the latter stages of the season, that he began to find the net with great regularity, finishing the season with 10 goals.

By then, the word was out. This lad was something special. They had missed him at twelve and thirteen, but now the scouts from pro clubs were sniffing about. Opposing defenders were resorting to desperate measures. The big boys of Sudbury closed ranks around their teenage prodigy. 'I think the thing he learned at Sudbury was friendship,' Des Lawlor reflects. 'He grew up with the team for a year. And if somebody was knocking John about, then one of ours would always go and have a quiet word. It wasn't a bruising side, but it was a team. We played one side, and they were real old bruisers. This guy just kept on kicking lumps out of John, but he didn't say a word. We thought, "This is crazy." So we said to our right-back, "Go and have a word with that full-back, will you?" Five minutes later, this guy's still kicking John. I said to ours, "Oi, I told you to have a word with him." He said, "But his nose is bleeding. I can't do any more, can I?" John just carried on playing. He's just a nice lad.'

The better Barnes played, the better his team-mates liked him. 'They respected him because of his ability,' says Lawlor. 'Watching him play football is a delight, but to play *with* him . . . he made their bad balls look good, and he was superb. You'd knock him a ball, and if it was a bit in front of him, he'd nip round someone and carry on. If John had not been such a good footballer, I think he would have been accepted, but not made such a fuss of. I know they were a real nice bunch of lads and the rest of it, but the more respect people

have got for your ability . . .' Sullivan finished the sentence for him:
'. . . the more they're gonna want you in their team.'

Lawlor and Sullivan consider that Barnes's personal qualities
also differentiated him from most other black footballers they and
the Sudbury players had encountered. 'They just took to him,'
reiterated Des. 'He's a really likeable lad. I personally think there's
a lot of black lads who've got a chip on their shoulder, but he just
wasn't that way inclined. Not at all. I think most people are not
worried about colour. They'll just get on with the business of
playing football and having a laugh.'

The implication here is that it was to the young Barnes's advantage that he did not choose to make an issue out of 'race', either
explicitly as a political position, or implicitly as a streetwise attitude,
the kind of combative identity that many of the black kids from the
Paddington tower blocks would have considered essential for their
daily survival. It is not that Lawlor and Sullivan are wrong about
him being different from the other black kids they dealt with. He
was, of course, in every way *except* the colour of his skin. The point
is that it was precisely those differences, enhanced by his brilliant
play, which helped him settle so readily into an all-white team in a
predominantly white league. He was more easily accepted as 'one of
us'.

So Barnes was seen as an exception. His distinctive family
grounding enabled him to contradict more easily the negative
expectations so frequently imposed upon all black footballers. On
the other hand, another slice of folk knowledge, commonplace in
the footballing fraternity, seemed to Ray Sullivan to be borne out by
Barnes's pace and obvious ability as a ball-player. 'He had natural
talent. His technique was outstanding, like a lot of the black kids.
Their technique is two or three years ahead of the equivalent white
English kids. I believe there is something in the theory that they are
naturally gifted. Natural athleticism. You could certainly play a ball
to John and some of the other [black] kids of his era, and their
control was brilliant.'

More than twenty years ago a number of studies were conducted
to try and establish whether or not black men and women were, in
general, blessed with greater inherent athletic gifts than whites.

Despite appearing to prove the case these studies have all been thoroughly discredited since. The fact that blacks seem to predominate at the highest levels of some – though by no means all – modern sports and sometimes to bring a distinctive style and technique to them, can only plausibly be explained as a combination of social and cultural factors, *not* genetic ones. But even so, at sixteen, John Barnes was perceived as having the 'natural ability' thought to be inherent in blacks. Also, at this stage, he had the opposite 'temperament' to that usually ascribed. In short, he seemed to the white men around him to be blessed with the best of both colours – a great natural player and 'a nice lad'. How could he lose?

Sudbury Court was undoubtedly a happy experience for the young John Barnes. He remained with them throughout a victorious season in which they lost only 3 of their 33 games, drew 4 and won the rest. They ran away with the Middlesex League Premier Division and though they were eliminated in the first round of the Middlesex Premier Cup, they won the other knock-out competition they entered, the Harrow Charity Cup, with a 1–nil final victory in the last match of the season. John Barnes scored the goal.

The schoolboy star was not, however, Sudbury's top scorer. Nor was he voted Player of the Year. That honour went to striker Pat Collins, who found the net 26 times that season. But what most surprised and delighted Des Lawlor and Ray Sullivan was the commitment of their teenage wonder to his team, despite the growing interest of scouts from professional clubs. 'The thing that struck me more than anything was his loyalty,' says Lawlor. 'Halfway through the season we knew that he was going with somebody. One of the people at the club had informed Watford. And then we had people from Ipswich come down and [Queen's Park] Rangers turned up as well. Rangers wanted to sign him on the spot. I couldn't believe it – he said he wanted to see the season out with Sudbury Court. I just couldn't imagine any sixteen-year-old boy with that sort of future in front of him turning round and saying that.'

Military men set great store by loyalty, and who would not be tempted to divine the philosophies of the Colonel at work here? But again, the circumstances for John Barnes were different. It was not his overriding obsession to have a career in English professional football, and anyway, his family was expecting to return to Jamaica. He simply did not see his future in England at all, something he himself confirmed in 1988 when profiled by the *Sunday Times Magazine*: 'My parents were preparing to go back, and I was going back with them. I was looking forward to home. Maybe I would have done something like computers or whatever. One of my friends had gone to Washington University on a scholarship, and my sister had a tennis scholarship. Maybe I would have finished up there; I wouldn't have regretted it.'

In the end, it was Watford who secured Barnes's services, and their success seems largely to have been due to their willingness to respect the young man's sense of priorities. They too assumed a laid-back attitude and, to the consternation of an eager Queen's Park Rangers, it paid off. The Colonel confirms that QPR asked his son to sign on as a professional right away, but that he declined in order to finish his season with Sudbury Court. He would not, Barnes explained, be available to play for their youth team on Saturdays. However, he did go to Rangers' ground a couple of nights a week to train. His arrangement with Watford was different. With them he had agreed that if ever there was a Saturday when Sudbury Court did not have a game, he would be ready to turn out for the Watford youth team instead.

One week, it happened. That morning, he climbed on to a coach at Watford and found himself being driven to, of all places, the Shepherd's Bush ground of QPR, to play against, in the Colonel's words, 'the same people he had been training with for weeks and had told he couldn't play for on Saturdays.' His reception at Rangers was frosty. 'He said the Queen's Park Rangers guy saw him, and if looks could kill he would have dropped down dead. He thought in his own childish mind, "Oh, I've really done it now." So he never went back to Queen's Park Rangers after that, although he quite liked the people there.' Des Lawlor confirms the story: 'When he got to Rangers, the guy just slagged him off. There was no way after that he was ever going anywhere near Rangers.'

Watford and QPR were not the only clubs interested in Barnes at the time. Nor were they the only ones which various people associated with Sudbury sought to alert. Ipswich Town had sent a scout down of their own volition, though nothing came of it. Des Lawlor, an Arsenal fan, had, he says, rung up his favourite club to bring the teenager to their attention. He asked to speak to someone in authority, but never got past a secretary who insisted on following standard procedure: How old? How big? What team and what name? Lawlor declined to volunteer the information: 'What he didn't want was pressure. I said, "No, I'm not interested in any of that. But I'll tell you what, I will give you his name. It's John Barnes. And one day, he'll probably cost you about half a million pounds."' No doubt a story that youth officers at professional football clubs hear every week. But in this case, the caller was right, except in the financial details. John Barnes would have cost Arsenal a lot more than that.

Sullivan and Lawlor also claim that Fulham missed their chance when Malcolm MacDonald was manager. A friend of theirs was a Fulham fanatic. 'He wrote to MacDonald about John and never heard a word back. So when John was picked to play for England Under-21s, he got all the newspaper cuttings and stuck them in another letter to MacDonald saying "see what you missed."' This time he did get a letter back, saying,'Yes, we admit we did make a mistake there. We did go and watch him. We thought, "good player, but we've got a better one on the books at the moment."' Ray Sullivan thinks the player in question was Leroy Rosenior, now at West Ham United.

So John Barnes joined Watford. If Ray Sullivan is right in thinking that he was not always consumed with ambition to be a professional player, the Colonel thinks that by the end of the 1980–81 season he was getting to like the idea. Watford offered him a contract at exactly the same time as the rest of the Barnes family were packing their bags for the trip back to Jamaica. A decision had to be made. It required serious thought, but in the end it caused no great agony.

'It wasn't all that difficult,' the Colonel maintains. 'It was difficult from the point of view that you're going back, and you're not sure what the hell Watford was offering him anyhow. Or whether he was good enough. So, yes, you worry about whether he's going to make the grade or not, that's what you're really concerned about. But the fact of the matter is, he certainly wanted to play professional football then. If you have a son of that age and you think, "This guy should go to university and become a doctor or an engineer", that's a different thing. But he was not an academic person. So from that point of view it was an easy decision.'

The Watford man who first contacted Colonel Barnes about his son was the former manager of Arsenal's 'double'-winning team of 1970–71, Bertie Mee. That Watford's initial interest came via a tip-off from a fan was extremely unusual, as Bertie Mee himself indicated to the *Sunday Times Magazine*: 'He is absolutely a one-off in twenty-eight years' experience. We act on a tip from a fan every two or three years.' At Watford, Mee had been important in building up the club's scouting system. So it was ironic that he should be the key figure in securing the services of the club's most talented player, after he had been missed by the system Mee had done so much to organize. One Saturday morning, he went along to watch the first half of a Sudbury Court game accompanied by the scout whom Sudbury's Watford fan had alerted. 'I looked at John Barnes for ten minutes, and I said, "I want his phone number and address. He's good enough for me." With an outstanding player, you can tell.'

The discovery of Barnes was a gift from the blue. It also re-acquainted Bertie Mee with a man he had never expected to meet again in his life. Their first encounter had not been under the happiest of circumstances. It had been in Jamaica and the circumstances were those of civil unrest. 'I rang up on the Saturday evening. Someone answered the phone and said, "Colonel Barnes here." I said, "Oh . . . *Colonel* Barnes. My name's Bertie Mee, from Watford Football Club." He said, "Really, Bertie? Well, what do you know?" He said, "You don't think you know me, do you? But you'll recall when you were with Arsenal and you were in Jamaica and you had a hard game and there was a bit of a riot, and we had to escort you off?"' Bertie Mee did. It had been a major incident during a pre-season tour. The Colonel had continued. 'Well, I was the team manager! Anyway, what can I do for you?' Mr Mee stated his business: 'About your boy, John.' 'I've heard he can play a bit,' said the Colonel. 'What about coming round tomorrow for a gin and tonic?'

It was a meeting of minds. Old pals and G & T. The Barnes family delighted Mee. At Arsenal his public image had been at odds with the growing tendency for successful managers to be flamboyant, outspoken 'personalities', men-of-the-people made good in the mould of Bill Shankly, Malcolm Allison or Brian Clough. By comparison, Mee was rather correct, economical in his speech and conservative in his dress – almost genteel. He was keen for footballers to shed their illiterate image. In his Foreword to the Arsenal midfield man Jon Sammels's autobiography, *Double Champions* (1971), he expressed his hope that the book '. . . should convince the public and grammar school boys that football has come into the forefront as a career, even for the academic. University graduates such as Steve Heighway and Brian Hall [interestingly, both Liverpool players of the time] . . . have set the pattern, and the influence of those who combine skill with intellectual qualities can do the game nothing but good . . .' So when he went round to make the acquaintance of the Colonel, Jean and John at what was their last home in England, he was quickly impressed. 'He was in a lovely mews property off Portland Place. Marvellous family. *Marvellous* family.'

John Barnes signed as a professional with Second Division Watford in the summer of 1981. A guardian was appointed, he was moved into approved accommodation, and waved his family goodbye. In return for nurturing their seventeen-year-old prospect, Watford paid Sudbury an undisclosed sum. Further amounts were received when he made his first team début, his first appearance for the England Under-21s and again on being awarded his first full international cap. But this was the last thing on the minds of Ray Sullivan and Des Lawlor when they went off to Watford to watch their former club-mate play in his first youth and reserve team games after only six weeks of pre-season training. They were chuffed to learn that he had not forgotten them now that he was edging towards the big time; there were always tickets on the gate. Lawlor and Sullivan, two very likeable men, are too modest to claim any credit for Barnes's development as a player. But when Lawlor took his place in the stand to see one of those early games, he witnessed something that made his heart sing: 'I remember saying to him time and time again at Sudbury, "Just shoot, you know. When you get through, don't worry about the others, just shoot. If it goes sailing wide, it goes sailing wide. But if you don't shoot, you don't score." Well, I think this game was about thirty seconds old. Watford kicked the ball forward, a guy headed it out, it came to John and he just volleyed it from about thirty yards. It screamed into the net . . . I thought, "I've been saying that for a year, you know, just shoot . . ." But his feet were always on the ground. He was just a nice lad.'

4
'Too Nice a Guy'

Between 1977 and 1982 Watford Football Club emerged as a *cause célèbre* of modern British football. It is not simply that during that period the small Hertfordshire club, which had never won a major title since its foundation in 1891, climbed from Division Four of the English Football League to Division One. To appreciate fully the achievement on the pitch, it is important to understand what was going on around it.

In the first place we are talking of paupers competing with princes. Never mind the thundering cliché that, at the end of the day, it's still eleven men against eleven on the field of play. The numerical equality required by the rules of the game pales in significance next to the vast differences in the wider contexts within which those two teams of men set about their work. By the start of the 1981–82 season, when John Barnes took his place on the Watford payroll, the wealth in professional football had long been heavily concentrated in the bank accounts of a handful of big-time clubs. Even compared to many of their Second Division peers, Watford were a humble concern. Money may not be everything in football, but it can buy you an awful lot of what there is.

The secret of Watford's rise from obscurity lies in a combination of factors, only partly to do with hard cash, a blend of pragmatism and idealism that proved in many, if not all, ways well suited to the early career of John Barnes. Three key individuals stood tall in the rise of the club into a footballing power above its station. They were, respectively, a former Lincoln City full-back, a mercurial millionaire rock star and a former National Health physiotherapist who spoke the Queen's English on TV: Graham Taylor, Elton John and Bertie Mee.

I met the last of these three on a damp December morning in his director's office at the club's Vicarage Road ground. A neat, genial gentleman, dressed like a bank manager from an Ealing comedy, Bertie Mee seemed pleased at the chance to discuss the philosophy of the game rather than the minutiae of his chairman's sex life. Behind his chair, a window opened out on to the pitch below as the 1988–89 Watford squad went through their training paces. Barnes and Taylor had departed the close season before last and Watford had been relegated to Division Two. It was the club's first major setback since the glorious rise from the Fourth, but even so, the ground's yellow paintwork still looked fresh and bright, a suitably cheery confirmation of Watford FC's continuing reputation as a cheery little club. Bertie Mee's reminiscences were cheery too. Watford, after all, had given a new lease to an already illustrious footballing life.

'I came to Watford to help Graham Taylor and Elton John create a club. I came in September '77. I think Graham had got here from Lincoln City [where he had gone on to become manager] in the August. I'd taken a year out to recharge my batteries and take stock of a few things. Graham had communicated with me when I was at Highbury because he wanted to come and work with me, but I couldn't fit him in at the time. He was still a young manager, a very, very young manager. But Graham is a very intelligent man and you'll probably realize that there's a big similarity between us in our philosophy and attitudes – Graham is very different to the average professional footballer. So I dropped him a line and said "Look, if I can be any help, fine." He was most enthusiastic to have me along.'

What Mee and Taylor had in common was belief in a rigorous outlook from their players towards *all* aspects of their lives, as befitted their idea of how *professional* people should behave. It is that philosophy which Mee believes he brought to Arsenal after he was promoted from physiotherapist to team manager in 1966, and which lay behind the side's 'double' triumph: 'Blowing my own trumpet now, I probably made Arsenal more professional than any other club,' said Mr Mee. 'But when I use that term in this context, I don't use it in relation to playing, but purely in relation to organization backstage. I was a professional, and very much opposed to the lack of attention to hygiene, diet, conduct, behaviour, drinking and so on. I restructured all that and produced a professional outlook because that's what the game obviously demanded and needed.'

When Mee spoke of 'professionalism', he explained, he did not mean that playing philosophy associated with the so-called 'professional foul'. No, what he meant was a willingness to shed those oafish working-class habits and replace them with an outlook appropriate to young men going up in the world. Arsenal's young players – of whom Brendon Batson had once been one – would be schooled in everything from which knife and fork to pick up first in expensive restaurants to how to contend with the carnal temptations of trips overseas. Mee took raw, new recruits from the backwoods on educational visits to the Tower of London and introduced them to the joys of personal pension schemes. He prides himself on having set an example that others would be expected to follow: 'I had to demonstrate behaviour patterns in order to get across this professionalism. I had to be dedicated, my staff had to be dedicated and that transmitted itself to the players.'

It is an outlook which corresponds precisely with the trademarks of Graham Taylor's management style. He and Mee set about restructuring the club in their mutual self-image. There was only a skeleton staff and no grass-roots network designed to scout local players or to bring the public in. Mee sorted out a youth development operation, the celebrated Family Enclosure was instituted at the ground, and Graham Taylor took it upon himself to get out and about in the town. Mr Mee, becoming animated behind his desk, set the policy in perspective: 'It's unusual for a football club manager to get out to schools and visit hospitals and get involved. Not easy. The demands on his time are very, very great. But Graham was particularly good from this point of view.' Taylor expected a similar dedication to public relations from his players. At his instigation Watford became the first club in the country to include a so-called 'community clause' in players' contracts. This required, among other things, that players should reside within the boundaries of the town, to become once more what footballers had been before the war; that is, as Mee put it, 'the chap next door'.

It was into this environment that John Barnes was introduced as a rookie professional, one where he was expected to help project the profile of the club towards the townsfolk it needed to woo if its success as a football team and a business enterprise was to be sustained. But where Watford's sales pitch was inviting, its playing regime was gruelling. It was a combination of which Colonel Barnes heartily approved. 'I think Watford did him a lot of good. He couldn't have gone to a better club: a family atmosphere and a manager who didn't put up with any nonsense. He could never play the superstar at Watford because Graham Taylor just wouldn't have it. From what he told me and what I could see they would send him off on fifteen-mile runs, and it was extremely rough, tough, rigorous training. I don't know if it was all that designed for playing good football. But whether it was snowing or raining or what, they went and did all kinds of hard work.' The Colonel nodded, approvingly: 'I'm all for that, the discipline part. I think it was a good background indoctrination for him.'

In the Colonel's opinion, combat is good for the character. 'He had, to my mind, a love-hate relationship with Taylor in that Taylor was his first boss and I think he admired Taylor a lot. But on the other hand, Taylor treated him like a little boy. So he always had this thing with Taylor. He had a lot of respect for him, but always sort of resented Taylor for keeping him in his place. And that was very good for him. I like that.'

As a player, Barnes Junior had not made such an instant impression on Taylor as he had on Mee. Taylor has been quoted as saying that in the first two games in which Barnes wore Watford's colours he had hardly been bowled over. Then, he suddenly found himself impressed: 'He hadn't really done very much when he played in a third game, a junior match at Orient. I was in the stand and I kept thinking to myself. "There is something there, but when will it explode?" Then all of a sudden a ball came over from the left and John hit it with the outside of his left foot from outside the area and the ball flew into the top corner of the net. That was it. That was enough to sign him. That was worth working with, a tremendous piece of skill at any level.'

If these remarks hint at the frustration Taylor would come to express frequently at what he perceived as the enigmatic qualities of the finest player he has ever managed, his opinion had risen swiftly enough for him to draft Barnes into the senior squad after only

three games in the reserves. His first appearance for the full
Watford side was at home to Oldham Athletic on 5 September 1981
– Taylor sent him on as substitute fifteen minutes from the end of a
1-all draw – and it was on 12 September that he enjoyed the
dubious distinction of making his full début against Chelsea at
Stamford Bridge, home of some of the most vocally racist fans in
English football.

If Barnes had been protected from the more overt extremes of
English football racism, then this was a baptism of fire. Brought into
the side to replace Watford's other black player, suspended goal-
scoring hero Luther Blissett, he was subjected to an experience
which he has clearly never forgotten. Six years later, after Everton's
fans had barracked him for ninety relentless minutes at Anfield, he
appeared on an ITV youth programme, *APB*. What did it feel like to
be subjected to such a tirade? Barnes offered a stock response, but a
telling one: 'It's like water off a duck's back to me, as it is to most
coloured players . . . I've been having that since six, seven years ago.
In my first game against Chelsea I had that, you know, when I was
seventeen.'

The almost ritual readiness of black footballers to make light of
racial abuse when asked to comment on it in public is often seized
upon by apologists for terrace chauvinism to trivialize the issue. The
'common sense' rationale Barnes himself employed for *APB* is
typical. 'A lot of it is done really to try and put you off. [It is] the
obvious way for them to have a go at me, because I'm a different
colour . . .' But it is worth weighing these comments from a player
who still runs out to boos and monkey chants week in, week out,
against those of Brendon Batson, a black ex-player now charged
with representing the best interests of his professional former colleagues. Barnes, when asked, has claimed that in the thick of the
fray, it is not possible to pick out individual comments or even songs
from the crowd. Batson of the PFA expresses a different view, a
cautiously dissenting one: 'We *are* conscious of it. Because if any
person is going to be subjected to ninety minutes of abuse, you'd
have to have a hide thicker than a rhinoceros to say it didn't affect
you. I always remember going to places like Leeds and West Ham
where they used to hurl bananas at us and what have you . . . and it

is so insulting. But what do you do? Do you react to it, then maybe
throw your game completely, and then be subjected to more of it?
You've literally got to grin and bear it. And I think that is one of the
problems in itself. If you grin and bear it, everyone thinks, "Oh,
well, you're accepting it." But I can assure you that black players
don't accept it.' Maybe Barnes was telling the whole truth as he saw
it or maybe he was being the practical diplomat, his father's son.
What seems certain, though, is that to have said anything different,
to confess to being wounded, would have amounted to an invitation
to further attack – the black footballer's Catch 22.

Barnes retained his place as Blissett's replacement in Watford's
next home game against Rotherham and was picked again, this time
alongside Blissett, for the following fixture at Wrexham. He became
an automatic selection from then on. And so the pattern of his
football life at Watford was swiftly set. Lots of blood, lots of sweat,
lots of pressing the flesh ... and, like every black footballer in
England, learning to live with a contingent of anonymous per-
secutors beyond the touchline at every game he played. In his fifth
full game, still too young to vote, he scored his first League goal in a
3–1 home win against Barnsley. He got two more the following
week against Orient (now Leyton Orient), another a fortnight later
against Norwich City and one more the week after that in a 2–nil
away win against Shrewsbury Town. His record to the end of
October spoke for itself. Barnes had become an integral figure in
the attacking strategy of a Watford side which had won 8 and drawn
1 of its previous 10 League games and had prevailed over two legs
against Grimsby Town in the second round of the League Cup.
With success, Graham Taylor's methodology was beginning to
reach a wider public. But while Watford FC's policy as a
community-minded business entity was earning critical approval,
the style in which they played enjoyed a less favourable press. It
plunged them into the centre of the great eighties debate about the
'long ball game'.

The genesis of the Watford method has been attributed to
another military man, Wing Commander Charles Reep. He described it as the 'Random Chance System'. It was, he said, 'designed
to drive a team on to furious, sustained attacks, home and away,'

and he drew it to Taylor's attention at the end of the 1979–80 season when Watford had only just avoided relegation back to Division Three. The Reep–Taylor Random Chance game was pragmatic rather than pretty, based more on physique than finesse. What the Brazilians have derided, famously, as 'track-and-field football' enjoyed high favour at Watford under Graham Taylor's regime and, whatever the aesthetic arguments, none could deny that it was effective in helping to make the team add up to more than the sum of its parts.

It is ironic indeed that a player of Barnes's craft and sophistication should have earned his professional spurs participating in such a system. When Watford launched an offensive, it usually went like this: welly, run and chase. The ball would be the recipient of some serious punishment as Watford set about hoofing the thing upfield, bypassing the midfield, and trusting in the law of averages: the more times the spherical missile could be projected into the opposition's goalmouth, the better the chance that Ross Jenkins or Blissett, big, fast and strong, would get themselves on the end of it. One of the most effective routes by which this could be arranged was by channelling the ball through the spaces on the wings, either directly or off the heads of the front men, and relying on the pace and crossing abilities of Nigel Callaghan on the right and John Barnes on the left. The Jamaican teenager covered an awful lot of ground before the spring of 1982, both on the touchlines of Division Two and the hillsides of Hertfordshire. It is, perhaps, a tribute to Barnes's sense of loyalty that he often found Watford's tactics wearisome to conform to, and yet defended them in public. 'I think they have been cruel jibes,' he once said in response to the team's critics. 'What is wrong with the fifty-yard pass? It can be a great tactic. People say it is the wrong thing for the game. Well, it is the right thing for Watford. So far it has brought tremendous success for the club in a very exciting period. Just as important, the spectators like it.'

The method served Watford well enough. They finished runners-up in the Second Division to Luton Town, so winning promotion to the top flight. They also enjoyed an FA Cup run which may have been brief but was no less glorious for that. In the third round they beat Manchester United by the odd goal at Vicarage Road and doubled that margin of victory at the same ground in the following round, to the dismay of West Ham. John Barnes started 35 League games and all Watford's matches in FA and League Cups. He also scored a total of 14 goals, fewer only than striker Jenkins with 15 and Luther Blissett himself who topped the Watford list with 22. Barnes's and Blissett's effectiveness could not fail to endear them to the Watford fans. They also met with the approval of Bertie Mee as PR men: 'In both cases they were first class here as members of the community. They *worshipped* Luther here. He was accepted. Colour', Mee asserted, 'never came into it.'

Blissett and Barnes make an interesting comparison. Blissett too was Jamaican-born, though his father, far from employing servants, was a Kingston carpenter. As the scorer of two outstanding televised goals that removed an earlier Manchester United team from the League Cup at Old Trafford in 1978, he had already come to national attention. Taylor, Mee, the Colonel and Barnes himself have all acknowledged the support Blissett was able to give his young team-mate in his earliest days. Blissett had already experienced, with shock, the nasty side of English football spectators. But his celebrity status at Watford helped pave the way for Barnes's own career. The most telling insight their relationship gives us into the circumstances of being black in Britain is that back 'home' Barnes and Blissett would have occupied different worlds. But with the potential for white hostility a fact of English life, racism re-aligned them on a common ground more unifying even than being members of the same football team.

But to those who knew them, the variance in background and personality between the two was clear. 'John was slightly different,' confirms Mee, 'a very educated lad.' Mee, who had been awarded an OBE for his achievements at Arsenal, where the directors included company chairmen and dignitaries from the Bank of England, enjoyed considerable social kudos. A sheriff of the City of London once invited him and a guest to attend a lunch with the Law Court judges. 'He said, "Would you like to bring a player with you?" So I took John Barnes along. Now if you can imagine that scene, all these judges sitting there in their red robes ... but his behaviour was absolutely impeccable. And of course he had a talking point because his sister was doing Law ... But I've seen John Barnes in all sorts of community involvements where he's conducted himself extremely well. And because of what he is, he has no problems.'

'*Because of what he is*' – a phrase which, if used in relation to most black footballers by most white football people, would be delivered, swollen with derogatory potential. Barnes, in Mee's eyes at least, was able to prove himself the exception to the 'common sense' rule. But if Barnes's capacity for escaping the straitjacket of other people's expectations must be seen as a victory for his own charm and social confidence, it is worth noting also that Bertie Mee himself proved something of an exception to the rule in the way he talked about Watford's two black stars. Of all the fifty or so individuals interviewed for this book, he was the only white one who did not reach, unprompted, for the sporting clichés that comprise a racial stereotype in football's insular little world, the only one who did not volunteer the popular myths about lack of discipline, natural athleticism, chips on the shoulder or dislike for the cold. And when he talked about John Barnes the footballer, he defined him as the product of an *environment* as much as of nature, of social background rather than biology. In fact, Barnes made Bertie Mee, OBE, positively nostalgic. And the historical parallels he drew were not with great black players of the past, but the lusty white, working-class wizards from English football's Golden Age.

'Barnes was brought up, by and large, in Jamaica,' Mee enthused. 'So he acquired all his skills in the dirt of Jamaica, in the same way that in the thirties, forties and fifties *we* all acquired *our* inherent skills kicking a ball around in the streets from morning till night, all our lunch hours, all the evenings and seven days a week during school holidays. So the Mannions, the Finneys, whoever you like, it was all those intuitive skills, all acquired at an early age at six or seven. And all those people needed was a little bit of organization. They were so adept and skilful that was all you had to do. Now when you reach the sixties, we in England had competition from television, then the pop scene. You can't kick a ball round in the street because of all the traffic. And you have a situation now where we're recruiting players that do not have anything like the basic skills that their predecessors had, because of the different environment they've been brought up in.'

Incongruous, perhaps, to hear the mastermind of the ultra-rational 'boring' Arsenal waxing lyrical about a player who reminded him of another time in England, a time before the big money, the big media business and the neuroses of the 'win' mentality. Mee's image of Barnes's early upbringing may be romantic, but it correctly identifies the influence of the Jamaican football ethos on his style. He draws a persuasive picture to explain why the things that make Barnes special may be impossible to separate from the things that so irked Graham Taylor. 'In terms of talent there's no doubt that John has got as much as anyone that's ever graced our game, including Stanley Matthews. And had he been in the era of Stanley Matthews then he would have been an equally outstanding player.

'But the game is a lot harder now. I don't mean physically harder, but more demanding over ninety minutes, which means physical effort and it means concentration. And John doesn't seem to be able to produce all his ability every time he turns out. It's only under certain circumstances and for small periods of time. In terms of nostalgia, yes, one would yearn for eleven people with his physical abilities, his skill. But a manager has to come to terms with whether you want someone with less inherent ability, like Kevin Keegan, who was invaluable within the team and gave you ninety minutes every time he turned out. And we're sorry, if anything, that because John's too nice a guy he's never realized his full potential. What you see him do for twenty minutes in ninety, as a manager and as an onlooker, you would want him to do for ninety. But he can't do that because of what he is.' A gentleman among professionals, perhaps – an aristocrat out of time. 'You have to tolerate it,' Mee explained. 'And it's difficult isn't it? It's ability-plus, and you can't coach that. Your most important job in management is to come to terms with those little situations that you can influence ... and the ones you can't.'

Graham Taylor tried and kept on trying. A man whose methods were based upon percentages and rationality, he found the fitfulness of the inexplicable hard to contend with. A disciplinarian, he did what came naturally, cajoling, hectoring, nagging Barnes to find consistency at the peak of his skills. There were long interrogations and there were rows. The response was not recalcitrance but a reluctant submission to authority and the love-hate relationship the Colonel described, the inevitable result, perhaps, of a non-meeting of minds: Taylor, the artisan, the dogged self-improver; Barnes, in spite of everything, the Corinthian, the artist, dependent on his muse. 'I think Taylor used to get at him if the team wasn't winning at half time,' revealed the Colonel. 'And I think Johnny felt, "This guy keeps treating me like a little boy". He got older and he got a place in the England team. I think he felt, "Ah, I'm not a little boy any more", but I think Taylor kept treating him as if he was still a seventeen-year-old . . . I felt it was a wonderful introduction into professional football.'

Whether it was the best way to help talent fulfil itself might be open to debate.

5
'Free Spirits'

19 May 1984 was the greatest day yet in the history of Watford Football Club. As 3 p.m. approached, Graham Taylor led his team out into the traditional faint spring sunshine of Wembley stadium to play in the FA Cup Final against Everton. John Barnes, hair grown out just enough to suggest a hint of a cool but conservative Afro, waved to the Watford fans from his place in a team file wending its way towards the royal handshake.

The odds were stacked against the Hertfordshire team. Their captain, the experienced left-back Wilf Rostron, had been sent off controversially in a League match and was consequently suspended on the big day. Regular centre-back Steve Sims was injured. Jenkins and Blissett had gone, the former on a free transfer, the latter to A. C. Milan for £1 million. Taylor had been unable to compensate completely for the loss of their cutting edge. By 4.45 p.m. an unmemorable encounter had been won by the blue Merseysiders, 2 goals to nil.

But despite the outcome, the occasion provided a stage upon which the Watford philosophy, in both playing and club terms, could be exposed to a national public. Mindful as ever of the proper decorum, Graham Taylor outlawed players' indulgence in the more outlandish money-making publicity stunts that have become a feature of Cup Final build-ups. Watford were keen to be seen to be doing the decent thing, the *professional* thing, as Taylor and Mee would define it. Anxious too to promote the personable image of the club's supporters, Taylor marked the build-up to the match by calling on them to participate respectfully in the traditional Cup Final singing of 'Abide With Me', instead of obliterating it with their own chants. In his Foreword to the following season's official Watford handbook, Elton John felt able to boast: 'Forgetting the result, I don't think Wembley has ever seen anything like our fans' behaviour.'

As an exercise in image-making, then, the Final saw Watford victorious. It also marked the beginning of the period in which John Barnes became widely recognized as a star. Though his Cup Final performance was not definitive, he made an impression on expert onlookers, posing a constant threat to the right side of Everton's defence. Danny Blanchflower, the great romantic, wrote in the *Sunday Express*: 'John Barnes shone all through the match. For me he was the best on the field.'

The Cup Final was a landmark in the continuing rise in Barnes's fortunes with Watford. It took place almost precisely a year after he had made his full England début in a drab goalless draw against Northern Ireland in Belfast, a fairly meaningless fixture in the now defunct Home International Championship. He came on as a substitute to replace, ironically, Luther Blissett. Bobby Robson, the new England manager, had introduced several emerging black players into his early squad selections and provided the press with the immortal quote: 'If the eleven best players in the country were black, that would be my England team.' Viv Anderson was already established. Regis was on the fringes and Blissett was well in the frame. To these, Robson added Mark Chamberlain, then of Stoke City, now of Sheffield Wednesday; Brian Stein and Ricky Hill of Luton Town; and John Barnes. It was the start of an international career which has proceeded as erratically as the national side's form, in a period where trauma, self-doubt and isolation have been hallmarks of the English football establishment, while chauvinism, malignance and brutality have continued to flourish among those who support it.

Following his début, Barnes won a string of caps in unexceptional circumstances. An experimental England squad toured Australia in a tournament celebrating that nation's centenary. Three games were played against the hosts' national side, in Sydney, Brisbane and Melbourne. Barnes came on as substitute in the first and started the other two on the left-hand flank. The England line-ups vanquished their part-time opponents in only one of the fixtures and that tamely, by the odd goal. The other two matches were unspectacular draws. In the autumn of 1983 Barnes was picked again, against Denmark at Wembley. The result was a miserable

1–nil defeat. For the next England game, away to Hungary in October, he was dropped. England won 3–nil. It was not one of the great introductions to the international stage.

Come the following (and final) Home International Championship in spring 1984, the first anniversary of his début, Barnes found himself out of the sides that played Northern Ireland and Wales, the first of which England won by the only goal, the second of which they lost by the same score. But, following his Cup Final appearance, the time was right for a rehabilitation. He found himself thrown in at the deep end, alongside Blissett, against the Scots at Hampden Park. England came away with a 1–1 draw, and although Barnes was substituted during the next England game, a 2–nil home defeat against the USSR, Robson still took him in his squad for a four-sided South American tournament in June, and picked him to wear number eleven in the opening match against Brazil in Rio de Janeiro's famous Maracana Stadium. It turned out to be Barnes's most famous England performance, a game which seemed to launch him into the international firmament. Instead it has become a symbol for what might have been.

Everything happened in the forty-fourth minute. Barnes received the ball twenty yards from goal and set off on a diagonal run which took him past a string of Brazilian defenders, all the time looking certain to lose possession and yet almost inexplicably floating onwards through the penalty area, deceiving the goalkeeper and tapping home. Something inexplicable happened in those moments, an illusion, a conjuring trick. The Brazilian defenders seemed hypnotized. Not even the man who did it could explain what it was. 'I don't honestly remember much about it,' he told reporters afterwards. 'I just put my head down and went.' England proceeded to win 2–nil, spurred by the first goal Barnes had scored for England in his seven fragmented appearances. The following day one Rio newspaper described it as the greatest goal ever seen at the Maracana, where Pele had regularly graced the stage – a compliment of almost onerous proportions.

It is in the light of that Maracana goal that John Barnes's subsequent footballing career has been judged, especially his England career. Between that goal and the 1986 World Cup he was picked by Bobby Robson seventeen times without ever recapturing the virtuoso mood or even really hinting at it. He started all the remaining five internationals in 1984, of which England won 3, lost 1 and drew 1, though the last two – against Finland at home and Turkey away – could hardly be regarded as first class opposition. Barnes scored twice in the 8–nil exhibition against the Turks. But he did not score another international goal until repeating the double against the same opposition at Wembley nearly three years later. In 1985 England played twelve international matches, including three in a four-cornered tournament in Mexico involving the host nation, West Germany and Italy. Barnes made appearances in nine of those games, but spent the whole ninety minutes on the pitch only twice. On three occasions he was taken off to make way for Chris Waddle, the talented Newcastle United winger now with Tottenham Hotspur. In three other games, the Waddle–Barnes swop was reversed, with the Watford man coming on wearing number twelve. He made another appearance as sub in England's best performance of that year, an unexpected 3–nil win over the West Germans in Mexico City, replacing Gary Lineker. His performances, in general, might be summed up as innocuous-to-adequate, and he did not appear for the final two fixtures of the year.

By 1986, it was clear that the Maracana promise had not been fulfilled. The six-game build-up to the Mexico World Cup saw Barnes come on three times as substitute for Waddle, who, nonetheless, had clearly established himself as Robson's choice as the most effective forward he had for operating wide and running with the ball. Barnes was relegated to playing the Newcastle man's deputy as Robson settled on an attacking formation built along traditional English – or hopelessly outmoded – lines depending on your point of view. Mark Hateley, who had scored England's second goal against Brazil, filled the role of the traditional centre-forward, a tall, physical target man. Lineker, soon to prove himself the footballing equivalent of a guided missile, was picked to provide pace, mobility and a scoring touch alongside him. A midfield of Ray Wilkins, Glen Hoddle and the combative Bryan Robson seemed to offer a blend of reliability, fitness and inspiration. Waddle would provide the derring-do. On paper, a plausible, flexible formula. In practice, it didn't work out.

England's World Cup began dismally. A 1–nil defeat against Portugal was followed by a torpid goalless draw with the minnows of Morocco. Bryan Robson was injured and Wilkins was sent off. Murmurs of internal dissent began to surface from within the England camp. The situation was only salvaged with a complete change of tactics. The muscle of Hateley was replaced with the skill and imagination of Peter Beardsley. Waddle was dropped and a tighter, more industrious four-man midfield set in place. With Bobby Robson's P45 only minutes from the post box, the new England went into a last-gasp match against Poland and beat them 3–nil. Lineker scored the lot. Advancing into the second stage of the competition, they despatched Paraguay by the same scoreline with essentially the same team and Lineker scored twice more. England were, at last, doing themselves justice. But after Paraguay came the quarter finals and some genuinely heavyweight opposition. England were matched against Argentina, an encounter so pregnant with significance beyond the touchline that even the British popular press could hardly fail to spot it. Not that we should congratulate them too loudly. After all, abusing Argentinians had been a favourite pastime among the British tabloids during the Falklands war. The *Sun*, typically, declared 'It's War, Sēnor'. In Mexico, meanwhile, the regular gang of inebriated England followers supped up, belched and readied themselves to goad the opposition's fans with a spot of *Sun*-style patriotic fervour.

But a footballing reprise of Argentina's military lament was never on the cards. 'We' might have had the guns, but 'they' had the footballers, and one footballer in particular – Diego Maradona. Streetwise, abrasive and built like an armour-plated spinning-top, Maradona was widely considered the greatest footballer in the world. Equal parts beast and beauty, he could bristle like a bull and move like a matador. He undid England in the first half with two goals of contrasting character, the first handled home outside the referee's line of sight – the infamous 'hand of God' affair – the second stabbed past goalkeeper Peter Shilton after a miraculous run from the midfield which left a string of England defenders lumbering. Blighty's artisans could not compete with such a combination of artistry and cunning.

Only one England player was able to hold a candle to the flair of Maradona's display, and he did not come on till the final quarter of the game. Consigned to the bench for the whole of the World Cup build-up, John Barnes was thrown into the fray on the left-hand flank as Bobby Robson's last-ditch gamble, joined by Waddle on the right. The Watford player responded with a cameo performance which showed he was capable of doing things with the ball that no other England player could. Barnes gave the team a glimmer of hope that the game might be saved, creating visible apprehension in an unsuspecting Argentine defence each time he got the ball. One fine cross enabled Lineker to pull a goal back. Then a delicious run down the flank saw him ease past his challengers and send the ball arcing across the front of the opposing goal, beyond the goalkeeper's reach and dipping down towards the far post where, homing in, Lineker failed by inches to make contact. In that brief moment, England's faint hopes glowed hot, then were extinguished. But Barnes had rekindled them almost single-handed against the team that eventually took the World Cup home to Buenos Aires in triumph.

In English eyes, Barnes's belated display had made the occasion tantalizing, even though England had been outclassed in most aspects of the game. In Jamaica, Barnes was proclaimed a hero, the island's very own World Cup representative, not just by national association, but by exhibiting a style that enabled him to purr past one man, two or three and still have the ball. But for everyone, his dazzling intervention once again begged the question that has been asked ever since the Maracana classic: why couldn't Barnes play like that for England all the time?

There is no straightforward answer to that question, no clear-cut explanation for a problem of unfulfilled potential that has assailed many other England internationals over the last twenty years. But the key to elusive solutions always lies in complex equations. All kinds of rogue factors can influence conundrums which can never be completely explained purely in terms of twenty-two big boys and a ball. Consider the scene on an aeroplane 30,000 feet above South America, back in the summer of 1984, just five days after John Barnes scored his immortal Maracana goal.

On board that plane were representatives of modern English football's four key factions. There were the players, up at the front with the team manager and coaching staff. Occupying the same part of the plane were the gentleman administrators of the Football Association, those musty, *petit bourgeois* bureaucrats responsible for the running of the national game. Pre-eminent among this contingent was the then FA Secretary, Ted Croker, the man who used to pull the little balls from the velvet bag in every ritual Cup draw. Behind this mixed bunch of athletes and officials sat the representatives of the British press, a menagerie of wide boys and public schoolboys, rheumy-eyed sporting scholars dreaming of better days, and unrepentant sensation-seekers out on a spree. A full house was completed by those gathered towards the rear of the plane. Some of the journalists had become aware of them making a nuisance of themselves at Montevideo airport, where England had played their second match of the tour, against Uruguay. Now, as the flight to Santiago got under way, it became clear they had boarded the same plane as the official England party.

'They were quite well behaved for a while,' remembers one of the travelling reporters, 'but there was a free bar on the plane. They got progressively more pissed, and then they started getting abusive.' The prime target for the England supporters' malice was Ted Croker. The core of their complaint was the composition of the England playing squad. 'They were shouting down the plane, "You fucking wanker. You prefer sambos to us." They just kept on. It was relentless.' John Barnes's goal against Brazil in Rio had sparked perhaps the most celebrated England victory since they won the World Cup twenty years before. Now he was obliged to sit there with two black colleagues, Viv Anderson and Mark Chamberlain, and impotently soak up the sound of naked racial hatred from the men who were supposed to be cheering him on.

Footballers notice crowds, their own as well as the opposition's. They all know which among them is loved by the paying public, which accepted, which most likely to be made the scapegoats for the failings of the side. Alan Mullery, quoted in *The Glory Game*, Hunter Davies's year in the life of Tottenham Hotspur, recalls his confidence soaring when he heard a touchline spectator christen him with an admiring nickname ... 'Come on, the Tank.' Mark Chamberlain has spoken of the thrill it gives him to feel the terrace roar swell as he takes the ball past defenders at speed: 'The crowd's cheering is like music to my ears.' Graeme Souness recalls in his autobiography that he knew he was never a favourite with the Liverpool crowd. They thought he was a bit too cool and cocky, the man who took the captaincy off Phil Thompson, their home-town lad. Think of a thousand football clichés about how our fans are like a one-goal start, how we need to get the crowd behind us, or how we wish they'd get off our backs when things are going wrong. Crowds matter to football teams because they want them on their side.

So what does the black footballer think when he finds his mailbag full of hate after hitting a hat-trick for his national team? This is what happened to Barnes's Watford colleague Luther Blissett in November 1982 after his triple strike in a 9–nil win over Luxemburg, the first black player to score for England. And what thoughts went through the heads of Chamberlain, Anderson and Barnes as the Bulldog contingent bayed from the back of the Santiago plane, hurling the vilest abuse, adapting the words of popular songs to become vehicles for still more? When the opposition crowd is against you, black footballers explain, it makes you fight harder, it makes you want to hurt them back in the only way you can. But when your own fans are your greatest tormentors, the very people who you expect to confirm you in your successes and to urge you to greater glories, what manner of bleak ambivalence is likely to flourish in the corners of a young man's mind?

'If the eleven best players in the country were black, that would be my England team,' Bobby Robson said. Let us imagine the response if such a situation ever came about. Let us consider the likely reaction of the thousands of England supporters who make it their business to stash away every penny they have to travel around the world and watch the national team perform in foreign lands. Draped in their Union Jacks, bellies bulging from their Union Jack shorts, directing derision at anything around them that is not 'English' in their terms, meaning anything that is not mean and macho, white and fair, of the Bulldog Breed. These are the hard core, the self-styled personification of all that made England great. Reliable consumers, hooligans, the bedrock source of the box-office profits that keep everyone in luxury cars, the ones who will go to the greatest lengths to get into a game. In all their beery bigotry, they are the most dedicated England fans of all, the ones who piss and puke their way across continents, 'on the march with Bobby's army', to goad the slimey 'Argies' and the dagos and the wops, to prop up bars and moan about the 'Pakis taking over'. Let us imagine how they, the most loyal fraction of the paying England public, would feel about eleven black players representing 'their' England, 'their' nation's team – especially when it fails to produce the goods.

Would the Football Association – would Bobby Robson – really wish to countenance the possibility of the English national side walking out to be greeted by barracking racists? English national football is an industry and inebriated, white ultra-conservatives are its core market. What price, then, eleven black Englishmen walking out for their country under the Wembley sky, standing for the National Anthem as the Union flags flutter from the turrets of the famous twin towers? It would take a very brave man to pick them. Signs of courage are scarce indeed in this sad scenario. The only place they can be found are among the young black Englishmen who have the nerve even to claim their rightful place in a white England shirt.

Barnes's England disappointments have not been for want of skill. He can do stuff with a ball that few of his peers can manage. He can run and cross and take defenders on. He can drag the ball back then push it through a gap in almost a single movement, sealing his advantage with a searing change of pace. Barnes has the ability, almost inexplicable, to contrive a fragment of space when hemmed in on the byline, enough, somehow, to send the ball winging across the penalty box with immaculate accuracy. He can bend free-kicks around the most solid defensive walls and bury the ball in the roof of the net. He can play the cutest backheel into the path of a team-mate while moving forward at speed. John Barnes can do all that and he did it frequently for Watford between 1981 and 1987, surrounded by defenders who knew he was the one Watford man who could be relied on to spoil their whole afternoon if they didn't keep stampeding him into corners, holding the lid on the cauldron. Stop Barnes and you multiplied your chances of stopping Watford too. He has had two defenders chasing him round the pitch since he was eighteen years old.

The First Division took its time to work out Barnes and his Watford colleagues. In their first season in the top flight, the team that Taylor built alarmed the purists but startled their opponents still more, finishing second to Liverpool in 1982–83 with Barnes a regular selection. He, Jenkins, Blissett, Callaghan and Rostron along with abrasive mid-fielder Kenny Jackett, ex-Arsenal full-back Pat Rice and goalkeeper Steve Sherwood, were the nucleus of a side that was much the same as the one Barnes had joined two years before, and was now about to make an historic, if fleeting foray into the UEFA Cup. In terms of results, their transition from a work-manlike Second Division outfit to Championship runners-up was a tribute to the club, the players, to Taylor and the Random Chance method.

But although Barnes was a vital member of the Watford side, did he flourish because of the approach Watford employed or in spite of it? Barnes was the man who could unzip your defence at the drop of a hat. But, for all that, he was not a *central* component in the Watford system. Taylor's method was crude but effective. The mid-field part of the pitch, that sector where the classic teams have done many of their greatest creative deeds, was dispensed with. Watford's attacking strategy was fundamentally long-range and airborne. Their mid-field men were there to disrupt the opposition rather than blind them with science. Welly, run and chase. Hump it forward to Luther's head and then look to pick up the pieces. Barnes and Nigel Callaghan spent much of their time feeding off the big front men, picking up the loose ball and turning it back in to the centre, getting to the byline or having a shot themselves. Though elegant, skilful performers, they often filled the role of scavengers.

In many ways it was an ideal situation for a man of Barnes's aptitudes and experience. He was young, very young at the start, and his obvious assets were pace, athleticism and outstanding skill on the ball. With the physical side of his game accentuated by Taylor's taste for a foot-slogging training regime, Barnes was well equipped to keep plugging away down the touchline, covering long distances at speed and then doing something priceless if and when the ball finally reached the ground. The tender youth was asked to fill an important role, but not a particularly responsible one. What was required of Barnes was that he let his flair speak for itself. Whenever the chance arose, he was encouraged to go past players, to perform spectacular feats and score dramatic goals. The nuts and bolts of the system were taken care of somewhere else. Barnes's job was to capitalize on the spin-offs from the Random Chance method transforming sow's ears into silk purses. For a teenage prodigy, it was about as carefree a commission as a top-class professional footballer gets. But while it suited Taylor's pragmatic pattern for Barnes to be employed as outrider and flashing blade, it is debatable whether so simplistic a function was in the best interests of his development as a player.

As Barnes worked his way into Bobby Robson's Under-21 team and then his senior side, Taylor came to expect a little more. He did not consider his star player to be sufficiently consistent. The easy-going attitude which had always helped Barnes to be accepted in the white footballing environment, became identified by Taylor as part of the problem. If things were going badly, it was Barnes to whom Taylor looked to instigate an improvement. It didn't always come. It sometimes seemed to Taylor that Barnes just wasn't that interested. The prospect of defeat did not seem to galvanize him. The fear of failure did not show in his eyes. Barnes has subsequently commented on Taylor's exasperation: 'We had long conversations about what he called my laid-back attitude,' he told the *Sunday Times Magazine*; 'He was really asking whether it was part of my West Indian upbringing.' Barnes's interpretation is consistent with a comment made by Taylor in 1987 to the *Independent* about Andy Gray, a black player who he by then managed at Aston Villa: 'Like a lot of lads with a West Indian background, he's a free spirit. You don't want to lose that, because now and again he'll hit an old-fashioned diagonal ball that will take your breath away. But I'm trying to stop him running about all over the place to get the ball . . . I want him to come off tired from mental application, rather than just plain knackered.'

Taylor employs the term 'free spirits' without malice, his perspective suggesting the benign face of a football philosophy which has, nonetheless, often worked against the full development of black players since their first innocent steps into the post-war English football fray.

The game did not exactly throw down a welcome mat. Black footballers found themselves assailed by white hostility and hamstrung by white assumptions. Brendon Batson can reel those off without thinking: 'no bottle, unreliable, don't like training, don't like the cold . . . All those ignorant views that have got no foundation whatsoever.' The idea that black people are somehow innately temperamentally wilful remains alarmingly widespread in the professional game, a continuing, stubborn presence despite an avalanche of evidence to the contrary. But then racism does not respond readily to logic. It is not, at root, a rational disease. A popular selection philosophy evolved among managers and coaches: because 'they' liked showing off and could not be relied on in defence, the best thing was to stick 'them' out on the wing where, because of course 'they' can run faster, 'they' might do something flashy once in a while. This weight of negative expectation was accentuated by the climate within the professional game that had developed after the Second World War. Bertie Mee looks back to a pre-war Golden Age when the virtuoso was fêted, his inborn talent left to bloom untainted by the dead hand of coaching manuals. The cream of English footballers were seen as representing all that was fine and lusty and heroic in the English working class. These players were applauded, not for their stolidity, but for their poetry and wit. An archetype emerged, romantic, but not without some basis in truth: great men who played for pride, for peanuts and for fun, who lived in a humble terraced dwelling near a pithead near you.

But the immediate post-war period inflicted a series of ruptures on this contented vision of effortless working-class wizardry. In

1945, with Berlin divided and the Cold War coming, Moscow Dynamo, the finest exponents of Soviet soccer, arrived for a prestige British tour. The contests between the mysterious Muscovites and some of England's best teams took on a distinctly jingoistic air, the flames fanned by newspapers whose expanding sports coverage was increasingly coloured by nationalism. Football people took up the theme themselves. And when the Russians comprehensively outclassed all those placed before them – including the mighty Arsenal in front of a full house at Highbury – the response of both newspapers and soccer spokesmen was bitter. Moscow Dynamo played in a very different style – cool, rational and based on strategy and teamwork. It was a measured, scientific approach. The vanquished English football body politic was swift to deride the Soviet style as anodyne and effeminate compared to the vigorous cut and thrust so prized in their own game. It was even claimed that the English teams had been asked not to tackle the Muscovites too hard in the interests of diplomacy.

But, for all this display of bravado, the writing was on the wall: English football had to adapt to a new world of tactics and technocracy, or die. In the years that followed, other changes transformed the nature of top-flight English football. The maximum wage was abolished. The media moved in. The win mentality began to take its grip and a 'professional' ideology evolved which insisted that only those within the game know what is best for the game. It helped to breed an inward-looking vocational philosophy which intensified the inherent conservatism of those who administered and made their living from football. With the success and sensibility of English soccer increasingly bound up with colonialist notions of national character, the first black players to step tentatively on to soccer's stage had a mountain to climb compared to what confronted their white counterparts. No wonder some of them lost heart.

Colonel Barnes puts his finger on it: 'It is to a large extent a question of confidence. Twenty years ago a black youngster brought in to, say, Tottenham for a trial would not have had the confidence because he would be so conscious of the fact that he was the only one! If he got a hard tackle he would not have stood his ground.' The Colonel believes that those days are long gone and in a certain sense, he's right. But it is too easy to pronounce, as players and commentators do, that racism no longer exists in the dressing-room because all everyone wants to do is win so the best players are always picked, never mind the colour of them. What defines 'the best eleven players'? Ask any ten football fans to name the best eleven in England and ten different answers would result. Team selection requires value judgements and these, especially in English football rhetoric, involve far more than an assessment of talent. 'Character', that is the thing, and it is still the widespread belief that black players do not have it: 'you don't want too many of them in your defence. They always want to beat three men instead of clearing it upfield'; 'they're fast, aren't they?'; 'all you've got to do is put a bit of pressure on them, get a goal up, and a bit of dissent creeps in – then they just cave in.' A random selection of casually racist views routinely held and blithely expressed by assorted white football men in This England in the late 1980s – and all of them somewhere involved in the career of John Barnes.

It is a terrible indictment of the intellectual poverty of the football establishment, its media, managers and moguls, that even Pele, the finest player the world has seen, was unable to elude this ludicrous typecasting. The popular belief is that the Brazilian teams of the late fifties, sixties and early seventies were all smiling, samba conjurors who brought the carefree flavour of Copacabana beach to the soccer stadia of the world. Pele is still widely taken to epitomize this 'natural' spontaneity. Yet there are few leagues in the world more physically punishing than those of Brazil. And no player knew how to punish opposing defenders with more concentrated determination than the best-known Brazilian of all. Pele did not only have the talent to take any defence apart but the wisdom to know how to use it. And he was hard – *very* hard. He had a body of steel and a mind like a steel trap. But all anyone can ever talk about are those euphemistic 'silky skills'.

It is against such a philosophical backdrop that we must assess the performances of black players and the periodic complaints that John Barnes is inconsistent, frustrating, lacks the proper temperament – derogatory descriptions routinely applied to Mediterraneans, Latins and blacks, coded metaphors for 'not like the

English'. A 'proper' Englishman is not moody, he is dogged and Teutonic; a 'proper' Englishman is not a magician but a durable exponent of the rearguard action, never more determined than when his ass is backed up against the wall (where, of course, no one can get near it). John Barnes is rather different. He likes to give his ass a shake and swerve his way past three men and still have the ball. He does it as often as, if not more than any other Englishman. The problem is, of course, that he does not manage to do it every time. The weight of expectations is immense, the concealed explanation for his failure to fulfil them is almost invariably bound up with the fact that he is black.

But never mind the evidence of their own eyes. All true, tin-hatted Englishmen know these 'darkies' are soft, inside and out. Add to that the fact that Barnes himself seemed, to a prejudiced eye, to provide a wealth of supporting evidence. Indeed, he *was* fast and skilful. He was also laid-back and inconsistent. He seemed to fit all the requirements of the stereotype.

The irony, of course, is that there could scarcely be a *less* typical black footballer than John Barnes. Not for him the extra daily weight of childhood expectation that someone, sometime, in the playground is going to do their best to kick you in the teeth, that someone, under their breath or behind your back, is calling you 'nigger', 'sambo', 'coon'. Not for the Colonel's son, tended by household servants at the Up Park family home, the niggling pressure of marginalization and exclusion. Not for him a looming future of unemployment and a demoralized underclass existence. As he went through his adolescence, football did not present the sole option for a working life blessed with exhilaration, job satisfaction, personal prestige and handsome material reward. There was no need to fight for that. It was his birthright, not his impossible dream. Football was just one way of claiming it.

It is hardly a surprise, then, that John Barnes sometimes seems free of the 'competitive', 'professional' urge to do or die. The facts of his life insist that if he does not do, he will remain very much alive. The call to duty implicit in the blood, sweat and tears philosophy that Graham Taylor brought to Watford might have struck a chord of militaristic recognition, but the demand for constant uphill struggle is not something familiar to his experience. This is not because black players, be they from Rio, Harare or Brixton, are innately 'free spirits', but because John Barnes is a young man from the Jamaican upper class, cast in an exported English Corinthian mould, for whom one off day on a Saturday afternoon is not the end of the world. That is nothing to do with race, but everything to do with class.

The pragmatic, modern meritocrat like Taylor could never quite figure him out. No amount of cajoling ever seemed to work. But then perhaps the problem with Barnes is that he is a bit too good at doing what he is told. When Bertie Mee compares his touch and flair to those baggy-shorted greatest Englishmen who played before the war, he is talking about those moments when the ball was at their feet. But what about when it wasn't? The distinguished sports journalist Ken Jones remembers Stanley Matthews on those afternoons when he didn't, at first, have things all his own way. 'If Stan couldn't get the ball, he'd go walkabout. He'd go back into defence and get it from there, just move about, leaving space for other people, always keeping the other guy guessing. The same with George Best. Unpredictable. You never knew what he was going to do next. Always thinking, always trying *something*. This is the kind of skill that most players acquire in the playground. But John doesn't seem to understand the way those things work. So when things are going against him, he doesn't know what to do.'

This is the difference between ability and wisdom, between the gifted and those who are shrewd as well. If the failings of Barnes are to do with ability-plus, as Bertie Mee insists, maybe the missing dimension is not a readiness to work, but the cunning required to *make* things work. Barnes is not a rebel. He was always willing to submit himself to the strictures of a system. He just lacked the survivor's savvy to make telling adjustments when the opposition sussed him out. If anything, his role at Watford magnified these shortcomings. The rigidity of the team pattern, the one-dimensional nature of its strategy, did not encourage players to use their heads. Individual initiative was not something players would indulge in lightly under Taylor's authoritarian regime. You didn't work things out for yourself, you did as you were told. Result? On bad days, John Barnes disappeared. 'Enigmatic' was just the politest word people used.

What the England fans see, meanwhile, is not the Caribbean Corinthian with all the ball skills but none of the streetwise ones; instead, just another of these black boys who plays on the wing and doesn't do the business. Watch Barnes playing for England and you do not see a confident man. Quality defenders get the measure of him quickly, forcing him on to his weaker, right, foot, easing him away from the touchline towards the midfield mincer, cutting off his supply. In those glum, anonymous Barnes performances there is a sense of contradiction. Denied the circumstances which enable his gifts to flourish, a fracture emerges between the beautiful ball-player steeped in the Jamaican traditions and a more deferential sensibility, the young man who has got so very used to doing what he was told that initiative and imagination desert him. And then there is that sniping media and those cold-eyed, resentful fans. Barnes puts his foot on the ball and passes back, a maestro gone to waste. The question to be asked is not just what is wrong with Barnes, but what is wrong with the England he represents.

Out of the spotlight, too, the young Watford hero, endured reminders that in many white people's eyes he was just another of 'those blacks'. A few days before the Cup Final, the Colonel flew to England intending to see the game. Father and son agreed to meet in a famous central London sports shop at one o'clock on the day of his arrival. 'I find it very interesting, you know,' said Colonel Barnes. 'I went to this shop and I must have been about fifteen minutes late. When I got there, it's the only time I can remember seeing him being cross in this way. I hadn't seen him in a year or so. But as soon as I walked in, he said, "I'm never going to come into this place again!" That's the first thing he said! There was a young attendant there, near by, and Johnny said to him, in quite a jovial way, "OK, my mate's here, so I'm gonna push off now." And then he said to me that as he'd arrived, there was a young black guy arrested for shoplifting. And the attendant had thought he was this fellow's accomplice. So this guy had said to him, "OK, we've nicked your mate, so you'd better push off too." He said, "I felt so embarrassed that I even went and bought something I didn't need, because every five minutes this guy would come back and say, "Look, I warned you. Your mate's been nicked, and you're gonna get nicked too."

'And you know, I felt two ways about it. First of all, the fact of the matter is, he was playing in the Cup Final in two days' time. If this young guy realized he was Johnny Barnes, playing in the Cup Final for Watford, he would probably have asked for his autograph. But as far as he's concerned, he's just a young black guy who is hanging around doing nothing; therefore he's a shoplifter. But then I said to myself, "Johnny feels a bit hurt about this, but it doesn't do him any harm. Because he's going to be playing in the Cup Final at age nineteen and he may be tempted to believe that he's a superstar, a big shot." Maybe an experience like that just helps you to keep your feet on the ground.'

It is salutary to consider the two separate identities that fame creates for the young, black Englishman. As a star, especially a nice, uncontroversial one, he becomes an honoured human being. Unrecognized, though, he is just another law-and-order problem. The hypocrisy is thrown into repulsive relief by the remarks of a man closely involved with Watford Football Club at the time John Barnes was there: 'Ah, yes, Ken Barnes, a charming man, not only for a Colonel, but for a Jamaican. One feels with him, as with John, that you're not talking to a banana man at all, but a civilized human being.'

PART TWO

Red, Black and Blue

6
'Liverpool is Rich . . .
but Liverpool is Racist'

Every visitor to Liverpool Football Club should inflict upon themselves the half-hour walk from Lime Street station to Anfield. Pick
your way through the one-way system, then up to Hall Lane and on
to the Everton Road. Watch the graffiti change denomination as you
go. On an archway entrance to an estate off Copperas Road, tall
white letters proclaim 'God Bless Our Pope'. Further on, the urban
centre falls away to the rear as you pass a bombsite of a children's
playground splattered with the initials 'EFC', donated by supporters
of Everton Football Club, and 'NF', donated by supporters of the
National Front. The city centre's proud colonial architecture
becomes a memory as you pass the grim Liverpool Provincial
Orange Hall, with its filthy Union Jack flapping from a flagpole
wrapped in barbed wire. The Everton Conservative Club looks like
an abandoned front-line fortress. There is, too, a Catholic church,
the Sacred Heart. 'No Pope', says the pale inscription daubed on its
walls.

Turn right into Breck Road. Post-war council housing estates fall
into the foreground, the white paint peeling, the grass uncut, the
inhabitants whipped by a wind that bursts across the brow of the hill
and snakes its way between the lumps of battered bricks and mortar.
Everything municipal is wrecked. There are shops, and then a
junction with a pub on the corner. At this point, at two o'clock every
other Saturday afternoon between August and May, a left turn on to
Oakfield Road feeds you into a flow of one-way pedestrian traffic.
This is the beginning of Anfield, Liverpool 4, and you are closing in
on the imperial palace of modern English football.

But for most of Anfield's patrons, Oakfield Road is not The Mall
and they are participants in no regal parade. Wiry, pinched,
hunched against the elements, the young men seem to take a
martyr's pride in wearing the minimum of clothes: tight jeans and

tighter T-shirts; the occasional grubby scarf. Proving something to themselves, perhaps, and to their mates. To the right, you can count off the network of back-to-back houses that leads all the way up to the turnstiles of the most famous football terrace in the country. The Spion Kop is named after a hillside in South Africa where, in one Boer War battle, British troops, many of them local, were crammed so close together they were decimated by enemy fire. But at Anfield the warriors live on, resilient, unvanquished, triumphant in their discomfort. Never mind the grime and litter and the boarded-up shops they have to endure *en route*, because, as they sing, 'We're on the march with Kenny's army', and no one can take that away from them. Those who pay their money to pass through the slit in the red brick wall enter into the presence of a glory which, for two cathartic hours, is theirs to celebrate, escalate and share.

To the semi-detached outsider, though, ironies run amok as up to 40,000 of Merseyside's proletariat pour in to worship at the shrine. They are mostly male. Liverpool FC is one of the city's few institutions automatically associated with success in the last ten years. But its wealth is not something to which its public can lay claim. The players who represent them are paid a basic weekly wage of over £1,000 and some, long-serving and pensioned up to the eyeballs, earn several times that amount. Yet the city of Liverpool has passed into the popular consciousness as a symbol of the worst unemployment, the deepest political crises and the bleakest social problems in the nation. Poverty is not a new condition for the citizens of Liverpool. A lack of self-confidence is, at least this side of the war. Contemporary citizens of this uniquely charismatic northern city have a habit these days of buttonholing visitors and asking what they think of the place: 'So do you like it here, then?' Bus drivers, shopkeepers and barmen all want to know. There is a rhetorical expectation in the question, but also a defensive edge. Twenty years ago, legend tells us, there was no need for Liverpudlians to seek such reassurance. They *knew* they were the best. They had the best buildings, the best pop groups, the best smart-assed one-liners and an economic past to piss on even London's finest.

The football teams weren't bad either. Over on the other side of Stanley Park, Everton had won the FA Cup in 1966 with a 3–2 beating of Sheffield Wednesday, one of the most memorable post-war finals. In the same year, Liverpool had provided Roger Hunt for Alf Ramsey's triumphant World Cup-winning side. Winger Ian Callaghan, who played one game, and full-back Gerry Byrne had also been in the squad. Gordon Milne and Peter Thompson were within an ace of inclusion too. The prominence of Liverpool players in the World Cup campaign was a marvellous tribute to the work of manager Bill Shankly since he came to the club from Huddersfield Town in December 1959 and transformed it into a monument to Liverpudlian pride.

When Shankly arrived at Anfield he found complacency, inertia and decay. The team were a moderate force in the Second Division, with a tatty ground, poor training facilities, little ambition and a board of directors whose pockets were deep. But backed by a new and enlightened chairman, local businessman Eric Sawyer, the Scottish protestant from the mining village of Glenbuck took a cleaver to the dead wood all around. The playing staff felt the brunt of its force. In his first year, Shankly got rid of twenty-four players and fought to be given the cash to buy some more – men in his own image to build a team befitting the city it served. Shankly knew what he wanted. He already had Hunt and Callaghan and soon signed Milne, a wing-half, from nearby Preston. But it was north of the border where Shankly found the two men who were the real foundations of the empire he was trying to build. In those days £37,500 was a lot of money, but Shankly persuaded the club to pay it to Motherwell in return for Ian StJohn, a striker with a special dimension of wit, able to make and take goals with equal subtlety. Soon after, Shankly was back in Scotland again, this time chasing a mountainous centre-half, still in his early twenties, called Ron Yeats; £30,000 prised him away from Dundee United. Shankly made him his captain, and for the next quarter of a century the massive 'Red Collosus' would define the character of Liverpool teams – big, hard, impregnable and canny with it. Handle with care.

Liverpool ended the 1961–62 season as Second Division champions, regularly drawing crowds of 40,000 to their home games. Two years later they became Football League champions, the first time for twenty-five years. The following season, 1965, they won the FA Cup, inflicting a 2–1 extra-time defeat on Leeds United, the team who would rival them most strongly as England's supreme football force in the seventies.

But Shankly had set the tone for an era with the first of a succession of Liverpool sides which inspired an extraordinary fervour among its own supporters for reasons which were to do with much more than just goals for and against. Although he was a Scotsman, Bill Shankly exemplified a part of the city's soul of which it was most proud, a part which the Beatles had launched upon the rest of Britain and then the world. By the middle sixties the global image of Merseyside culture had become an infectious blend of caustic wit and working-class grit, a city with a swagger and no room for frills. Shankly, a man whose voice spoke of gravel in his guts and whose eyes betrayed a comic streak that made him a media star, helped define the hard-bitten humanity that enshrined the city in myth. With him as its prime personality, football became as central to the Merseyside legend as its comedians, its poets and its rock 'n' roll bands. All aspects of Liverpool's fame found a common voice on the Spion Kop. Its passion was raw, its humour somehow generous and unforgiving all at once. BBC's *Panorama* documented it as if discovering a lost tribe: it really did sing the songs that Lennon and McCartney wrote, and, most famously of all, the one Gerry and the Pacemakers took to the top of the charts in October 1963 – 'You'll Never Walk Alone'.

But if Liverpool's popular culture was selling an irresistible image to the world, it was one which – as images do – told only a part of the truth about the town. In much the same way as Liverpool and Everton Football Clubs and their fans celebrate a kind of civic solidarity in combat, so the character of the city in which, it seemed, all working Merseysiders shared, belied a history of strife whose legacy lingers, inflamed by the onset of a decline so deep that no amount of bravado can conceal it.

The roots of Liverpool's particularity and self-esteem lay in the Victorian age, when only London could top its turnover as a port. Tony Lane, an ex-merchant seaman, has described the symbols of its economic power:

The city was at its peak in 1910. Victoria, only recently dead, had not long before been translated from mere monarch to Empress. In Liverpool, especially, the promotion must have seemed right. Red-ensigned merchant ships carried half of the whole world's waterborne trade and the most potently famous ships of British mercantile power, the liners of Cunard and the White Star, were operated from grandiose head offices on the Liverpool waterfront. Liverpool was the gateway of the British Empire.

With so much of its male employment centred on the doings at the docks, a large proportion of Liverpool's working-class males became accustomed to irregular wages, long periods away from home, or both. Dockside labour was required or not, according to the arrival and departure of ships. Seafaring men could be out on the water for weeks, on the way to America, the West Indies, Europe and Africa, returning with strange and exotic cargoes, and money in their pockets to burn in bouts of homecoming hedonism. The so-called Victorian values of caution and thrift had little place in the homes of returning seamen, because, with no way of knowing what tomorrow might bring, it was incumbent upon them to make merry while they may. It is a sensibility that survives, made more logical, not less, by the onset of job insecurity on a devastating scale. It is Liverpool's charm and its trauma that nothing can be taken for granted. Often, it has seemed as if only the football teams are winning at home.

But the vagaries of port employment were not the only reasons for Liverpool's volatility and its endlessly shifting population. Its apparent prosperity and opportunities for casual labour made it a magnet for outsiders seeking employment, such as London is for citizens of the beleaguered provinces today. Bill Shankly was not the first Scotsman to bring his labour to Merseyside, or his influence to Liverpool Football Club. Nor was Ron Yeats the last. But the greatest influx of English-speakers were the Irish. It has been calculated that in 1847, between 1 January and 1 June 370,000 Irish men, women and children – one-and-a-half times Liverpool's population at the time – came pouring off the boats in flight from the potato famine, bringing with them typhus, cholera, starvation

... and Catholicism. This to a town where 12 July is still celebrated with Orange Parades and the ancient Anglican cathedral looks across at its modernist Catholic counterpart, with a chill, Calvinist air.

But in today's Liverpool, religious sectarianism is a shadow of its former self and footballing affiliations have corresponded only fleetingly to those of faith. Liverpool is much like Glasgow, but not in this respect. There the situation is clear-cut: Celtic is the team of the Catholics, Rangers that of the Protestants. To this day, Rangers, traditionally the most insular of British football clubs, do not field Roman Catholic players despite the arrival of a revolutionary management regime that has imported a string of Englishmen. Celtic have been less set in their ways, and there is a joke about the first Protestant to play for them in an 'Old Firm' Glaswegian Derby. For the first forty-five minutes, the Rangers fans set about the new man with a vengeance, taunting him even more mercilessly than the rest of the Celtic team. At half-time, the Protestant slumped on to his bench, astounded at the fervour of the hatred directed at him. 'Don't worry,' said one of his team-mates; 'You get used to it.' 'It's all right for you to say that,' replied the Protestant. 'You *are* a fucking Fenian bastard.'

On Merseyside, though, the roots of both big clubs can be traced back to the very same church. The man who first brought football to Anfield was a local businessman and politician called John Houlding. His field of enterprise was brewing, his political leanings Conservative and Unionist.

In the beginning there was no Liverpool Football Club. Its jagged line of descent starts with the formation of St Domingo's Football Club in 1878, a recreational affiliate of a new Methodist church in the area. The club proved popular, took on a life of its own and changed its name to attract players from a wider catchment area. It re-christened itself Everton, after the district it served. A new pitch was secured when Houlding negotiated the use of a nearby field owned by fellow brewer, John Orrell, in exchange for a small rent. Houlding went on to become the dominant figure at this newborn Everton FC and remained so until 1892. It was then that he fell into dispute with the other members of the club over an increase in the rent. The malcontents upped and left, and purchased new premises for themselves at nearby Goodison Park where Everton Football Club has remained ever since. Houlding, then, was left with a football pitch, but no team. His response was to recruit a whole new set of players with the help of his colleague, John McKenna, an Irish Conservative and Freemason, who signed up a string of mainly Irish Glaswegians drawn from both sides of that city's religious divide. With them, Houlding set up another club at the Anfield ground and call it Liverpool Football Club. Effectively, then, the same Orangeman went down in history as the founder of both the Merseyside giants.

Despite the split, close links have been maintained between the two clubs ever since. On his death, Houlding's coffin was borne by players from both sides, and over the years, a substantial number of players have turned out for both clubs, including several of current or recent vintage: Steve McMahon, Kevin Sheedy, Dave Watson, David Johnson. As for their shared denominational roots, neither side has imposed any hard-and-fast rule. Many of Shankly's 1965 Cup-winning side – among them Chris Lawler, Tommy Smith and Gerry Byrne – were local Catholics. But, predictably, both boardrooms have remained strongholds of local Toryism, while on the playing side a robust Scottish Protestant ethic has been passed down, via Shankly, through generations of iconic hard men from Yeats and former Rangers half-back Willie Stevenson, to Graeme Souness and so on to the key figure of the current regime – it is hard to imagine Kenny Dalglish at Mass.

There was a period when Everton became identified as the team the Catholics supported. It probably peaked in the fifties when their side contained a large number of imported Irishmen. Tommy Smith, educated at a Catholic school, was told by his headmaster that he was going to 'the wrong club'. One Liverpool fan of the same generation, born and raised a Catholic, attributes his deviation from the rule to a rebellious father whose twelve older siblings had all followed the blue party line. Many fans of both teams are aware of this unwritten tradition, whether they conform to it or not. Even as recently as November 1988, a piece of graffiti scrawled above a turnstile at the Anfield Road end read: 'No Fenian Twats'. A city's bigotry does not die overnight.

*

You can ask them about that in Liverpool 8. Speak with the people who live there, the black and the white, and they will tell you that one division in the city of Liverpool remains as razor sharp as the religious divide is now blurred. Everyone knows about the Liverpool of myth, but did anybody know, before the summer of 1981, that a part of Liverpool was black? That was when the borough of Toxteth, where Liverpool 8 is contained, became a synonym for 'riot'. Black Liverpool's invisibility to the wider world was an index of its exclusion from the rest of the city's social and economic life. And as Liverpool lore went global a quarter of a century ago, so its public profile remained exclusively Caucasian. And that went for the football culture too.

In the sixties, you could count the black footballers in the top flight of the entire Football League on the fingers of one hand. Ironically – and perhaps tellingly – the two First Division clubs whose teams were not exclusively white were those whose supporters later earned reputations for containing substantial racist minorities, Leeds United and West Ham. The Yorkshire club had two ex-patriate South Africans, Gerry Francis and, far better known, the diminutive winger Albert Johanneson who played in the 1965 Cup Final against Liverpool. Johanneson was a quick, slight, delightfully skilful player but he had a reputation as a faint-heart. Chris Lawler, who marked him for Liverpool at Wembley, recalls being instructed to put Johanneson under physical pressure early in the game, to mark him closely and stop him getting the ball: 'that's what I was told to do, you know. 'Cos if you did let him play, he *would* play – he was very quick. But if you put pressure on him, he'd pack in. He did get abuse from other players. It was too much for him.' This added to the tension of the occasion made the South African crumble. The other Leeds men did little to assist Johanneson. They just moaned. There were no substitutes in those days and Johanneson's broken spirit effectively reduced them to ten men.

What nobody ever thought about was the ordeal Johanneson faced playing with white men at all. An upbringing under the cosh of apartheid had taught Johanneson deference. He even touched a metaphorical forelock to the Elland Road groundsman when he wanted to do a spot of extra training on the pitch. In 1964, a British-made movie called *Zulu* went on general release, detailing the resistance of British troops to a bunch of African 'savages'. That season, Johanneson turned out for Leeds against Everton at Goodison Park. The Merseyside fans, taking their cue from the film, bombarded Johanneson with their version of Zulu chants and plenty of nasty remarks. There is a famous clock at one end of the Goodison ground, whose face carries a selection of adverts. After the game, one of the Leeds players remarked that Johanneson could have recited every word of the copywriter's text, so anxiously had he willed the hands to tick round to the final whistle.

At West Ham in the sixties, there was a black full-back, John Charles, and Clyde Best was in Ron Greenwood's side for several seasons from 1969, a powerful striker and a Bermudan international who had been brought to the club's attention by his home country's national coach. He has been described as a ringer for Sonny Liston. He had the face and the physique. But Best was a self-effacing man, with little of the legendary American boxer's belligerence. He was a constant target for racial abuse from the terraces and from opposing players. Like Johanneson, he had a tendency to disappear from games. His diffidence dissuaded him from making a fuss.

Best was capable of brilliance and he became an early role model for a new generation of black British youth. However, neither he nor Johanneson were, of course, typical of the nation's black population. The majority of these citizens had arrived in the fifties as immigrants from the West Indies, uninitiated in the 'mother country's' ways and with their sights set on higher things for their sons than careers in professional football. Brendon Batson, who came to England at the age of nine, believes that many parents earnestly dissuaded their sons. He remembers the family pressures on him to find what they considered a more respectable way of life: 'My mum had no idea what it meant to be a professional footballer. She was very concerned about where my future lay. When I was getting married, my wife's father, who still lives in Grenada, said, "Well, how's he going to earn a living?" And while there's always been the talent there, parents would actively deflect their children from going into professional football.'

Liverpool, though, was another country. Six per cent of the present population are black, and the roots of that community were established in the south of the city at least a century ago. Its founders were West African sailors who disembarked in Liverpool and decided to stay. Post-war immigration from the Caribbean simply boosted a black population for whom scouse was already the universal language and football was the game that young men played, on the streets and in the parks and playgrounds. And yet black Liverpool did not feel that it *belonged*. The familiar grim patterns of discrimination had long been set in place, in housing, in employment, in all facets of social mobility and social life. Nowhere did this exclusion become more glaring than on the hallowed turf and teeming terraces of Anfield and Goodison Park, the arenas of Merseyside self-esteem. Black Liverpool was conspicuous by its absence, not just a numerical incongruity but a symbol of a diminished way of life.

But this was just one more chapter in a longer, bleaker story. The wealth of Victorian Liverpool did not come from nowhere. It, like the original citizens of Liverpool 8, came from Africa and it came in human form – as slaves. Thomas Jefferson, the founding father of Liverpool, was a slave trader. No city in Europe could rival Liverpool as a slave port, a key geographical point in a triangle of misery linking Africa, England and the Americas. The trade was enormously profitable. The gains from it underwrote the banking system, the great textile industries and all that generated surplus value in this metropolis of the north. Today, that crucial chapter of Liverpool's history is written out of the official civic memory. Ferdinand Dennis, in his book *Behind The Frontlines*, noted that the municipal museums have documented the slave trade either apologetically or not at all. He continued: 'The slave trade, of course, benefited the whole of Britain. Not all, though, appreciated that George Frederick Cooke, an eighteenth-century tragedian, was one. Booed and hissed by a Liverpool theatre audience one night, he retorted: "I have not come here to be insulted by a set of wretches, of which every brick in your infernal town is cemented with an African's blood." Cooke's dissatisfied audience fell silent.

And it is a silence which still seems to pervade Liverpool today. The past is not only another country, but it is one too far away to be seen.'

Bill Shankly was a trader too, and a businessman, though of a very different kind. Even so, the upshot of his dealings confirmed the invisibility of black Liverpool. One of the greatest changes he made was in persuading his directors to let him go into the transfer market. But of the eleven white men who walked out at Wembley to play Leeds in 1965, five were native Liverpudlians – Byrne, Callaghan, Hunt, Lawler and Smith – and of the other six, two more – Gordon Milne and Peter Thompson – had been brought from nearby Preston North End. So, Yeats, StJohn and others nothwithstanding, English north-westerners dominated the team. But there were no black Liverpudlians riding down Wembley Way to represent their city that day. Throughout the seventies, as Liverpool asserted itself as a financial as well as a footballing power, the side was still well blessed with locally born players. The club captain till 1980 was centre-back Phil Thompson, a wiry son of Kirkby and proud of it. There was Terry McDermott who joined via Newcastle, establishing himself under Shankly's successor, Bob Paisley, as one of the most subtle midfield passers in the League. Jimmy Case, like Thompson, was a product of the Anfield youth policy, an authentic Liverpool hard man in midfield with a ferocious right-foot shot. Of the twelve who went out to represent Liverpool against Manchester United in the 1977 FA Cup Final, seven – Smith, Case, McDermott, Johnson, Callaghan and the flying winger Steve Heighway – where drawn from Liverpool and district, while Joey Jones had been signed from nearby Wrexham and Emlyn Hughes was Barrow-born and purchased from Lancastrian neighbours Blackpool. All of them were white. And though a son of immigrants, Viv Anderson, was on the brink of being capped for England, though Batson, Regis and Cunningham were putting West Bromwich Albion on the map, though black players were filtering through the youth ranks and into the first teams of most of the top London clubs, and blacks were actually becoming statistically over-represented in the professional game, Liverpool did not have a black player even remotely in contention.

There weren't many in the crowd either, fewer, even, than at most League clubs. And it is on the terraces of Anfield and Goodison Park that we find the clearest clues as to why there were none on the park. At Everton, the 1966 FA Cup win is remembered for the solo winning goal by winger Derek Temple. But the other two, the ones that brought Everton back to level after Sheffield Wednesday had taken an unexpected two-goal lead, were scored by a little inside-forward signed from Plymouth Argyle for £20,000 – Mike Trebilcock.

A Cornishman, Trebilcock's racial make-up seems to have remained a mystery to his fellow players. He was dark-skinned but not very, not so you would automatically think of him as black. His hair, though, was black and curly. He has been described as a 'coffee-coloured Cornishman', whose looks indicated that the Spanish influence characteristic of his native county's genotype was particularly pronounced in his case. Whatever, to some of his more vocal home supporters, he looked black enough to have a special song bestowed upon him: 'We've got the best nigger in the land'. Compliments do not come much more backhanded than that. It expressed an attitude which sent a clear message to the black citizens of Liverpool 8: 'Keep Out'. Trebilcock played only a handful of games for Everton before emigrating to Australia. His heroism is largely forgotten now, and his name lives on as an uneasy footnote in the history of Everton FC, the forgotten man who saved them from the jaws of a Wembley defeat.

The acute colour-consciousness of the Goodison scene had manifested itself before and it concerned one of the greatest goal-scorers English football has ever seen. In the 1927–28 season, centre forward William Dean scored a total of 60 goals, a record which has never been beaten. Dean is better known by his nick-name, 'Dixie', not, however, a moniker he cared for. In fact he detested it. He insisted that 'Billy' was how he should be addressed, and anyone calling him 'Dixie' to his face was likely to be corrected. The received wisdom is that he earned the con-tentious nickname because of his complexion and crinkly hair. The term 'Dixie' derives from the southern United States where, at that time, the black population was concentrated, an impoverish-ed pool of cheap rural labour. When people called William Dean 'Dixie', they were not always being polite, and Dean once recalled being the target of a racist remark from a Tottenham supporter. Friends and relatives of Dean have since indicated that 'Dixie' was actually a corruption of a childhood nickname, 'Digsy'. Yet the widely held explanation for the 'Dixie' variation seems to speak for itself.

What then of Liverpool FC and its swaying, singing tribute to Liverpudlian togetherness, the massed ranks of raw-boned English warriors, on the famous Spion Kop? The name of that immortal terrace was not the club's only South African connection. The long history of trading and colonial links with the Boer regime was manifested in a succession of Liverpool line-ups with a number of white South Africans turning out for the first team between the wars. Goalkeeper Arthur Riley toured Britain with the South African national team in 1925 and signed as a deputy to the legendary Elisha Scott. In 1926, Gordon Hodgson arrived and set a club goal-scoring record that remained unbroken until Roger Hunt broke it in 1961–62. The winger Berry Nieuwenhuys joined in 1933 and was still playing after the Second World War, making 236 League appearances in all. Liverpool signed at least six other white South Africans in the twenties and thirties, all on the recommendation of an agent they had working in that country.

The sixties came, the Beatles came and Shankly came. Liverpool FC geared up for a quarter century of imperious success. Ron Yeats led the Reds out at Anfield to droves of white Liverpudlians and a tiny handful of intrepid blacks keeping their fingers crossed. There was one black kid called Paul and he was football-mad: 'At an early age I was only really interested in football. And like most children, I was only really interested in supporting Liverpool or Everton. I supported Liverpool because my brother was a Liverpool supporter. At that time, Jimmy Melia was playing, and Ian StJohn, Milne, Callaghan, Yeats, Thompson. I used to go a lot.'

Today, Paul is a social science student and community activist. He was born in Liverpool 8, but much of his childhood was spent with his family – mum, dad, two brothers and a sister – in Norris Green, a grim, dishevelled district in the north end of the city. Paul's early life was not typical of black Liverpudlians, because Norris Green is decidedly white, whereas Liverpool 8 is mixed. Because of that, most of Paul's friends were white. He would go off to Anfield with them on Saturday afternoons and stand in the boys' pen with all these other white kids he didn't know. The impact of his experiences there has stayed with him: 'I don't think there was an occasion when I did not have to defend myself – *physically* defend myself.'

Paul had not gone to Anfield with his eyes wide open. His upbringing, as one of the only black family in a white part of town, presented him with a dilemma. He could accept a situation in which no day of his life would pass without some white peer or other calling him 'nigger', an insult that lands with the full weight of centuries of degradation, dehumanization and terrorization behind it. He could, in theory, have taken it on the chin and done so till the day he died. Or else he could take issue with that situation. He could decide that no one had the right to subject him to a goading reminder of the things that word implied, and the threat implicit in them. Paul chose the latter course. He pursued it at school, on the street and on the Anfield terraces.

But there was a price to pay. 'I had a grounding in not having the support of black people around me. I had learned to stand up and defend myself. So to make the transition from the black environment to the white environment, I had to go through a character change. I had to assume a machoistic tendency instead of the humanitarian one of getting along with my fellow human beings. And of course, in white quarters I became to be regarded as someone who was carrying a chip on my shoulder, that I had some point to prove. That wasn't the case. But I found that the more macho assertion I could give off, the more respect I got and the easier time I had. The racist remarks, the racist actions would prevail, but they became less overt.'

Paul described the informal racial geography of Liverpool, the unwritten rules designating those parts of the city which blacks had learned to regard as potentially most hostile. He used the word 'apartheid'. It was not, he explained, a term he employed lightly, and he justified his use of it with examples of what happened to himself and other black people who breached the colour line that was not, officially, there. There was always a choice to be made.

Paul could, for example, accept a nightclub bouncer denying his entry after half a dozen of his white mates had already gone in. He could, after all, just hang about outside. Or he could argue about it. And if he did decide to argue, well, perhaps he would finally get his way, which might make it easier for other black people to get in in future; and so on, one dogfight at a time. Or maybe the police would come and take them away, and everyone would say, "Well, you know what these blacks are like."'

'Among my age group at that time, this was very prevalent,' said Paul. 'Anything you were alleged to have done, you inevitably ended up being charged with. If I had any ten black friends sitting here with us now, there would be maybe two who hadn't been to prison following some trouble or disorder with the police. And these people are no different from me, in that they are able to converse and articulate how they feel. They are able to defer gratification. You know . . . they are not barbaric. And it is a bit unnerving when you look round at those peers and realize that most of them have been through some form of corrective institution. And I'll bet you ten to one that my father was more of a disciplinarian towards me than yours was towards you.'

Paul describes a Liverpool experience that does not fit with the Liverpool legend. There was no black input into the tenets of the ubiquitous scouseology that was Liverpool's biggest export in the sixties. 'Liverpool is racist,' Paul said, quietly, 'but the people do not think of themselves as racist. And it's sad, because the people here are rich . . . rich in their own sense of being Liverpudlian, and this goes for black Liverpudlians, or Irish Liverpudlians, people that have their roots in Scotland, or Arabs and Chinese. There are Chinese that speak just the same scouse as me or a white counter-part. The language and culture of Liverpool is one that is unique in Britain because the people here have struggled. They have always been able to ask questions. They've always been enquiring and do not just accept the statements of authority as necessarily valid. And they gain knowledge through this enquiry. They learn from verbal experience, because they don't take everything as read.

'But it is difficult for me to talk about my upbringing in Liverpool when I'm a black scouser. I identify with both those things, because that's what I am. But you belong more with your blackness than with your Liverpool accent, because you don't have a sense of belonging to the framework defined by the accent. You're intrinsically bound to being just on the periphery. So I'm proud that I'm black, firstly. And secondly, I'm proud to be Liverpudlian. I cannot say more or less than that. And white people retort by saying that black people are racist . . . Black people can be *prejudiced* but they can't be racist. And when there is prejudice, it is born out of years and years and years of suffering. And denial. Which makes them feel inferior. Some black people *do* feel inferior, and others feel intimidated. Whatever else, you just don't feel equal, you don't feel *right*. And the people who carry these labels are the same ones who were fighting in two world wars. My father was a merchant seaman delivering cargo during that period. My mother's brother was killed, torpedoed. Her other brothers served in the navy. My grandfather served in the First World War. So our involvement here is just as great as our white counterparts. We've died. But what have we inherited, for all that dying?'

Not a seat in the Anfield grandstand. Not a place on the terraces either, unless you enjoy having to spend a good part of your time looking about you to see who was shouting this or throwing that or trying to pick a fight. 'I stopped going,' shrugged Paul. 'I found that it was an intolerable situation to find yourself in, when you were prone to racial abuse from all sections of the ground, from *both* sets of supporters. It just defeated the object of going there.'

The crowds at Anfield and Goodison Park celebrate their sense of being Liverpudlian, an identity bound up with decade upon decade of heels dug in against the odds, of perennial survival that is not quaint or glamorous at all. It is a matter of profound tragedy that running through those Saturday afternoon exhibitions of solidarity there is a distorting streak of brutality which confuses working-class Liverpudlian staying power with ignorant, lumpen white power. It is a definition of whiteness that underpins the isolation of black Liverpool from the humour, the poetry, the music, the football.

Stand in Liverpool's central shopping precinct any Saturday morning and see how long it takes before you see your tenth black citizen, as white Liverpool mills around you in droves. You do not see six in every hundred. You do not see sixty out of the thousand shoppers the eye can take in at a glance. Even in the fast-food burger bars, which, in most major British cities, have become black employment ghettos, you will be lucky to see more than one person scooping French fries into cartons who is not white. Then, at two o'clock, take a ride up to Oakfield Road and back to the one-way pedestrian traffic, hustling, heads down, towards Anfield football ground and try the numbers game again. It will take a long time to get to ten. There is a passion for football in black Liverpool, but you'll be lucky to get a whiff of it round here. You need to go to Liverpool 8 for that – and a flavour of the greatest staying-power of all.

7

'The White Nigger'

An unofficial resident artist has painted all the street name plates in Liverpool 8 the Rastafarian colours of red, green and gold. He did it in the months following the 1981 uprising, after the riot police had retreated from the streets and Michael Heseltine had gone back to his country house in Surrey. The symbolic implication of the artist's action hardly needs spelling out. It is hard to hold a conversation with the citizens of Liverpool 8, black or white, and remain oblivious to a deep-seated militancy that is their response to too many years labouring under a stigma they do not deserve.

It is a sensibility which informs the Liverpool 8 football scene too. Its most illustrious representatives in recent years have been a Liverpool and District Sunday League team called Almithak who completed the 1987–88 season victorious in all three local competitions they entered and also reached the quarter-finals of the Football Association's national Sunday knock-out cup. Almithak are just the latest in a line of powerful amateur sides from the south end of the city, going back at least to the early sixties when a succession of teams named after pubs and community centres developed formidable reputations in the local leagues. The Windsor, Stanley House, The Bedford, who also won the coveted Sunday treble: these are just the names which emerge most frequently from the folk memories of Liverpool 8's unsung soccer enthusiasts.

Almithak were born of a merger between Saana FC, who represented Liverpool's Yemeni community, and Dingle Rail, a team sponsored by a nearby British Rail station who won the FA Sunday Cup in 1981. The bizarre genesis of Almithak is a reflection of the difficulty teams from Liverpool 8 have in attracting the kind of financial backing they need for kit, balls, travel and the other expenses of running an amateur side. It was the interest of Yemenia Airlines that prompted both the merger and the name. In return for

1 Barnes in classic dribbling action versus Tottenham Hotspur,
26 March 1989.

2a The Colonel's boy in his first season at Watford, 1981–82.

2b A shot at goal versus Everton, FA Cup Final, 1984.

3 A winter fixture with Watford, sporting the gloves favoured by some players to combat extremes of cold.

4 Peter Beardsley and John Barnes behind the Kop on the eve of their first season at Anfield. Note the 'NF' insignia scrawled on the noticeboard.

5a National Front graffiti on the Kop's entrance gates, summer 1986, some months before the speculation that Barnes might join Liverpool.

5b More racist graffiti on the Kop's red-brick outer walls. 'Munich 58' is a goading celebration of the plane crash that killed a number of Manchester United players.

6 Kenny Dalglish, pensive in the manager's dugout.

7a Howard Gayle playing for Liverpool against Bayern Munich,
22 April 1981.

7 Disdain? Resignation? Contempt? A shaven-headed Barnes
backheels a banana off the Goodison Park pitch during the second
half of the 5th round FA Cup tie against Everton,
21 February 1988.

8a A corner kick taken in the full glare of the Anfield arena.

8b Scouse hero: Peter Beardsley runs back as Barnes, with Nigel Spackman, is mobbed by Anfield pitch invaders after a Liverpool goal in the acrimonious 3–3 draw with Manchester United, 4 April 1988.

9 One of Barnes's first games in a Liverpool shirt, a pre-season friendly away to
Celtic, 9 August 1987.

10 In full flight.

11 Barnes flummoxes two Wimbledon defenders in League action, a feat he
   rarely repeated during the Cup Final later in the season.

12a Goal: Barnes beats Southampton goalkeeper Burridge for the opening strike
in a 2–2 away draw, 12 December 1987. Barnes scored Liverpool's second too.

12b The Newcastle posse piles in.

13a A Chelsea defender does the 'professional' thing.

13b Mudlarking at Vicarage Road as Barnes returns to Watford, 13 February 1988. Liverpool won handsomely, 4–1.

14 (Main picture) Parading the League Championship trophy.
(Inset) Despair that he cannot do the same with the FA Cup.

15a Barnes of England, selected to
play against Brazil in Rio's
Maracana Stadium, 9 June 1984.

15b On the way to defeat against
Holland, European Championship,
15 June 1988.

15c Glory in the Maracana, Barnes's finest hour in the national team.

16a Pre-match confidence in the Anfield dressing room, 1987–88 season.

16b Barnes's apprehension shows as a police officer instructs referee Roger
Lewis to halt the 1989 FA Cup Semi-Final against Nottingham Forest at
Hillsborough. In the shocked aftermath of football's worst tragedy, Barnes's
concern for the bereaved confirmed his personal popularity among many
thousands of Merseysiders.

a spot of financial underwriting, the team assumed the moniker of a Yemeni town, ostensibly a kind of Anglo-Arabic twinning arrangement. From time to time, observers from the Yemeni embassy turn up to check on Almithak's progress and report back home. They must be delighted with the results, but Almithak's success owes little to the Middle East. Their powerful chemistry cannot be explained without reference to the spiritual condition of living in Liverpool 8. For the black players in the team, the experience of racism is fundamental to their outlook on the game. Their visits to Anfield as spectators have done little to discourage it.

'I used to go to every evening game,' said one player, winger Stevie Joel. 'When they played, say, Tottenham when Garth Crooks was playing, he'd get a hell of a lot of abuse. I used to stand there with a couple of mates and you'd feel half an inch high. And I'd paid money to go there and watch. It got to the stage where I used to look at the fixture list and if Liverpool were playing someone who I knew *didn't* have a black player in their team, I'd go. But if they were playing someone who *did*, I wouldn't. Because you can't fight 40,000 people.'

Eugene Lam plays on the left side of Almithak's midfield, a man whose industry and determination would endear him to any set of supporters. He too had learned, back in the seventies, that Anfield was not a happy place for a black person to be: 'I can remember a time when a few of us was there and the other team had maybe two black players. And the Liverpool fans started chanting and shouting at them and then started doing it to us. It seemed like half of Liverpool was pointing at them on the pitch and then pointing at us. It's not a nice feeling at all.'

Almithak's player–manager Steve Skeete had his bad times as a teenager too. He remembers going to Anfield, a red scarf round his neck, cheering on the home team with everybody else. So far so good. Afterwards, though, it was a different story. 'I'm outside, looking for the number 27 bus, and I hear them: "Get the nigger!" They ran me from Anfield, all the way up to Hall Lane, about a hundred of them ... Liverpool fans. The same team that I was supporting.'

Skeete is a veteran of the victorious Dingle Rail side of 1981.

Before that, he had turned out as a youngster with Stanley House alongside Paul, the self-defined 'black scouser' who grew up in Norris Green but later moved down to Liverpool 8. Paul's surname is Gayle. His younger brother, a kid called Howard, was Skeete's best friend. Between them, the two youngsters built quite a reputation for themselves. 'Me and Howard was so good,' reflects Skeete, dispensing with false modesty, 'we'd end up dribbling *each other* to see who'd score the most. We'd already beat the other team.' Howard Gayle was a winger, skilful, strong and very, very quick. Skeete, a tall, lean man, whose size had earned him the nickname 'Bull', was his partner in attack. Lobbied by the Stanley House manager one of Liverpool's scouting staff invited Gayle and Skeete for trials. Soon they found themselves asked along to Melwood, Liverpool's training ground, to work with other youth team pretenders a couple of nights a week.

The trips to Melwood were major events, not simply because of the connection with such a famous club, but because it required a journey to the wrong side of town. Even the briefest foray outside of home territory could not be embarked upon lightly. 'We couldn't go out of Liverpool 8 without there being five or six of us together,' says Skeete. 'We couldn't go beyond Smithdown Road without fighting with the skinheads down there. So it had to be a group of you. And then the police would be thinking you were up to no good. That's how bad it was in them days.' It was no surprise, then, that when Skeete and Gayle turned up at Melwood they stuck out like sore thumbs. 'There was only me and Howard. We was the only two black guys there. We knew a lot of the other lads from playing against them, but, you know, we felt a bit out of place. We'd never been anywhere like that before. We were only used to our own teams out on Sefton Park.'

Skeete's relationship with Liverpool FC was short-lived. Part of this he blames upon himself. 'I missed the odd training session. I might go on the Tuesday night and miss the Thursday. I was probably messing with some girl or whatever. Then I stopped going altogether.'

There was more to it than that, though. Skeete had a perspective, an attitude about himself, about life and how he was going to deal with it. Mirroring, as it did, the combative realities of his everyday existence, the same absolute necessity to contend with bitter experience that Paul Gayle described, it was not a sensibility likely to endear him to an establishment as white and conservative as Liverpool FC. 'I was put at centre-half, and that was too easy. I wanted to score goals, be where the glory was.' Skeete lived up to his nickname. As a young man he bulled himself up. 'I used to think I was better than anyone I was playing against, and anyone playing in Liverpool Reserves.' But he was put in the B team or A team, junior XIs, basically 3rd and 4th teams where raw prospects are tested out. 'I thought to myself, "I'm wasting my time here, man." Maybe my attitude was wrong. I don't know. But I feel my face didn't fit. I think a lot of it is down to that even this day now. Your face has got to fit. Don't matter how good you are on the field.' Skeete believes there is a moral to this story, but his own pride demands that you have to coax it out of him. 'At that time, in 1974, I would say it was a white face. I don't know about now. But back then I would.'

Not long after, Skeete got an offer from Manchester City to go and train with them. At Maine Road, right in the heart of Moss Side, a black youth did not need to look around and ask himself deep and troubling questions about why he seemed to be the only one, and wonder what that might say about his chances of making the grade.

At Man. City it was great,' Skeete recalls. 'Dave Bennett, he was there. Roger Palmer, Alex Williams. There was at least half a dozen black players already. I felt more at home and I stayed for like, six months. These were guys of my own age that I could associate with and feel comfortable with, and that was really important, especially at that time.' Dave Bennett went on to make his name as the architect of Coventry City's famous Cup Final victory over Tottenham Hotspur in 1987. Alex Williams represented Manchester City in goal, becoming the first black man to wear the green jersey in the entire Football League. Steve Skeete, meanwhile, was substituted in a Manchester City youth game after a spot of heavy partying the night before. 'In the previous couple of months, I'd been getting fed up. Were they going to offer me a contract or not? Then they took me off in this game. I could not believe it. Me, being a spoiled little brat, I got changed, went back to the club, got me apprentice's money – £65 a week, or something – got off and didn't go back.'

Maybe Skeete paid the price for his bullishness. But as he puts it himself, 'It was pride more than anything. They seem to want to hold you back. That's what I felt, even at Man. City. They only want to tie you up to them so that you're under their control, so you do what they say. And a black man won't accept that. You've got to fight for your freedom,' he explained, with a shrug.

Such fierce independence might not win the approval of white football professionals. But Liverpool 8 has learned that it is part of the armoury of survival. As Paul Gayle's younger brother was to learn, professional football set up a tension between personal dignity and career success. It was not one that could be easily resolved.

Initially, Howard Gayle fared better at Liverpool than Steve Skeete. He battled his way through the Youth team, into the A and B teams, then the Reserves and, in 1977, he became the first black player to sign as a professional for the club. At Anfield, it was a time of change and anticipation, with Liverpool on the brink of becoming the mightiest football force on the continent. Bill Shankly had retired and his long-serving deputy, Bob Paisley, had stepped up to replace him. By the end of Gayle's début season on the payroll, the European Cup had come to Anfield for the first time. It marked a significant leap forward for Liverpool FC. During the four years that Gayle was with them they won the European Cup three times, the Football League Championship three times, and the Football League Cup (subsequently the Milk Cup and the Littlewoods Cup) once. Their domination of domestic and European football not only elevated them to still greater sporting prestige, but also magnified their power as a business enterprise.

Already among the leading box-office takers in the country, their income from gate receipts was boosted by the prestige fixtures generated by cup runs, especially in European competition. Prize money filled the coffers still further. Financially, Liverpool FC were about to move into the big league, continuing an expansion which had already seen them grow from a local company into a national one, and now, they hoped, would enable them to operate on the international market as well. Inevitably, this meant that competition among locally-bred youngsters became even more intense in a city that was well and truly football mad. Increasingly, the club was looking not only beyond Merseyside but even abroad to replenish its stock of players, be they raw recruits or established stars. It was a situation which emphasized the already considerable pressure on Howard Gayle as he strove to make a name for himself.

At first, Liverpool offered him a contract on amateur terms. 'It surprised me at the time,' says Gayle, 'because I was training and playing with young professionals at the club and I was doing as well, if not better. But I bided me time, and I spoke to them again a few months later and said, "Look, have you considered me being taken on a full-time basis as a professional?" They obviously had a chat about it, and I signed up.' Gayle was one of a generation of young Liverpool recruits that included locals David Fairclough, Kevin Sheedy and Sammy Lee, Irishman Ronnie Whelan, and a teenage signing from Chester, Ian Rush. Not bad for a bunch of reserves. 'I was elated just to have the feeling, to say that you were a part of Liverpool Football Club,' Gayle recalls. 'For lads who've been brought up here and watched the Liverpool sides through the years, to sign with them is a dream. When you come from Liverpool, you don't just want to be just a footballer, but a footballer who plays for Liverpool or Everton.'

Gayle signed professional terms knowing that he bore the aspirations of a disenfranchised community on his shoulders. In no way could he be regarded, or regard himself, as just another foot soldier in the famous Red Army. With black players already making inroads into the First Division throughout the rest of the country, Gayle knew that his experiences at the club would either confirm or contradict a widespread belief among Merseyside's black footballers – that Liverpool FC was an institution where suspicion or downright hostility were fundamental to its attitude to blacks. He needed no reminding that he was breaking the mould. 'Everybody made that clear to me. It was constantly in the press when I broke into the first team – the first black player to play for Liverpool. It was a landmark as far as black people were concerned. And I was proud to represent the black community of Liverpool.'

Howard Gayle entered Anfield formed by experiences and bearing responsibilities that he was neither willing nor able to forget at the drop of a pay cheque. There were things he had to handle within Liverpool Football Club the same as anywhere else. He already had his method worked out. Like his brother Paul he had resolved to confront hostility, not appease it. In his everyday life he had drawn a line which others might not cross. To let them, in Howard Gayle's book, would be a betrayal of yourself, your friends and, ultimately, of all black Liverpool. Gayle did not erase that line for the benefit of the club and there were plenty of people around ready to make him defend it. 'You'd get little jibes of other players. And I'd stand up to them. I'd stop it there and then. Because if anybody's calling me a name ... I wouldn't let it happen on the street. And I'm not going to let it happen there. It's just a method, an instinct, the way I've been brought up.'

There is a category, defined by an expression, into which black people who will not tolerate certain kinds of behaviour are put by others who think they should. Howard Gayle was quickly condemned to it by some of those around him at Liverpool. It is the view of a number of ex-players and onlookers that the problem was all his: 'Howard had a chip on his shoulder,' they say. They have other things to say about him too: 'he was a very bitter person, Howard'; 'he was a bit, you know, black power'; 'The main problem with Howard Gayle was his temperament. He was in too much of a hurry. He wasn't prepared to wait'; 'he was a silly little sod'. But Gayle believes this reputation was the price he paid for refusing to sacrifice his own self-respect. 'Once one thinks he can get away with it, then they all want to do it. And you become a victim of your own personality then. Sometimes it's hard to know the times when people are having a joke. It's difficult sometimes to draw the line between when they *are* having a joke and when they're taking the piss. But by stopping it straight away, you don't have to make that comparison ... you don't have to draw the line.'

There was just one other black footballer on the scene at Liverpool at the same time as Gayle. Indeed, Lawrence Iro had been training at Melwood since before Gayle and Skeete were invited, beginning at an earlier age but, because he was still at school, on a less regular basis. Iro, too, was a pacy schoolboy forward, but though a native Liverpudlian, he came from a different social background. As isolated black men in a white footballing environment, the similarities and differences in their outlooks are instructive.

Lawrence Iro's mother and father were immigrants. Originally from Nigeria, they had come to Britain to study and build their careers. They were anxious for their Liverpool-born sons, Lawrence and Gus, to improve their minds as well. Professional football did not seem to them like a very good idea. Lawrence's headmaster, at his school in the district of Allerton, agreed. Illustrious old boy Steve Coppell, the Liverpudlian who played for Manchester United, had got a degree as well as many England caps. However, the ex-Everton centre forward Joe Royle (now manager of Oldham Athletic) had left without taking his exams. So the head had introduced a rule – no boys from Quarrybank Comprehensive were to represent Liverpool Schoolboys, the showcase for the city's budding talent.

But there was no keeping Lawrence from the game, and his exploits for the school team and in weekend junior leagues led to an approach from John Bennison, then, as now, a member of Liverpool FC's scouting staff. 'Everton were interested as well,' Iro recalls, 'and some other, little clubs. But Liverpool most of all.' What made the difference was a visit from the club's Youth Liaison Officer, Tom Saunders. A former headmaster himself, Saunders put Mr and Mrs Iro's minds at least partially at ease. 'When they want you to sign as an apprentice, they go to your parents to get their permission. He said, "OK, carry on with your studying, and we'll see what happens."'

At the age of fourteen, the young Iro began going to Melwood to train during his school holidays. There would be about sixty players of various seniorities working out, and fifty-nine of them were white. 'I enjoyed it,' Iro reflects, 'but I did sort of feel . . . you know, I was the only one. There was a fair amount of alienation. A couple of others sort of drifted in and out, but until Howard Gayle came, I was the only one who stayed. If there was a hint of racism there, I didn't feel it then – I was probably oblivious to it at that age. But I did wonder why I was the only one. Obviously, there were other black players in the city who were good. And yet, I must admit, it made me quite happy in a way. Because it seemed that out of all of them, I was the one they felt shouldn't be missed.'

Iro's sense of incongruity was only a matter of mild mystification to him for the first couple of years. But as adulthood drew closer, so did the nastier conventions of the grown-up game. He began turning out for the B and A teams, getting into more competitive situations. Things began to change. 'It wasn't until sixteen or seventeen that I started feeling it more. You would begin to get stick from the people who were watching or from the players themselves.' Iro learned to count to ten, to grin and bear it. 'When there's only you to take it, it's not so easy. I used to laugh at them, basically. I think you've got to be really tough-skinned to take the level of stick you might have to take. You would be expected to take a certain amount from your own team, and I think you would do as well, providing that it was a joke. But I think in some cases the lads do sometimes go over the top with it.'

So when is a joke not a joke but an insult masquerading as one? And when does even a joke stop being funny? Lawrence Iro is a black Liverpudlian from the lower middle class. He and his brother are affable, confident young men, sharply dressed, two of the precious few black Liverpudlians holding down good jobs in the centre of the town. Lawrence is a partner in an insurance company. His brother is a solicitor's clerk and used to referee in his spare time. Lawrence played a few games for Liverpool Reserves before taking up non-League, semi-professional football instead. It was not the end of the world. Lawrence could afford to smile, just as he was able to feign laughter in the face of racial jibes. But Howard Gayle was from Liverpool 8 and an angry young man. It made his definition of comedy a little more stringent. He could not afford to be laughed at by anyone.

To imagine the effect of Gayle's resistance properly it is important to understand the conventions of the male sporting dressing-room in general and Liverpool FC in particular. Communication tends to take place at the level of relentless banter. At Liverpool it has become a tradition that the players themselves reinforce a roughshod egalitarianism. Stars have never been permitted to get above themselves. Prima donnas have been swiftly suppressed.

Chris Lawler is not the only ex-player who believes this accounts for a large measure of the club's success. The patter sets the tone for an often caustic comradeship, building a team spirit which chimes with the neurotic demands of traditional masculinity. It's a man's game, and so on. Sensitivities cannot be tolerated and any sign of weakness or deviation from the norm is quickly lampooned. Your willingness to succumb to this ritual ribbing – or, maybe, this humiliation – with a smile was essential to your initiation into the team, the way your place in the pecking order was defined. Where was your threshold of tolerance? Were you one of the lads? It was not an audition with which Howard Gayle was ready to co-operate.

'There would be incidents, just in games during training. Like, you might kick someone or get stuck in to each other. If it was two white boys, they'd just be laughing at each other. But if it involved me, it's so easy for them to jump up in a moment of temper and go "You black so-and-so" or whatever. And I didn't care who it was, whether they were apprentices or whether they were senior players at the club. Most of them had the sense to see me for what I was. But there's always the minority.'

Gayle made it his business to try and set certain terms on which he related to his team-mates. When it came to racial remarks, it was not a question of asking nicely: 'It would be more of a confrontation than that. 'Cos if I just said, "Don't call me that," and they knew I didn't like it, they'd call me it again. So I had to say it in a manner which would get home to whoever it was. A few of the lads, they knew what a joke was. But when you get someone saying things and it isn't a joke, they're obviously going to be drumming for support.'

Among the playing colleagues with whom Gayle had disagreements was Tommy Smith, a Liverpool legend, 'The Iron Man of Anfield', a pillar of the establishment. You kept your shin pads on when Tommy was around, even if you were sitting in the stands. Born just round the corner from Anfield, Smith was generally regarded as the hardest man in the English game. Whether in midfield, where he began in the Liverpool team, as central defender or full-back (where he finished), this was a gentleman whose ferocity in the tackle was frightening. Even the assorted tough guys of Don Revie's Leeds United – cultivated scrappers like Giles,

Bremner and Norman 'Bites Yer Leg' Hunter – treated Smith with respect. All footballers get nicknames, and Tommy Smith's complexion earned him his. But no one ever – not *ever* – called Tommy Smith 'Beans on Toast' to his face.

Meeting Mr Smith is an education. He went to Anfield at fifteen, choosing professional football as a career despite winning a scholarship to study architecture. The reasons were partly financial. His father had died a year before and the County Council could offer his mother only £1 a week to compensate for the loss of income. Liverpool, on the other hand, offered £7 a week. Smith was big for his age, five feet nine and eleven stone. Shankly gave him a run in the Reserves. Two years later he was turning out for the first team, a Liverpool legend in the making.

As a new boy, though, Smith says he was a shy, retiring character. He describes his initiation among a bunch of seasoned pros with the nostalgia of one who survived it: 'When I joined Liverpool I got treated like a bit of shit. They used to say: "Hey, you, clean me boots!" Talk about taking the piss. One of them said to me once: "Go and get a square ball." You're nervous enough anyway. You end up going over to the groundsman: "Er, like, can I have a square ball?" Get off, you know. You had to get over to the older pros that you had enough ability inside you, that you had enough bottle.'

When Howard Gayle came to Liverpool, he was subjected to comparable examination. Colour was the obvious target. His relationship with Smith was volatile, to say the least. Smith has his own explanation for it. 'He was wary of me. Howard suffered from a black man's attitude towards the white man. See, everybody thinks whites have got an attitude towards blacks. In reality blacks have got a problem with the whites. Howard, unfortunately, was the only black man at Liverpool at the time. Nobody got on to him or anything! He just had a grudge. He thought he was the only one to get it, the sole benefactor of all the piss-taking. In the end it got the better of him.'

Tommy Smith's theory of race relations is a classic contradictory example of blithe xenophobia laced with protestations of innocence. His conversation is candid, his remarks delivered almost mildly, in a tone which insists that certain things in life are self-evident. In spite of his best efforts, words like 'coon' and 'nigger' soon begin to fall from his lips. The possibility that he might have been talking to, say, the husband of a black woman never seemed to cross his mind. 'I'm not prejudiced,' he explained, 'but if a coon moved in next door, I'd move, like most white people would. If me daughter come home with a nigger I'd go mad! But I'm only being truthful and normal.'

It seems to be Smith's understanding that racial tensions occur because people have stopped regarding blacks as second-class citizens. Those 'coloured people' whom he considers his friends have achieved the distinction by learning to, in Smith's own words, 'think like the white man.' He had his own special epithet for them. In time, Howard Gayle was awarded this bizarre, backhanded plaudit too. 'I used to call Howard "the white nigger",' says Smith. 'Now that is a compliment. It was the only way I could find to describe that I thought he was OK.'

The accolade was not bestowed, however, because Gayle did an ideological U turn. On the contrary, it was because he proved he was ready to fight. 'I had my run-ins with Tommy Smith early on,' he recalls. 'But once I stood up to him, he was great after that. He looked after us after that, 'cos I think he was ignorant, really, until he seen how I was gonna stand up for myself and just wasn't gonna take it.' Lawrence Iro's assessment of the Iron Man is similar, glowing even. He went on to play under Smith's management as a part-timer at Caernarfon Town. 'Tommy Smith is a fabulous bloke because he's clear-cut. He's the sort of person where you've got to be able to take a bit of stick from him. That's his nature. He is a genuinely nice fella, and he's one of those that would back you up. But if he was to kick you and you ran away, he'd go and kick you again. That's the way Tommy is. It's as simple as that.' But none of this vindicates Smith's unspeakable perspectives, which contributed to making Gayle's situation next to impossible. Fighting back was the way he earned Smith's respect, but the same determination to defend his dignity earned him many of his peers' disdain. The only moral here is that a stab in the front is easier to deal with than a stab in the back.

The same rough-cut rules of engagement could not be applied to some of the players Howard Gayle encountered on opposing teams.

It was only on the field of play that he had to compromise, because if he didn't, he was going to lose. It is a lesson in injustice which every black player has had to learn. 'I've been sent off twice in my career,' Gayle explains. 'The first was at Liverpool, in the Reserves against Derby. I got into a fight with somebody who called me a "black pig". It was quite funny, actually, because I was expecting a bollocking when I come off, but the team manager was laughing. He said, "That's the fastest left and right hook I've ever seen."'

Lawrence Iro understands this particular no-win situation too. 'Once you start showing that it's affecting you, and then it affects your game, then they know. People will say, "Listen, just have a go at him. He'll lose his rag. He'll either turn round and hit you, and the ref will send him off, or his game will go." You've got to not let them realize that. So if they're saying all sorts to you, you just laugh at them.'

The staff at Liverpool FC were not unaware of the particular difficulties facing black players. By the second half of the seventies, racist terrace taunts were a routine occurrence at most football grounds, and Gayle was given the obvious advice: 'You can't fight the crowd.' But he had worked that out for himself. The same was true of wind-ups from opponents. 'It doesn't happen to me so much now, because people tend to know me more and they give me a bit more respect. It's usually when you're just coming in, a raw young lad. That's when they do their shouting out on the park. Once I got sent off I realized that it was doing me more damage than anybody else. And it just inspired me more. It made me play better, 'cos I knew that scoring goals would sicken the people that were doing it, kicking me or whatever. You just go and score a goal and give them a little wink as you're running past them. That does the job. There's nothing else you can do.'

Such is the professional code of football. Eat shit, it's part of the job. Find a silver lining if you can. And your capacity for eating shit is one criterion by which most football people make their value judgement regarding who does or does not have that quality upon which English football likes to pride itself – 'character'. It is when we match Howard Gayle's definition of 'character' against that of the football establishment that we begin to gain some insight into how the dice were loaded against him. Consider the politics of the field of play. Rule One: don't retaliate when opponents bait you. The ref. will send off you, not the other guy. Rule Two: don't lose your rag with the crowd when they shower you in spit as you back away to take a corner kick, when they goad you with monkey chants and throw bananas on the pitch just to let you know that they think you are no better than an ape. Rule Three: don't get upset when your own team-mates behave in exactly the same way.

Break any of these rules, and they say you've got a temperament problem. What price a lone, black teenage scouser building a career in a world like that?

8

'We Were Selling Football'

The office of Peter Robinson, Liverpool Football Club's chief executive, lies among a maze of carpeted corridors, bare save for one bulging trophy cabinet and a collection of framed newspaper cuttings, recalling decades of glory days. Directions were provided by a hard-pressed female switchboard operator who seemed to be acting as receptionist as well. The telephone did not stop ringing during a ten-minute wait on the padded vinyl seat in the red-carpeted foyer. She spoke in frenetic fragments of sentences between taking calls. That close-season morning in the summer of 1988, she and Mr Robinson appeared to be running the entire multi-million pound operation between the two of them. It was the chief executive, though, who was the more relaxed. That is not so surprising. After all, Mr Robinson is one of the few men working in English professional football who can honestly claim to feel secure in his job.

'I came here twenty-three years ago through a newspaper advertisement,' he revealed. 'I was twenty-nine at the time.' A round-faced, balding man, he speaks in a tight-lipped executive purr which cannot wholly conceal the remains of a Northern accent. 'I was at that time secretary of Brighton. Liverpool wanted an experienced administrator, and I had been in football starting as an office boy.'

Mr Robinson's predecessor had hanged himself from one of the stanchions holding up the roof of the Spion Kop. The circumstances surrounding his demise remain unclear. Since replacing him behind what was then the secretary's desk, Mr Robinson has seen the accomplishments of Bill Shankly steadily built upon, supported firstly by chairman Eric Sawyer, the managing director of Littlewoods Foodstores, and subsequently by today's incumbent John Smith, formerly a brewer, subsequently a local magistrate, a Conservative Party supporter and, until recently, chairman of the

Sports Council. By common consent it is Smith and Robinson who, in business terms, have really run the Liverpool FC show since consolidating their positions in the seventies. The Littlewoods group meanwhile, retains a major financial interest. Its chairman, John Moores, is the biggest shareholder in both Liverpool and Everton. 'Liverpool is a limited company with 12,000 issued shares,' Mr Robinson explained from behind his desk, 'so it's very similar to any other limited company where the directors are elected by the shareholders.' Mr Robinson expressed his admiration for Mr Sawyer, approving of the entrepreneurial philosophy he brought to the club. 'I think he called himself a shopkeeper, and he always likened it to a shop where you'd got to have attractive premises for people to come into and then you'd got to have the best commodities to sell to them. We were selling football.'

Mr Robinson talked for a while about money and the reasons why Liverpool Football Club had been able to invest very large sums of it in the summer of 1987 on players such as Peter Beardsley (£1.9 million from Newcastle United) and John Barnes (£900,000 from Watford) while others, up and down the land, were perpetually on the brink of bankruptcy. He responded with a piece of vintage self-made rhetoric. 'On the spending of large sums of money I would point out that we've only spent what we've generated ourselves. Nobody gives us one penny piece. We have to exist totally as a commercial operation. We have no benefactors anywhere that help us.'

These remarks were made three years after the Heysel Stadium disaster in which the 1985 European Cup Final between Liverpool and Juventus was overshadowed by crowd confrontations leading to the deaths of thirty-nine Italian supporters. It resulted in an indefinite ban on English teams competing in any of the three European club competitions and an additional three-year penalty to be imposed upon Liverpool if and when the blanket sanction was lifted. The Brussels catastrophe was a major trauma for the club, emotionally and, of course, financially. Mr Robinson expanded on this second aspect and indicated, with carefully measured candour, how the club has continued to prosper, albeit at a more modest pace.

'We had to take steps and we didn't know what kind of effect this was going to have on the public. Initially we lost quite a lot of season ticket holders who said that they weren't going to come along in view of what had happened. So we carefully looked at all our financial obligations and we believe that we were very prudent in the first few months afterwards. Apart from going into the transfer market for Steve McMahon, we didn't spend on players or very much on capital. Then it quickly became apparent to us that the public weren't holding the club responsible in any way and I think we opened up the season following Heysel with a gate of nearly 40,000 against Arsenal. And those gates have progressively increased over the three years. But I think Europe is missed because, literally, the ground was rebuilt out of profits from Europe. We were in it for twenty-one years, we were very successful and most of that money was ploughed back in.'

Just before the Heysel disaster, Liverpool Football Club was close to commissioning a major expansion to the Kemlyn Road stand. An adjoining plot of land had been purchased some years before, together with the row of terraced houses that stood on it. All the occupants but one have subsequently moved and the buildings on it demolished. The sole remaining resident is an elderly lady, living at Number 26. Her house stands conspicuously amid the surrounding asphalt, supported by two boarded-up premises on either side.

It is a source of considerable irritation to the club, though Mr Robinson managed not to let it show. 'We said we wouldn't forcibly move anyone out,' he said, reassuringly. 'Ninety per cent of the people wanted to go rather than live there. And so we made arrangements with them that were satisfactory to both, and the people gradually moved out. We got to a situation round about 1984–85 where we had planning permission, so we were very close to being in a position to do it. We were actively discussing extending the stand which would give us another four-and-a-half thousand seats. But with the Heysel situation, the cost of that was something like two-and-a-half to three million pounds, so it was something that we shelved. We didn't really think we could take on that sort of commitment immediately following Heysel. We were making on average somewhere between a quarter and a half million pound net profit from Europe over the last few seasons. So we've lost that. With Europe you also negotiate the sale of the television rights and the perimeter advertising. Now I believe we are not only missing out from the gate return point of view, but television fees and perimeter advertising rights have increased dramatically over the last three years. So we would now be making much greater profits from Europe.'

A blow to the stand plan, then, but not a fatal one: 'We've no clear indication when we might be permitted to play in Europe again,' Mr Robinson said at the time. 'But in the light of what has happened in the last three seasons and the tremendous support we are drawing, we are now again, if I may use the expression, blowing the dust off the plans.' The extended stand would be, said Mr Robinson, a logical commercial move in the light of trends he had perceived in the composition of Liverpool's home support. From the addresses of those purchasing season tickets and entering programme competitions, he has surmised that 'around 50 per cent of our support comes from thirty miles away or more.' Proceeding from this, he invoked the footballing version of the new received wisdom of eighties leisure capitalism: 'I think more and more people are wanting to sit. It may seem strange for me to say this of a city which is supposed to be very depressed with such high unemployment. But we embarked upon a policy in the seventies of providing more seats. We seated the Paddock and then we seated Anfield Road. We reduced the capacity of the ground from 56,000 to 45,000, but our seats increased from 11,000 to 21,000 and it's quite remarkable that in the season just passed, every seat for every game has been sold. It's the Kop area of the ground that we're not filling, i.e. the standing area. So it proves to me that disposable income has increased for the people who are working and they're in an age where they want more comfort. Obviously,' he conceded, finally, 'those who do not have a job are finding it more difficult.'

It is Mr Robinson's view that Liverpool was probably the last English professional club to be able to support itself through gate receipts alone. Today, he estimates that 70 or 80 per cent of their annual income is taken through ticket sales and at the turnstiles.

The remainder comes through a variety of commercial ventures – shirt sponsorship, advertising, merchandising and the perpetually vexed subject of television rights – but it is the fans who continue to provide the financial bedrock. Asked to define the relationship between the club and its supporters, Mr Robinson thought for a moment. He then responded with a platitude: 'Technically, clubs are legal companies and they belong to the shareholders. But from the trading point of view the income of a football club comes mainly from the turnstiles. So the club *really* belongs to the spectators.'

In the light of this definition, and with the Hillsborough disaster almost two years in the future, it is interesting to consider how those who follow the Liverpool team had had the most impact upon the policies pursued by the club's executive. The answer was through acts of hooliganism resulting in death. One direct result of the Heysel disaster was the instant curtailment of ground improvement plans which would have made the Anfield stadium a more upmarket leisure facility and probably thrown the Kop's lack of cost-effectiveness into sharper relief. It is increasingly ironic that the logic of Mr Robinson's outline of Liverpool's future plans should hint that it would make better business sense if the low-priced Spion Kop terrace was upgraded to a seated area too. After all, it was not those who could afford to buy seats who defined the unique Anfield atmosphere that everyone says is worth a goal start. It was the not-so-ordinary working scouser who did that. Now that the working scouser is not working any more, he may find himself priced out of the market. The Hillsborough carnage appears to have brought this possibility closer. If it wasn't for the Heysel carnage, it might have happened already.

The club's initial, panicky response to Heysel was extremely revealing in the context of these business priorities. With some justice they claimed that throughout the twenty years Liverpool had competed in Europe, no serious disturbances had occurred. The reputation of Liverpool fans had been equally good at home, the most notorious pockets of hard-core hooligans being associated with big clubs who had suffered a fall from their former grace: Chelsea, Manchester United, Leeds United, West Ham. But the deadly involvement of such a disruptive element within Liverpool's own ranks appeared to leave the club's top brass in a state of disarray. The concept of accountability threw them into a spin. One journalist, who has enjoyed a close relationship with the club for many years, describes a post-Heysel press conference held after the Liverpool party had returned from Italy.

'It was a new situation. After the actual game, the manager was there, maybe the chairman, and they were talking to the football lobby. Nobody asked embarrassing questions, and if they did, they were batted away easily enough. But when they arrived back at Speke Airport there was a press conference and embarrassing, awkward questions *were* being asked. And it was no longer the football lobby that were asking them but the hardened frontline news reporters. And Smith and Robinson just did not know how to cope with it. They just didn't know how to take criticism. They were totally lost.'

The response of the Liverpool top brass in Heysel's immediate aftermath told us much about their conception of their own paying public – their market. They clutched at a romantic portrayal of it like a lifebelt. Mr Smith suggested evidence of National Front involvement organized by agitators from elsewhere, outside Liverpool. He couldn't imagine the average Liverpool lad getting involved in something like that. But the popular image of the rough Liverpudlian diamond with his heart of gold was beginning to sound like a cliché, one which, like all clichés, may have roots in reality but has a tendency to blossom into fully fledged fantasy.

Mr Robinson inclines to a similarly forgiving explanation of this apparently uncharacteristic outbreak of exported Merseyside misbehaviour. 'On that theme, and this may be ironic in the light of Heysel, but we've no evidence that hooliganism has ever been organized either at Liverpool or Everton. Police tell me this. There are statistics showing that at other clubs there has been an organized element. Liverpool has not been without its hooligans, but there is no record of it having been organized.'

He offered these thoughts a few weeks after the end of a season in which John Barnes had been the brightest star in a championship-winning side newly fashioned by current manager Kenny Dalglish. His accomplishments had been recognized by his peers in the Professional Footballers Association and by the Football Writers Association when both elected him player of the year. Football followers were looking forward in the eager hope that he would reproduce his club form for England in the European Championships in June. On the Anfield terraces it had been a remarkable season too. The traditional abuse directed at the black players of visiting teams had all but ceased with the adoption of a new home hero, who was young, gifted and definitely black.

Mr Robinson agreed that a part of Barnes's success had been due to a good diplomatic job off the field as well as a sparkling one on it. 'Oh, I think he's contributed greatly to improving racial relations,' he declared with enthusiasm. 'He's a highly intelligent young man and he's become involved in various activities locally. He's been like a breath of fresh air about the place. If there were any racial activities before, I don't think there are now.' Mr Robinson accepted that racial taunts had been a feature of Spion Kop rhetoric over the years. It was his view, however, that 'it's very difficult to prevent if a group in a crowd of 40,000 decide they are going to chant something'.

Further, it is his conviction, chanting notwithstanding, that racial hostility has never been a serious problem in the city: 'I've lived in Liverpool now for twenty-three years and I've never sensed that there is great racialism here. I've always put it down to the fact that Liverpool has been a port and it's had its many communities for hundreds of years, so it's not like some of the other cities of England where the coloured population is of more recent times.'

He is therefore puzzled that so few black people come to Anfield to watch. 'It's strange, I don't know why they haven't come to football here. We have a very large number of Chinese season ticket holders, and you see quite a sprinkling of them at games. But for some reason, which I can't answer, we've never had a large black following here. And that hasn't increased much with the coming of John Barnes.'

Mr Robinson's perplexity on this matter is hardly unique to him, but that does not make it any less depressing. A degree in sociology is scarcely necessary to sense at least the possibility of a connection between the chorusing of slogans such as 'Kill, kill, kill the nigger', and the apparent reluctance of black people to expose themselves to an environment where, for years, pre-Barnes, such sentiments were openly expressed. It would not require much in-depth research to conclude, if only from the Liverpool 8 insurrection, that serious racial tensions existed within his adopted city and that the behaviour of some of Liverpool FC's supporters reflected and exacerbated them. Maybe he had simply not read and digested the results of two pieces of work by the Sir Norman Chester Centre for Football Research into the soccer culture of Merseyside, undertaken in the wake of Heysel. If he had, he might have been surprised by the degree of awareness of racist attitudes at both Anfield and Goodison Park as reported by Liverpool's secondary school children – and by the way that significant numbers actively identified with those attitudes as being integral to their affiliation for the Liverpool team and the contempt they felt for others.

'On Saturday, I went to the match to watch Liverpool v. West Ham. A coloured person inside the ground was standing in front of me and started shouting in a very loud voice, "Scouse divvies", and a lot of other coloured people joined in so a young skinhead jumped out of his seat and started shouting, "Kill the nigger" and his friends . . . started singing, "There is no black in the Union Jack so all the niggers fuck off back". And to this chant almost half the ground stood up and joined in.'

That was one experience as recalled by a fifteen-year-old boy. Another male youth of the same age described the growing hostility between Liverpool and Manchester United fans and the way that racial malice was a central component of that hatred:

'Manchester United are probably our worst enemies because of the closeness of the cities, rivalry of the two clubs and the colour of a few Manchester United fans during the last few years . . . The National Front are infiltrating the terraces and causing hatred towards black players, both of which Man City and Man United have had many. Now, to see a black man or a black woman at a football match is a very unusual sight.'

A third teenage boy elaborated on the intensity of the dislike between some Liverpool and some United fans, but from a different perspective: he deliberately participated in it. He went on:

'I am in a racist organization. From going to Liverpool matches I have come to hate black people. I am in the APL. We want all immigrants out of this country. Our motto stands for Anti-Paki League. We want all the Paki scum out.' The latter essay was submitted to the CFR researchers complete with the APL symbol and the slogan: 'LFC – Wogs Out'.

The football culture of Merseyside has, for twenty-five years, represented one of the most passionate distillations of Liverpool's collective grass-roots identity. To support Liverpool or Everton is not simply to consume an afternoon's sporting entertainment, or even to follow the fortunes of a team. It is to participate in a ritual celebration of all the working-class characteristics that Liverpudlians of red and blue alike recognize as marks of distinction. The things that have become clichés, the wit, the knowingness a streetwise cut above the average – these account for part of it. Everton in the sixties was known as soccer's School of Science. Liverpool's players were canny and cultivated. But there were other qualities which the Merseysiders prided themselves on too, Liverpool in particular: dogged, resilient, nothing airy-fairy, and, if required, ready to mix it with anyone.

At Liverpool that reputation was formed under Bill Shankly. 'If you're going to fight for something, fight till you drop. That was Shanks's way of playing the game,' says Tommy Smith. In European competition, the qualities of true-grit solidarity-under-fire came to be contrasted with the perceived cynicism and sneakiness of the club's great European rivals, especially those from Italy. The Heysel confrontation has a historical explanation. A notorious previous European Cup encounter between Liverpool and an Italian side had taken place in 1965, the Reds' first foray into European competition. The opposition was Inter Milan and the two teams met at the semi-final stage. Travelling to defend a 3–1 lead from the Anfield leg, Liverpool's players were subjected to an all-night barrage of motor horns and church bells on the eve of the game. Some dubious refereeing helped Inter to a 3–nil win and led to persistent rumours that the official had been bribed. The incident has entered the folk memory of the Liverpool FC fraternity, preserved with a prejudice echoing the English football establishment's habitual characterization of Mediterranean teams – excitable; untrustworthy; fatally flawed by the so-called 'Latin temperament'.

Liverpool supporters and Liverpool teams would never count-enance such defects in their own ranks. Even at the height of their fame great individuals like Roger Hunt, Kevin Keegan and Kenny Dalglish never put vainglorious whims before the good of the team. Craft was encouraged, great skill highly prized, but unbridled ostentation – now, that could be a mixed blessing. The florid, intuitive player of extravagant gifts but dubious consistency was unlikely to be tolerated under the Anfield regime. After all, he might give the ball away. There had been eloquent flair players, running wingers like Peter Thompson and Steve Heighway whose job it was to go past opponents if they could, and the crowds had warmed to them. But these were also team men and tempera-mentally seen to be sound. Nothing suspect about them.

The Liverpool teams of Shankly, Bob Paisley and his short-lived successor Joe Fagan were united by this philosophy. If the club's Orange foundations had never been flaunted or actively promoted, on the field of play the Protestant work ethic was alive and well: blood, sweat and discipline a plenty, with no unnecessary ritual – and, of course, home with the silverware year after year. Given the unyielding stereotype to which they were routinely compared, black players were assumed to be about as suitable at Anfield as a ham sandwich in a synagogue. They, like all those swarthy Continentals, were generally regarded in English football as flashy, superficial and untrustworthy.

One football journalist recalls discussing the matter with Bob Paisley: 'If you ever talked to Bob Paisley and you asked him about various coloured footballers in private conversation, he'd say, "The trouble is, these sort of people, they don't tend to get stuck in, and they tend to get discouraged very easily." I don't think he was the least bit racialist . . . he just thought that in his experience, coloured footballers tended to get upset when things started going wrong, and drop out of the game. So he tended to be looking at them rather more critically than he'd look at other people.' Paisley is not recalled as expressing these views with malice. Simply, he was adhering to the prevailing wisdom of the football world at the time. At Everton, the same attitudes prevailed. Brian Labone was Everton's centre-half and captain throughout most of the sixties and early seventies, when Harry Catterick, an old-school disciplinarian, was manager of the team. He confirms that all the usual assumptions, about bottle, about reliability, about how 'they' won't go out when it rains, were commonly held in the Everton dressing-room. Gordon Lee, the Goodison manager from 1977–1981, was well known for his dislike of foreign players and black players, and in the opinion of former Everton stars, would never have signed one. It was hardly a break with tradition. Trebilcock, the Cup Final hero, had gone almost as soon as he arrived. Cliff Marshall, the local black winger, had failed to make a major impact. Some say that Marshall had all the skill but lacked competitive will. Others say that his spirit was so sapped by intimidation from crowds and opposing players he was emptied of the desire to play.

Liverpool meanwhile, were the last club likely to take what they would have perceived as a risk. Their rituals were established, their preparations routinized to the point of fetishism. 'I'd ... suggest that something as simple as superstition could be at the heart of the matter,' wrote former club captain Phil Neal. 'I reckon some of the coaches fear that a change in the training pattern could burst the Anfield bubble. It's a very old-fashioned club in many respects.' The system was the thing and the players Liverpool liked were the sort who would conform to it. And, of course, you couldn't rely on these 'coloured lads', could you? Everyone knew that.

It was into this environment that Howard Gayle took his Liverpool 8 sensibility, a native scouser and yet an outsider in a revered institution of his own home town. Gayle was a winger, a ball-player, a guy who could beat one man, beat two men, beat three men. He had a lot of ability. But, not, apparently, enough for some. 'It's quite ironic that we've not had a lot of coloured players,' Mr Robinson reflected, lightly, 'but the local community hasn't really thrown an outstanding one up. It's rather strange that it's happened in other areas. We had Howard Gayle who was locally-born. He had a good spell here but he really wasn't up to the standard that we required.'

It is not a point of view that everybody shares. 'At the age of sixteen or seventeen he was a very good player. He had the toughness and everything. I know for a fact that at Liverpool they were very disappointed that he didn't come through.' This is Tommy Smith's assessment of Howard Gayle's talent. Lawrence Iro, who knows both Gayle and John Barnes, offers a comparison of the two. 'OK, John Barnes is a great player, and he's got that little bit of craft. But Howie was fast . . . faster than John Barnes will ever be.' Another of Gayle's team-mates, goalkeeper Bruce Grobbelaar, expressed a high opinion in his 1986 autobiography. But in the end his explanation for Gayle's failure to flourish is much the same as Smith's. Grobbelaar is the latest South African-born player to appear in a Liverpool shirt. Having moved to Rhodesia as a child, he had been drafted into the army there, and fought against the black guerrillas – 'terrorists', as Grobbelaar calls them – fighting to bring down Ian Smith's white supremacist regime. After a spell of goalkeeping in North America, Grobbelaar became a celebrity the hard way at Anfield. His early performances were littered with mistakes in vital games and he earned the nickname 'The Clown'. Subsequently proving his prowess as a marvellously gifted 'keeper, his attention-seeking activities on the field of play have made him a favourite with the Anfield faithful and have seen him hailed by the football media as the kind of individual who, to them, is meat and drink – a 'personality'.

But despite his early brushes with the derision of Liverpool partisans, Grobbelaar seems to have remained blissfully oblivious to the sensitivities of those around him. The passage in his ghosted book devoted to his relationship with Gayle speaks volumes for an inability to understand that there are some things some people should never be expected to laugh about, especially coming from a white South African: 'I do know that . . . Howard Gayle was none too keen on me. There is always a lot of chat and winding up in the Liverpool dressing-room, and the first team players, quick to pick up on my "Jungle Man" nickname and my military service background, warned the coloured Howard Gayle that I would be after him.'

Grobbelaar goes on to describe an incident involving himself, Gayle and Olympic decathalon champion Daley Thompson who visited the team in training one day. The episode revolves around a racial 'joke' Grobbelaar made to the two of them, an astonishingly crude personal remark. 'Daley promptly fell into fits of laughter,' Grobbelaar reports, 'but Howard was not at all amused and found nothing to smile about.'

Thompson is a man whose consciousness with regard to his own colour is, by his own account, entirely different from that of Gayle. In fact it is not a characteristic by which he choses to define himself at all. But, then, it is not colour itself that has required race to become an issue among black people, but the attitude of whites to the characteristics they believe go with it. The peculiarities of Thompson's upbringing appear to have shielded him from the worst of the institutionalized diminution of black people's lives that is routine in Liverpool 8. Of racially-mixed parentage and educated in an otherwise all-white private school in Sussex, he has been spared the worst that British racism can offer. Submerging himself in sport, his strange, solitary lifestyle increased his isolation from the rest of the world. He rationalized 'race' to himself as a non-issue and took a dim view of other black athletes who did not. A revered figure in his chosen career, Thompson had spent his whole life refusing to acknowledge that racism, or anything else, could stop him from getting to the top. What else was he going to do but laugh?

But for Howard Gayle, racist 'humour', from Grobbelaar or anyone else, was not something his own heart would allow him to tolerate. He talked back. He fought back. He knew how to turn a cutting phrase himself and did not leave the talent untapped. But Gayle's resistance was not acceptable to some of those around him and there is no doubt that he paid for it. 'The funny thing is that I rather liked Howard Gayle,' wrote Grobbelaar, 'and if he hadn't carried around a great big chip on his shoulder he could have become an English international . . . If we were to allow [his] ability to take over and express himself in football terms he could still be a truly outstanding player.'

'Get rid of that chip, and you'll go far,' is how one club insider recalls Gayle being addressed by an illustrious Liverpool player. And how he was put to the test. One year at the players' Christmas party a comedian was hired to entertain. As part of his act the comic walked up to where Gayle was sitting and emptied a bowl of flour over his head: 'Now try walking into fucking Toxteth,' announced the funny man, or words to that effect. Gayle kept his cool. But the effort required to keep smiling in the face of such attentions would try the patience of a saint.

There are many who claim that Gayle was no angel. Under Shankly and Paisley, Liverpool players who got their names in the papers following this indiscretion or that seemed inexorably to find their way first on to the subs' bench, then into the Reserves and on to the transfer list soon after. People's memories of Gayle are fogged with speculations about one dubious propensity or another – speculations, though, are all they are. The club, meanwhile, put pressure on him to move out of Liverpool 8 and break contact with the area altogether. But though Gayle agreed to live somewhere else, he was not willing to desert his friends, whatever reputation the club attached to them. He was not willing to abandon his roots to keep Liverpool happy, not physically, not emotionally, not politically. The club could not begin to understand why.

So was it lack of ability that counted against Gayle or was it a question of 'character'? What word in English football parlance is more pregnant with value judgements? Consider the different things 'character' would have meant to Howard Gayle from Liverpool 8 compared with every other person in his vicinity at Liverpool Football Club. For them, 'character' meant submitting to the culture of the club. For Gayle, it meant the opposite. It could only count against him.

Howard Gayle played just five times for the Liverpool first team. The first, in October 1980, was a run-out as substitute away to Manchester City. The second could not have been more different. Liverpool were embroiled in a contentious European Cup semi-final with the formidable West German champions, Bayern Munich. The first leg at Anfield had seen the home team held to a goalless draw. Afterwards, the Bayern captain Paul Breitner had been reported as describing Liverpool's tactics as 'unintelligent'. Liverpool prepared for the second leg determined to make Breitner eat his words, but they had problems. Injuries had forced them to draft in a couple of reserve defenders. Howard Gayle made it on to the substitutes' bench. In a furiously combative atmosphere Kenny Dalglish, the ace in Liverpool's pack, limped off the pitch within a few minutes of the start. Manager Bob Paisley, in what has been described by the then team captain Graeme Souness as 'an inspired use of the tactical substitution', sent Gayle on with instructions to take on the German defence.

Bayern, it seems, had no prior knowledge of this young fringe player, dribbling with the ball at high speed in a manner that was utterly untypical of the usual Liverpool style. 'Howie ran them ragged,' wrote Souness. And for an hour that is precisely what he did. The Germans resorted to kicking him. '[Liverpool] might have had a penalty just before the half hour,' wrote the *Guardian*'s David Lacey, 'after Gayle went sprawling after being tackled from behind ... Gayle's strength and speed were of sufficient concern to Bayern for them to foul him regularly.' Jeff Powell, writing in the *Daily Mail*, enthused: 'Liverpool ... found in Howard Gayle a substitute of such remarkable confidence ... while he was unsettling Bayern with his black muscularity and aggression, the survivors were piecing together a performance of immense concentration, enduring discipline and inspiring morale.' Note the seemingly automatic association of 'aggression' and 'muscularity' with the racial category 'black'. But even so, a consensus around Gayle's performance emerged, from press and players alike. 'Howard's performance was outstanding,' says David Johnson, who played alongside Gayle that day. 'It was gritty, it was hard and it was courageous.'

Ten minutes from the end, Johnson, struggling with a torn muscle, lobbed the ball hopefully infield towards the Bayern goal. Ray Kennedy came through from midfield to score a priceless away goal. In the dying seconds, Karl-Heinz Rummenige equalized, but the away goal counted double and Liverpool were through to the Final against Real Madrid. Bayern had never been beaten at home in Europe and they had very nearly won at Anfield. It was an extraordinary performance, a Liverpool true-grit classic.

But for Howard Gayle the night ended in bitter disappointment. After being booked for retaliation – and Gayle insists the referee was conned – he was removed from the fray twenty minutes from the end and replaced by Jimmy Case. 'I was told', says Gayle, 'it was to prevent me from being sent off.' Paisley's logic was that he could not risk being reduced to ten men with extra time on the cards. It might have been an arguable case, but it was hardly a vote of confidence.

Others, though, hailed Gayle as a rising star. The following Saturday he played a full first-team game away to Tottenham. With Johnson and Dalglish both walking wounded, he linked up with the nineteen-year-old Ian Rush in a new-look attack. The match ended in a 1-all draw, Gayle scoring for the visitors. His last two first team games were both at Anfield, where he enjoyed 'a good reception'. In the first, against Sunderland, he was substituted in a lack-lustre 1-nil defeat. In the second, against Manchester City again, Liverpool won by the same score and Gayle hit the post with a powerful header. Robert Armstrong in the *Guardian* filed the following report on the Tottenham match: 'A few more goals of quality by Gayle, who swept Lee's pass into the net after 25 minutes, and Johnson may have more than injury to overcome to regain his place. The impressive pace and timing of Gayle's runs, which bemused Bayern Munich, could well restore a dimension and width to Liverpool's attack missing since the dropping of Heighway. Significantly, both Gayle and ... Rush have ... shown they possess the nerve and flair required for the major occasion.'

It was not an assessment with which the club concurred. At the end of the season they offered Gayle a contract with just a cost-of-living wage rise – hardly a hint that he featured in their future plans. Wounded, Gayle reconsidered his position and asked the club to circulate his name. He went to Fulham on loan and had spells at Newcastle, at Sunderland, where he fell out with Lawrie McMenemy, and at Birmingham City, where he fell out with old-guard autocrat Ron Saunders. He ended up at Stoke City, a shadow of his former self. It was not until Don Mackay took him to Blackburn on a free transfer that his career picked up again and his gifts of pace, strength and timing began exerting themselves once more.

To many at Liverpool, Gayle's subsequent career simply proves that the club was right to let him go. To others, that heroic night in Munich will stand for ever as a clue to what might have been, with confidence, with encouragement, with a little bit of faith. Gayle's performance has made its mark in two different histories of Liverpool Football Club. One is within the club establishment of staff and supporters as the night the local black kid turned a vital game – a footnote in the record books; funny he didn't last. The other belongs in the folk memory of black Liverpool's disenfranchised football lovers. It is the story of the night that Liverpool Football Club decided that a black boy from Liverpool 8 could not be relied on to do his home town proud.

9
'A Law Unto Himself'

The first speculation that John Barnes might be selling his services to Liverpool came with a glut of newspaper reports in the early spring of 1987, six years after Howard Gayle had left. The *Liverpool Echo* reported that the Football League champions were 'poised to pay a club record fee of more than £1 million' for Barnes, whom Watford had 'given the go-ahead to leave'. This, and other stories, marked the onset of a three-month transfer saga in which nothing was half so fully revealed as the capacity of all parts of the English football industry to talk an awful lot while saying nothing at all.

As far as the press were concerned, the temperature of this already hot big-money story was considerably heightened by the identity of the man Barnes was being touted to help replace – Ian Rush. It was already known that the 1986–87 season would be the celebrated Welsh goalscorer's last before moving to Juventus to fulfil the terms of a deal clinched the previous year, yielding the Merseyside club the record sum of £3.2 million. Liverpool had already purchased another central striker – John Aldridge from Oxford United – the previous Christmas. They had been playing him primarily in the reserves, apparently grooming him to step in to the Rush role. However, with player-manager Dalglish now well into his thirties, it was clear that further reinforcements were required. Before long, Peter Beardsley, the Newcastle and England forward blessed with many similar attributes to Dalglish, also became linked with Liverpool. But for the last six weeks of the season it was the Barnes story that counted, with every aspect of the potential move documented and dissected – except, of course, those that no one, as ever, really wanted to talk about.

The events – or, for most of the time, non-events – of the period between the negotiation becoming public knowledge and Barnes's first appearance at Liverpool were more remarkable for what was read into them than what actually occurred. The business facts of the matter now seem plain enough. Dalglish wished to purchase the services of both Barnes and Beardsley, add them to those of Aldridge, and create an entirely new offensive thrust to the Liverpool team. On learning of Barnes's decision to turn down a new contract with Watford, reportedly worth £1,000 a week, Liverpool entered into talks with Graham Taylor and made an offer in the region of £900,000. It has subsequently been asserted by Dalglish that both parties agreed a deadline of 8 June 1987 for Barnes to make a final decision, pending the possibility of offers from other clubs. Liverpool, then, were first in the queue. It was merely a question of waiting to see if anyone else joined it. In the end, no one did. Dalglish got his man and John Barnes became the first black player ever to be transferred to either of the two big Merseyside clubs, agreement being formally reached at a motorway rendezvous halfway between Watford and Liverpool on 9 June.

But it was the fall-out from this limbo period which tells the real tale of modern football. It was a period in which Barnes's anxiety to make the right career move ran uncomfortably against the grain of his public relations instincts and the vigorous partisanship of Liverpool FC's supporters – a characteristic of which Barnes would enjoy both the generous and the chauvinistic aspects in the space of barely four months and only the same number of games.

The player himself made no secret of the fact that he saw his best possible future option as being with a continental club. Barnes likes Italian football and watches lots of it on TV via a satellite dish. To that end, his agent Athole Still, a former Olympic swimmer, had compiled a video showcasing his client's talents and distributed it to a number of Italian clubs. It was reported that more than one such team had already taken the trouble of watching Barnes in action, among them Fiorentina, Napoli – the home of Diego Maradonna – and Roma. A number of French teams were also mentioned briefly in despatches. None, however, went so far as to make an offer.

Meanwhile, the impression that Barnes was less than wholeheartedly enthusiastic about the prospect of joining Liverpool was greatly strengthened by newspaper stories quoting him as expressing a preference for one of the two biggest London clubs, Arsenal or Tottenham Hotspur. On 3 June the *Echo* produced a quote: 'If I cannot go abroad, I would prefer to stay in London with a club like Arsenal or Spurs, and I simply cannot believe they are not interested in signing me.'

Whether these remarks were actually made by Barnes in this or indeed in any form at all, we shall probably never know. Certainly he was careful to distance himself from them in subsequent public statements. But it would be very surprising indeed if he had not thought long and hard about the size of the task that awaited him should he opt to sell his house in Hemel Hempstead, pack his bags and migrate to the heartland of the penurious side of the north–south divide.

First, there was the hate mail. It is unclear precisely how much of this there was, but Peter Robinson admitted that 'about half a dozen letters' were sent to the club, expressing the view that 'we should not sign a coloured player'. At the press conference following his signing, Barnes was quoted in the Liverpool *Daily Post* carefully absolving his new home crowd from any connection with the poison pens, saying, 'I haven't had any bad mail from Merseyside whatsoever, in fact I'm dying to get out and play for the public here.'

The precise contents of Barnes's or Robinson's postbag may remain shrouded (though in the light of the volume Grobbelaar has claimed he received after his early goalkeeping gaffes, 'half a dozen' seems remarkably restrained). The outbreak of graffiti in the vicinity of Anfield did not; at least, not once the club's latest investment had signed on the dotted line. One morning it was discovered that a person or persons had painted slogans on the walls at the Kop end. The interlopers' handiwork had an unmistakable message: no blacks welcome here. Police were called and a trap set to catch the perpetrators if they returned. They did not. The club, meanwhile, hushed up the incident. The local press did not report it until after the new boy was successfully signed.

The local Liverpool sports lobby was a little less tardy when providing a platform for the secretary of Liverpool FC's official Supporters' Club, Bob Gill. Quoted in a piece headlined 'Barnes Saga Leaves Fans Stunned', Gill dipped into the Golden Past: 'In Shankly's time [this deal] wouldn't have dragged on more than a day, let alone three months. Most of the fans believe Barnes was given too much time. It appears now that nobody else wants him, so he has finally decided to unload himself on us. That's the way it has come across. Most players would jump at the chance to join a club like Liverpool and he is no different.'

This story, written by chief football writer Ken Rogers, appeared in the Liverpool *Daily Post* on the morning of the day Barnes actually signed, lending local authority to the sensationalized accounts that had appeared in the national tabloids. The following day's coverage of the happy event saw the club's spokesmen, Robinson and Dalglish, seeking to defuse the situation before the assembled pressmen. 'There has been some speculation in various newspapers about this signing,' said Dalglish, 'but we can assure the public that John wasn't using Liverpool as a makeweight in any other negotiations.' Barnes said a little piece that would have been after his father's heart: 'I can't wait to play here in front of the fans. It's a marvellous move for me and a great challenge. When it was made plain I wasn't going to Europe, there was only one English club for me and that was Liverpool.'

Good local politics, but was it the whole of the truth? It is understood, for instance, that Barnes consulted with other black professionals before finally making up his mind. Those he spoke to are said to have encouraged him to go. They knew he had the talent and the temperament to make a go of it and break down a barrier on behalf of all England's black players. Ray Sullivan, Barnes's old tutor at Stowe Boys and Sudbury Court, sensed Barnes's trepidation too. 'I saw him the night before he signed. He'd just had his medical that day and I'm still certain in my mind that he was reticent about going up there. It was a major step for him, for one because of the black thing. I sort of said as much to him without quite saying it, you know. I said: "You realize Liverpool's traditions and the background up there? It's not like being in London." I think he was aware that it wasn't going to be plain sailing. He was very much aware of the demands there were going to be for instant success. Arsenal would probably have suited him a lot better. I said: "Are you really sure that Liverpool is the best club you could go to? It's different being a big fish at Watford and being one of the team at Liverpool." But he'd obviously made his mind up.'

And, as Sullivan correctly points out, no one – not Arsenal, not Tottenham, not anyone – had made a bid for him except Kenny Dalglish. It was Liverpool or nothing. He had to make it work.

Two days later, the new boy was making the most of his plunge into the Merseyside spotlight, exploiting a photo opportunity by meeting fans queuing for season tickets and finding a few well chosen words to complement the snapshot with a bunch of beaming scallies: 'Over the last few years I've built up a tremendous respect for the entire Liverpool set-up. They have always had a tremendous side. It's never been about one player, but a blend of qualities. I believe they are the best club in England, on and off the field.' He continued to take the wind out of the supposed 'saga': 'I can understand how the Anfield fans must have felt, but I know that for me the Reds have always been the biggest club. The Kop are famous in their own right, but it is the atmosphere in the whole ground that I find so marvellous. I will do my best for them in a red shirt.' Spoken, once again, like a diplomat's son. Now all he had to do was repeat the performance with his boots on.

On the Merseyside football network, news travels fast. Even signing autographs for a bunch of fans in the car park by the Shankly memorial gates was enough to send good vibes rippling across the city; the word was that John Barnes was sound. Booked into the busy Moathouse Hotel, a regular meeting and eating place for the players, he became an immediate celebrity as he went about his daily business, his visibility compounded by being one of the few black men to be seen in the centre of town. His impeccable manners and amenable style were duly exercised in local pubs and nightclubs. One local story concerns an insult directed at him by an Everton fan in a bar. Barnes, with bodyguard in tow, went over and introduced himself. A short while later, one shamefaced Evertonian and his mates were, as the storyteller put it, 'eating out of his hand'.

The Colonel's son introduced himself to Merseyside with a low-key charm offensive. He had no proclivities for leading an intemperate lifestyle or for smacking tormentors in the mouth. But if Barnes was making a shrewd job of salvaging what was an unpromising situation, the fact that he was in that situation at all cannot be fully explained without reference to a new, rogue factor in the Anfield works – the extraordinary Kenny Dalglish.

The media consensus about the distinguished Glaswegian (certainly before Hillsborough) was that he was a facetious, taciturn misanthrope from whose evasive public utterances even the most mendacious headline writer would be hard pressed to contrive a sensation. The viewpoint of some who know him slightly better is that Scotland's most capped international is a creature of high integrity, murderous dedication, alarming single-mindedness and incorrigible caprice. 'Kenny is just a law unto himself,' says one former member of the Anfield staff. 'Nobody ever knew what he was going to do next.'

The appointment of Dalglish to the manager's chair in 1985 was made in circumstances which, in their way, were almost as onerous as those Barnes had to face. Following Bob Paisley's retirement in 1983, the manager's mantle had passed down the established line of succession to Joe Fagan, who had joined the club as assistant trainer in 1958 and been promoted to Paisley's deputy when Shankly retired. In Fagan's first season the team won three major titles. Under the imperious captaincy of Souness, they took the League Championship for the third season in succession and also the Milk Cup after a replayed Final against Everton. Finally, Liverpool found themselves facing the daunting prospect of a European Cup Final against A.S. Roma at the Italian side's own Olympic stadium. With the score 1-all after extra time, Liverpool took the trophy following a tumultuous penalty shoot-out.

The following year, though, struggling to replace Souness in midfield, Liverpool approached the end of the season with no major domestic trophy and the European Cup offering their only hope of adding to their mountain of silver. Fagan, aged sixty-four and feeling the strain, had made his intention to retire at the end of the season known to his employers, but not to the players or public. Opting to move down a generation, the Liverpool board decided to appoint Dalglish player–manager for the following season. The main impetus for this came from Smith, in discussion with Robinson, Fagan and Paisley. It was, though, to the consternation of all when news of Fagan's impending departure broke just as the team were on the brink of their ill-fated encounter with Juventus at the Heysel Stadium in Brussels.

Rumours of the new appointment began circulating among the players even as they kicked their heels in their hotel. None could quite believe it, least of all full-back Phil Neal, Souness's successor as team captain and the man who has won more honours with Liverpool than any other player. Neal subsequently claimed, in a prickly autobiography, that chairman Smith had as good as promised him at least some sort of job as he approached the end of his playing days. He expressed his astonishment that Dalglish was given a job he clearly coveted himself: '[Dalglish had] never given any indication that he harboured managerial ambitions . . . Off the field . . . he was a quiet, complex sort of character who kept himself to himself and spent most of his afternoons resting in bed. No one could really claim to know him well and so none of us had any knowledge of where his true ambitions lay, none of us that is except the chairman!'

And so, with the farce of a match completed and the bodies of thirty-nine Italian supporters scarcely cold in the Brussels morgue, the world's press converged upon the rumoured new Liverpool player-manager, demanding all they could get from a man who gave nothing away. The upshot for the transfixed British public was an early TV example of that euphemistic term, 'being economical with the truth'. Had the players known about events on the terraces *before* they went out to play? Dalglish answered 'No'. In reality, though, some of the players had been weeping in the dressing-room as kick-off time approached, with news of fatalities steadily filtering through.

Things improved for Dalglish after that, and rapidly. In his first year as player-manager Liverpool won the FA Cup and League Championship 'double' for the first time in the club's history. It had been an uncomfortable first half of the season. In playing terms, Dalglish's first move was to start experimenting with the team formation. Jan Molby, a Danish international, was brought in as a sweeper, Continental style, for a number of games. It was not a great success. Liverpool spent the first half of the season trailing the early leaders with Dalglish, nursing a troublesome knee injury, declining to pick himself. But when his ostensible successor Paul Walsh was confined to the treatment table, Dalglish, relying on his remarkable footballing intelligence to make up for his restricted fitness, came back into the side and masterminded an unbeaten surge to the top in the second half of the season. In May, the Reds again went to Wembley to meet the men in blue from across Stanley Park in the first-ever Merseyside FA Cup Final. They vanquished them by a margin of 3–1. The player-manager's boyish beam as he held the trophy aloft will never be forgotten.

The following year, though, was less successful. Everton, under the guidance of Howard Kendall, took the Championship; Liverpool lost a disappointing Milk Cup Final to Arsenal during which Dalglish failed to impress in his twenty minutes as substitute. With Ian Rush departing to Juventus, a huge gap was about to appear in what remained of the team that Paisley had built. The steps Dalglish took to fill it probably stand as his finest achievement in management, a testimony, perhaps, to Liverpool's spending power, but also to his own assessment of what a good football team should be.

Shankly, Paisley and Fagan had all been half-backs in their playing days, men whose value to a team would be counted more in strength and dependability than distilled in poetry. The qualities of vigour and organization which were the hallmarks of Liverpool's success stemmed directly from their own approaches to the game. But while Dalglish's ferocious win mentality and his reluctance to suffer fools were in keeping with that tradition, his own exquisite talents give him a dimension of understanding with which his illustrious forebears could never have been intimate. At his best there was a profound geometric perception about Dalglish's style which enabled him to retain possession in the most unpromising circumstances and deliver the ball to team-mates with flawless precision. A goalscorer of unerring cool, his capacity for finding the net was only one part of an armoury of skills which made him the nerve centre of the Liverpool attack for years. It was often said that he lacked great pace, and he certainly could not compete in that department with his brilliant striking partner, Rush. But the subtle economy of his skills and the intelligence with which he employed them stood as incontrovertible evidence that football in its purest form is not the product of an athletic technocracy, but the realization of talents that are not entirely explicable, a thing of beauty, an art.

Tottenham Hotspur's manager David Pleat did not bid for Barnes. Nor did Arsenal's George Graham, though he gave it a lot of thought. Perhaps they did not wholly believe in a talent which had not been consistently fulfilled over seven seasons for Watford and England. But Dalglish did. In fact, he obtained backing from his board to the tune of nearly a million pounds to go with the flow of his own judgement – this being that, in the appropriate setting, precious jewels can be relied upon to shine.

It is a tribute to Dalglish's singularity that Barnes had all the characteristics of a wholly atypical Liverpool player. Heighway and Thompson notwithstanding, this was an empire built on *passing* the ball. Barnes was famous for running with it. Never mind the pedigree of individuals, the Liverpool citadel was constructed on the concepts of rationality, not of intuition. And yet Barnes was criticized for fading out of games when his muse deserted him. The Anfield faithful were not much used to welcoming wayward aristocratic ostentation. And Liverpool embodied all the qualities which the football culture had regarded for decades as the antithesis of what the black footballer offered. 'White' values ruled from turnstile to team sheet. So what was this 'black' man doing here?

If anyone did whisper that question in Kenny Dalglish's ear, he plainly declined to hear it. His imperviousness to received wisdoms which he considered to be flawed had already been established. The club's hierarchy could bear rueful witness to that. When Dalglish assumed his new managerial role, he planted his feet under the desk with a resolution that sent everyone into a panic. A local pressman recalls his and his colleagues' first encounter with Dalglish in his new hat. It was a formal introduction to the regime at which the manager made his position absolutely clear: 'He said: "You don't know anything about football, and I don't know anything about writing. So we should get along just fine."'

Then there was an unpublicized fracas after a game at Watford, involving Dalglish and a man with diametrically opposed attitudes towards publicity and the media. The caustic Kenny and entrepreneur extraordinary, Jimmy Hill, were never designed to be pals. In his role as TV pundit, Hill had taken it upon himself to criticize Liverpool's approach to the game a few weeks before. Entering the inner portals of what was then John Barnes's club, Dalglish spied his critic on the other side of the room. It did not take him long to cross it and metaphorically invite the astonished mediacrat to 'stitch that'. It was not behaviour which the Anfield brotherhood regarded as at all becoming in this most undemonstrative of clubs. Chairman Smith, it is said, thought it necessary to advise his new appointment against similar intemperance in future.

Whatever, within a a very short time, Dalglish began exercising his iron will upon an Anfield power structure whose unwritten rules yielded surprisingly easily to anyone who did not care to recognize established protocol. People started collecting their cards. Dalglish fired likeable Reserve team manager Chris Lawler. Phil Thompson was brought back as a more abrasive replacement. Another long-serving backroom staffer, scout Geoff Twentyman, was also relieved of his duties after a row with Dalglish. He went off to join the Souness dynasty at Glasgow Rangers. But the most startling stories of all concern Dalglish's relationship with Bob Paisley.

Though it is rarely articulated publicly, Paisley enjoys an ambiguous status among players and pundits alike. Statistics have secured his standing as the most successful club manager British football has ever seen, and they can scarcely be denied. His secret, though, remains a mystery. In an era when football managers loom from the mass media as garish, motor-mouthed caricatures, Paisley never projected much of a personality at all. Distracted, diffident and inclined to mutter in his dense Newcastle accent, his television appearances were hardly comic vignettes in the Shankly tradition. In a classic example of public image jerry-building, the media scratched about and finally succeeded in presenting Paisley as a cosy fireside character, an avuncular soccer sage in a zip-up cardigan.

But Paisley was nobody's cuddly toy. He dominated the playing side of the club with a combination of ruthlessness and complete incorrigibility. Former players offer only mundane explanations for his winning ways: he was a good judge of a player; he inherited a system and knew how to make it work. One ex-Liverpudlian just shook his head: 'It's hard to talk about that because the man inherited a team and his opening words were, "I didn't want the job in any case". But he bought very wisely, he ran the club wisely . . . if he watched a game afterwards he could tell you every pass, every run, every move, every mistake. He remembered everything. But his ability to man-motivate or put his knowledge of the game over verbally was non-existent. It was down to the players to try and suss out what he was on about.'

When Dalglish took over from Joe Fagan, Paisley, by this time a club director, was re-activated as his adviser behind the scenes. The two of them went back a long way. It was Paisley who had brought Dalglish to Liverpool, a £440,000 purchase from Celtic to replace Kevin Keegan. But as Dalglish tightened his grip on the reins, their relationship deteriorated. Paisley had always tended to work collectively with the club's hierarchy. Forays into the transfer market tended to be discussed as a group. Dalglish, though, was determined to prove himself his own man. A story has circulated that one match day morning Dalglish took it upon himself to eject Paisley from the team coach, telling him he should travel with the directors from now on. The tale may well be apocryphal. But the existence of ill-feeling between the tight-lipped Geordie and his former protégé has subsequently breached even the high-gloss veneer that Liverpool Football Club prefers to turn to the outside world.

It was the latest in an unbroken sequence of discordant separations from the managerial chair. Bill Shankly himself left under a cloud, in conflict with the board. From the day of his retirement to the day he met his maker he was never welcomed back to the club he built, never invited to travel to prestige away fixtures, never offered a place of honour in the directors' box. He died an unhappy man. Fagan's sadness in the wake of Heysel speaks for itself. Paisley, however, did not exhibit the pain of separation until the team Dalglish built was running away with the League. It was only then that Paisley's infamous statements appeared in the press, claiming that the current First Division was the weakest he'd ever seen and putting John Aldridge's back up by saying that he would never have signed him.

Such a break in the Liverpool ranks was a measure of the extent to which Dalglish had seized the whip hand at the club. He had built a team in his own image and done it his own way. The signing of Barnes was a symbol of his steely determination to do things as he pleased, whatever demons it might unleash. It is a tribute to Barnes's sporting talent and personal equanimity that he confronted the fall-out from Kenny's ambition with such panache and grace.

10

'Black, or Something?'

With John Barnes on the payroll at last, Liverpool Football Club finally had to face the writing on the wall. It was on 2 July 1987 that the *Daily Post* ran an article at the top of page three headlined 'Reds' Crackdown On Race Hate Graffiti'. Credited to a '*Daily Post* Reporter', it announced that the club had 'launched a "clean up the terraces" campaign to welcome new signing John Barnes – after being accused of racism.' Two photographs accompanied the article: one, a head shot of the new signing smiling; the other, a view of a main exit gate from the Spion Kop upon which had been clearly sprayed two large sets of the initials 'NF', the slogan 'White Power' and the message 'No Wogs Allowed'. The piece quoted Brian Thompson, an art teacher and a member of the Liverpool Community Relations Council. For him, the *Daily Post*'s coverage represented, at last, the kind of publicity over the issue for which he and others had been lobbying in vain in the two years since Heysel.

Thompson's indignation had been roused by the apparent willingness of the club to tolerate large quantities of racist graffiti painted around the ground. Chairman Smith had seen fit to blame National Front activitists for fomenting the Brussels disaster, but the club over which he presided seemed content to ignore that organization's daubings all over the premises. Thompson began by visiting the ground: 'In some places the letters were four and five feet high. In other parts it was just things that people had written when standing waiting to get in, written on a single brick. I made complaints at the ticket office and at reception. I left messages for whoever was responsible for it, saying there had been a formal complaint by a member of the public about this graffiti and how it wasn't being attended to. But no attention was paid.'

At this time, Thompson was working as an art teacher at the University School, an inner-city Liverpool comprehensive. He decided to involve some of his students in a more vigorous attempt to jolt the club into action. It was, by coincidence, the day that the Popplewell Report into the causes and motivations of Heysel and other football-related violence was published. Thompson, framing the exercise as 'a practical example of peaceful but direct action', went back to Anfield with a dozen or so black and white children, some boys, some girls. 'We went there, looked at the graffiti and took photographs of it. Then we went to speak at the ticket office and asked to see the stadium manager. When eventually he came over to us we made the complaint, but he wasn't really taking it seriously.

'I was with one of the school students, a girl called Beverly, and the guy was saying, "Oh, it's terrible isn't it? They write lots of silly things like 'Everton Football Club' and things like that." Then this girl Beverly cut in and said, "Listen, we haven't come here to talk about stupid things like Everton Football Club. We've come here to deal with racism." And she put this guy on the spot. And he was visibly shaken by the fact that a young black girl could speak so articulately and forthrightly. We told him then that we'd taken photographs of the graffiti and unless some action was taken we were going to release them to the press.'

This had the desired effect, at least in the short term. Later on that day the school was contacted by the club, and assured that something was going to be done about it. Soon after, Thompson and the school delegation returned to the ground and discovered that, true enough, large areas of the racist graffiti had been removed. 'That was fair enough,' says Thompson, 'and we didn't do any more about it. Then a year later, which was January 1987, we went back up to the ground. The situation was worse, and some of the graffiti was still on from the year before.'

This time the campaigners decided to dispense with niceties and launch a public campaign. They took more photographs, compiled them into a display with text, and circulated copies of their material to various relevant bodies, including the local papers. All this was undertaken, of course, well before the first speculation about Barnes's transfer had appeared in the press. Given this, it is interesting to consider the way Liverpool's local papers dealt with the subject.

In the first place, they did nothing. It was not until the signing of Barnes had been completed and the start of his first season loomed that the *Daily Post* considered the business of racist graffiti worth reporting. When the 'Clean Up' splash eventually appeared, the reporter quoted Brian Thompson's view that the black community in Liverpool felt unwelcome at the ground: 'You hardly ever see a black face in the crowd at Anfield, and why? – because it's not safe for them to go there.' The response of chairman Smith was reported as follows: 'Nonsense.' He expanded upon this view: 'How many black people do you see at football matches in other parts of the country?' It was no kind of reply to Thompson's point. In the first place many clubs have attracted larger proportions of black supporters than Liverpool despite having much smaller black populations. And the fact that black representatives are still statistically tiny, despite the conspicuous numbers of black players, says more about the extent of racism across the country than the lack of it at Liverpool – and this from the recently appointed Chairman of the Sports Council.

Dalglish's policy with regard to race was to adopt the 'colour blind' position. 'He's not a black player – he's a player,' snapped the Boss in response to one impertinent post-match enquiry early in the season. It was a posture he maintained with great care in all his public statements. In a handsomely produced 'diary', *The Liverpool Year*, Dalglish, ghosted by *Daily Express* reporter John Keith, wrote: 'The fact that John happens to be the first Black player Liverpool have bought was something that had not crossed my mind until it was pointed out to me. At Liverpool we are not concerned with race, creed, or the colour of a person's skin. The only thing that matters to us is whether a player we would like to sign is available and keen to join us. And in John's case those things applied.'

Dalglish reiterated this in a rare and exclusive interview serialized over three days in the *Daily Mirror* in November 1988. As the most successful manager at that moment in the English game, as well as the most tight-lipped, three double-page spreads' worth of opinion from King Kenny was gold dust, even if the paper did feel obliged to flag a veiled apology for the lack of snide remarks about other figures in football: 'Dalglish lifts the lid off soccer but does it without resorting to the outrageous statements that bring only disgrace to the game.' On the second day of the 'World Exclusive' Dalglish spoke of the new players he had brought to the club, starting off with you-know-who.

'The signing of Barnes is something I've never regretted. I know that he was good enough. I certainly had no qualms about signing him because of his colour. It didn't even cross my mind. It's always been a hallmark of my time in football that I would never judge anyone on their colour, creed or religion. All that concerns me is their ability.' So far, so good, and entirely believable, coming from a Protestant who became a hero at Glasgow Celtic. Then the going got a bit more contentious: 'It makes no difference, either, to anyone who supports Liverpool. I don't understand those people who say we don't have black players at Anfield.' Dalglish reached for the thin thread of historical precedent: 'Don't forget Howard Gayle ... and don't forget his performance in the European Cup semi-final against Bayern Munich.' Dalglish might rest assured that over in Liverpool 8 that perfomance will never be forgotten, especially for the way it ended.

But this is not to imply that Dalglish's perceptions, uttered to the *Daily Mirror*, were necessarily anything less than well intended and sincere. What they tend to confirm is that Dalglish is a rigorously rational thinker in his assessment of the game. Coming from a younger generation than his predecessors, one that included many black contemporaries, he was far less prone to the old superstitions. Dalglish represents the players of English football's first multi-racial era coming to managerial power, a new wave of professionals who were ready to vote a racially-conscious black contemporary, Garth Crooks, into the Chairmanship of the PFA in 1988. Dalglish, too, has grown out of a period in which the religion of the balance sheet has outstripped many of the more ethereal values, left over from the Victorian industrial society. In this new sporting meritocracy every player enjoys a similar status, as a commodity and a provider of labour. Bigotry may be set aside in the interests of points in the bag. Dalglish looked at Barnes's specifications and liked what he saw. He had seen Barnes play enough to know that this player possessed a dimension of ability which, when applied to full capacity, would be too potent for any opposition to consistently resist. He not only recognized, but also placed the highest value on, the evident fact that John Barnes was capable of doing things with a football that few players in the English League could match – and that, he knew, was the greatest gift, the greatest asset.

Dalglish looked at Barnes and saw a footballer whose skills he wished to acquire, and whose personal reputation was unblemished. The 'colour blind' position takes some swallowing. But it is not difficult to believe that Dalglish elected to dismiss it as a criterion for assessing the worth of the player.

Liverpool also believed Barnes could be developed and improved. Dalglish considered that, for all his reputation, Barnes could be slotted into Liverpool's traditional passing pattern, and that his classic winger's skills – running, dribbling, crossing – could give it an extra dimension. In Beardsley and Aldridge he had two more components in a new attacking repertoire that might properly compensate for the loss of himself and Rush. Beardsley's talents were abundant: an ability to find and exploit space in and around the penalty area; superb ball control; an unselfish capacity to create and the imagination to recognize creative possibilities; a potential, not yet fully exploited, for producing goals out of thin air. Aldridge, meanwhile, was simply a consummate craftsman. Not the most artistic or the most skilled, he had, nonetheless, squeezed the maximum profit from relatively limited resources. He knew the angles and anxieties of the penalty area intimately. He had already proved that he could score goals in any team. Dalglish knew the players he wanted and how they could be made to work together. The cheque book did the rest.

And so John Barnes became Liverpool's first black signing. He and Dalglish had their picture taken together with the Anfield turf in the background, two handsome men, the white Glaswegian Protestant with his arm around the black, Anglo-Jamaican Catholic. On 15 August 1987 Barnes ran out on to the pitch at Highbury, North London to play his first competitive game for Liverpool against

Arsenal in front of 54,703 spectators. After nine minutes he crossed the ball from the left towards Beardsley, who flicked it on towards Aldridge who headed it past Lukic in the Arsenal goal. For Dalglish, vindication could hardly have come more quickly. The Londoners fought back to equalize by half-time. But five minutes from the end, full-back Steve Nicol headed home a long-range header after a free-kick by Barnes had been inadequately cleared: 2–1 and the final whistle was blown. Liverpool's travelling supporters went home delighted, any doubts about the wisdom of the manager's summer shopping spree already on the retreat.

The swing in Barnes's fortunes was already assuming the proportions of a melodrama. It took an extra, and ironic, shove in the right direction thanks to the dire condition of the Spion Kop. It was discovered that the main sewer running beneath the famous terrace had collapsed and that a large part of the Kop's surface area was dangerously unsafe. Somebody at the club made a joke which hinted at the terms of Barnes's acceptance in the dressing-room: 'We'd have cleared it out before, but we didn't have a spade till this season.' But while Liverpool Football Club was investing nearly £4 million in new players, the ground was falling apart.

Eighteen months later, it would not be quite so easy to make jokes about crumbling stadia. Jokes about 'spades', though, were all the rage for a while. The rest of 'the lads' soon found out that 'Barnesie' wasn't the sort to get upset about, you know, colour and all that. Aldridge, in his end-of-season biog, makes reference to it: 'The boss brought a touch of humour to the team talk today. He had a board with little figures on it to explain the moves we had been practising in training.' They were all red except for a black one, and Kenny said: "This one is you, Barnesie." John doesn't mind,' continued Aldridge, 'and there is no racialism at Anfield. Some people said that John might have trouble being the first "big money" black player to play for Liverpool, but the fans love him. Who wouldn't, the kind of football John plays? We all get on great with him. There is no animosity. He calls us honkies and we all take the rise out of him. There is no animosity and the spirit in the dressing-room couldn't be better.' Lots of goals, and no 'animosity'. That's the military attaché's boy.

He needed to be like that to survive in the Anfield dressing-room. There is piss-taking and parody in most such masculine gatherings – no other form of communication is permitted. But Liverpool always have been seen as that bit different. The pressure to conform carries everyone before it. 'They're very funny, the Liverpool players,' says one who experienced them at close quarters for years. 'They have a very dry sense of humour. When people join, they may not have it but within a couple of months they will find they have *got* to have it. Nothing is taken seriously. They just have to take the piss out of everything and everybody and that's the way they are. Everton have got a sense of humour, but it's not the same. If you go up to Bellefield [Everton's training ground] after they've finished and they're having lunch, everyone's very quiet. But you go to Liverpool and they're all just taking the piss out of each other. Anyone just walking in would rather be with the Everton players, 'cos they're far more like ... human beings – people you would want to talk to. But there's just something at Liverpool. It's very tight. When you're new you have to cope with it, and when you do, you're there for ever. But I think that's very hard, because it comes over a period of time and you need a lot of patience. But John fitted in as if he had been there the season before. Normally, it takes about a week, where they'll all sit alone and have their lunch. They'll say a few things, but they won't actually get right into the team. But John did.'

People were very conscious that Barnes was stepping across the threshold of a white football culture, and not just at Liverpool. Everton's players had lots of 'jokes' to offer. One Liverpool fan, a luminary of the amateur leagues with contacts at both clubs, recalls his first visit to Bellfield after Barnes had been signed. A number of Everton players went out of their way to rib him about it. The word 'nigger' was casually used.

At Liverpool, Barnes had his strategy worked out. On his first day at the training ground he sat at a bench with a couple of his new team-mates. Cups of tea were put before the two established players. Barnes looked up at the woman who brought them. He said: 'What am I, black or something?' Everyone fell about.

It is a very significant story. Other black footballers, professionals and amateurs alike, say they could not have made that joke. They just wouldn't have felt right. For them, Discrimination is not something to be laughed about. But John Barnes is different. Maybe being the product of a black nation's top brass enabled him to make a joke like that. Maybe £900,000 of Liverpool FC's pre-tax profit gave him the confidence to reduce prejudice to a laughing matter, to initiate breaking the ice in an institution where twenty-five years of unbroken habit demanded that you had to conform or go under. Barnes pre-empted his own initiation. He gave permission for his team-mates to, for better or worse, relate to him in the traditional Liverpool way. I'm black. It's a joke. Everyone relax. 'Barnes has got a brain,' says the Liverpool insider. 'But to use it there's got to be someone serious to use it with, and you're not allowed to be serious. If John was on television and he gave a serious interview, he would get some stick. And it's hard to take that sort of stick when you're trying to be part of the team. You've got to act like everyone else does.'

After that, there were lots and lots of jokes. Jan Molby, the huge, scouse-talking Danish midfield man, had earned the nickname 'Rambo' from the Anfield crowd. The dressing-room gang soon thought of some more nicknames that rhymed. Beardsley, a hunched, diminutive figure, not widely considered handsome, was christened 'Quasimodo'. Guess what they thought of for Barnes? So there was Rambo, there was Aldo, Quasimodo and, of course, there was Sambo. Ho-ho. The football columnist of *Today* even made a cheery reference to it in his programme notes for a sub-sequent game against Wimbledon: 'Sambo has samba'd down the wing . . .'

Still, 'John doesn't mind . . .' But then, if he did, it wasn't the done thing to say so. 'John being black is not even considered, or that he could be having problems or whatever,' says the Liverpool insider. 'It just isn't seen as an issue. They've seen what goes on, but they've not done anything about it. He's coped by himself, he's not had any help from anyone.'

But by this time, fate and even the Anfield plumbing was with him. Liverpool's first four scheduled home games of the season had to be postponed. Barnes and company, then, could continue to bed-in beyond the Merseyside spotlight. It was a delicious acclimatization. By the time the new-look Liverpool finally came to Anfield, the Koppites were in a frenzy to see them. Especially Barnes.

The victory at Arsenal turned out to be the first in an opening sequence of 29 unbeaten games. It continued in style a fortnight later at Coventry, where Liverpool won 4–1. Barnes did not score, but the Liverpool *Daily Post* noted the signal from the fans: 'The chant that signalled acceptance rang out from the appreciative army of Liverpool supporters. "Johnny Barnes, Johnny Barnes, Johnny Barnes" they roared . . .' Kenny Dalglish wrote in *The Liverpool Year* that 'a very heart-warming aspect of the afternoon was the way in which the large number of Liverpool fans who travelled to High- field Road gave tremendous vocal support to John Barnes and Peter Beardsley. Both players told me afterwards that it gave them a great lift and that they are now bursting to make their Anfield débuts as Liverpool players. But we've got one more away-day before that.'

It was at West Ham, a 1-all draw. Not too bad. But the week after was all joy. The team ran out for their first home game of the season with the Kop turnstiles already boarded up forty minutes before the kick-off. It was a monumental Anfield occasion, and there was one man in particular the masses had come to see. Patrick Barclay in the *Independent* wrote: 'The roars that enveloped John Barnes while he warmed up for his appearance at Anfield had a clear message: however long the England winger may have pondered the decision to join Liverpool from Watford, he was more than welcome.

'His response will live in the memory. For decades to come every home début will be measured against Barnes's against Oxford on Saturday . . . Not since Kevin Keegan in the early seventies has the Kop formed such an instant bond . . . His performance was ren- dered all the more astonishing by its proximity to perfection. A player of Barnes's type, who runs with the ball and commits opponents, expects to win some and lose some, to trade errors for the confusion he prompts. Yet in 90 minutes I cannot recall his conceding possession once.'

An important clue to Liverpool's approach lies in their training style. It could hardly be more different from what Barnes endured at Watford. Most of the work is done with a ball in the form of five-a-side games. It is within this format that the players learn and re-learn the value of creating fluid, passing triangles, the classic geometric pattern of the game. Trap, pass, move ... and keep on moving. Find space to create space for someone else. *Then* the man with the ball can do something with it. *Then* you can dismantle your opponents' defence, swiftly, cleanly and as sweet as can be. *Then* you can go for goal.

Against Oxford United Barnes not only conformed to Liverpool's most sacred tenets, he thrived upon them. His own, special potential was suddenly unleashed and he brought to the Liverpool pattern a whole dimension of his own. He crossed for Aldridge to score against his old club, in front of the bank of supporters whose ranks he himself had occupied as a boy. Then, in the thirty-seventh minute, Barnes cut inside and was fouled. The free-kick was tapped sideways, primed for his left foot. Barnes sent the ball swirling around Oxford's defensive wall and past goalkeeper Hucker, a spectator from the instant the shot was struck. The second half was, almost inevitably, an anti-climax. But, as the players left the field at the end of the game, Barnes turned back from the tunnel to receive the adoration of the Kop. The message was, 'You're in.'

PART THREE

Out of His Skin?

'Everton are White'

On 29 October 1987, London Weekend Television transmitted late evening highlights of the season's first bristling contest between Everton and Kenny Dalglish's new Liverpool team. The occasion was the third round of the Littlewoods Cup and Liverpool, with Barnes as their chief inspiration, were unbeaten in all competitions since the start of the season.

Anchor man Nick Owen, dressed in immaculate suburban casuals with a haircut to match, billed the evening's entertainment as 'the most passionate tie of the round.' He added that so many Merseysiders had been disappointed not to get tickets that a giant TV screen had been erected at Goodison, enabling the game to be viewed live by a further 12,000 supporters, just across the park. The occasion was that big.

Owen gave way to match commentator Martin Tyler, shouting to make himself heard above the Anfield furore, as the opposing supporters did their best to chant each other down. As minorities go, Everton's were hardly silent. Tyler noted that this was the first derby game in twenty in which Ian Rush had not appeared and drew our attention to the outstanding form of Everton's centre-forward, the Scottish international Graeme Sharp. Referee Vic Callow from Solihull set the match in motion. The familiar frenzy of blue and red ensued. Tyler settled into his commentary style, pitched at a level of barely suppressed hysteria, spiked with a tremor of impending mayhem.

It was not altogether inappropriate. The match was like a war of attrition. The action was concentrated in the centre of the field where a vigorous engagement involving Peter Reid of Everton and Liverpool's McMahon was the focus of the proceedings. It was the footballing equivalent of trench warfare, the kind of out-and-out contest which apologists like to assure us is the proud hallmark of

British football today – 'it's a man's game'. Viewers settled down before a chaos of ferocious tackles and hurried back-passes which continued unabated as everyone waited for the single moment of luck, inspiration or catastrophe that alone would break the deadlock. It happened in the eighty-fourth minute. The ball came to the advancing England right-back Gary Stevens who cut boldly inside and took a pot shot from twenty yards with his weaker, left foot. The ball struck Gary Gillespie, Liverpool's Scottish centre-back, and was deflected past Grobbelaar into the net. That was the end of that. Over at Goodison Park, it later transpired, the 12,000 big screen viewers had actually invaded the pitch. Tylor signed off. In the studio, Nick Owen beamed blandly. The nation reached for the on–off switch, another night of media-sport successfully endured.

But the real story of the night had not been told. Viewers with an ear for spectator noise (a mere backdrop to the commentator's spiel in TV's version of sporting events) might have detected the dominant nuance of the support voiced on Everton's behalf and the way it rose to a crescendo when the action involved John Barnes. Every time the Liverpool winger got the ball he was loudly and vehemently booed. Every time he advanced towards the corner flags at the Anfield Road end he was showered with abuse. Photographers stationed along the goal line were astonished by the violence of the language directed at him, clearly audible to the players at the edges of the field. Barnes took corner kicks in a hail of spit. Meanwhile, a substantial section of Everton's fans assailed Liverpool's new hero with chants, prepared specially for the occasion. One, based on the popular campaign anthem 'Here We Go', was changed to contain just the relentless repetition of a distortion of the home team's name: 'Niggerpool, Niggerpool, Niggerpool'. The other, based upon the lament 'What A Load Of Rubbish' goadingly proclaimed: 'Everton are white! Everton are white!'

The blue choir made their feelings known, and it was a symbolic demonstration. Liverpool versus Everton in the Littlewoods Cup was not just a football match. It was a night when all the skeletons in Merseyside football's closet stepped ghoulishly into the spotlight. Despite the failure of ITV's match commentator and programme presenter to draw attention to it, the brutal undertow of prejudice to which Barnes's mere presence was provocation could no longer be ignored.

All this was in no sense a sideshow, the foible of a vocal handful. 'It dominated the match,' recalls Patrick Barclay. 'There's no getting away from that. The sheer volume of bananas, which are not cheap in a city taking longer than most to get out of the recession, showed how much the Everton supporters wanted to make their point.' Some, such as BBC Radio Merseyside commentator Graham Beecroft, would not go that far. He agrees, though, with many others, that it was a prominent feature of the evening's entertainment. Other radio commentators felt moved to remark on the verbal assaults. Clive Tyldesley, of Liverpool's local commercial station Radio City, was moved to condemn it on air. So too was Radio 2's Alan Green, backed by his expert summarizer Denis Law. The booing and chanting came across the airwaves loud and clear. There was no mistaking what was, in short, the most intense display of terrace chauvinism involving Merseyside football fans since Heysel. It was a squalid episode.

The incidents struck a nerve in the city of Liverpool. There may have been barely a mention in the morning papers' match reports, but that did not prevent many Liverpudlians making it their business to speak out. The tremors from the taunting of Barnes were felt beyond the walls of Anfield, a tribute to the game's emblematic power. The following day, Graham Beecroft sat in on BBC Radio Merseyside's daily phone-in, *In Town And Around*, responding to a string of calls 'all of them expressing their abhorrence at what had happened'. Clive Tyldesley received many letters responding to his interventions, some applauding them, some not, but all supporting their sentiments. Barnes himself has spoken of people apologizing to him in the street: 'People up here were shocked. They'd not seen anything like that up here before.' Even so, Barnes had certainly experienced such treatment on Merseyside as a Watford player. Two fifteen-year-old boys quoted in the Norman Chester Trust report remember it well: 'Blacks are usually the main people to be picked on at football. On watching Watford play Everton at Goodison Park, the black players were getting chanting from the fans like "You black bastard", this being chanted like a war cry, or "Ooh, ooh, ooh", the noise that a gorilla makes.'

The stunned aftermath and public indignation after the derby match served a purpose. Indeed, it brought about what some might describe as a miracle – a major club Chairman making a useful contribution to society. The gentleman in question was Everton's Phillip Carter who, at that time, was also the Football League President. By a freak of the fixture list, the Merseyside rivals were due to meet again at Anfield just four days later, this time in a League match. A Sunday fixture, it was to be broadcast live by the BBC not only in England but to an audience of many millions all around the world. Mindful that the behaviour of many Everton fans threatened to bring further disrepute upon the English game in general and his club in particular, Carter made a statement which harmonized nicely with the news priorities of the national tabloids. It helped spice the build-up to the sabbath clash to print headlines such as the *Daily Mirror*'s of Saturday 31st: 'Stay Away You Scum'. Carter's remarks were quoted at length, together with pictures of Barnes. Even the *Sun* managed to squeeze in a reference on an inside page, a footnote at the end of a sensationalized report alleging that Jan Molby wanted a transfer: 'The Kop's current darling, black flash John Barnes . . . was belted with bananas. Carter said last night, "It is deplorable. It is important for football in general and Merseyside in particular that everyone conducts themselves correctly this weekend."'

By this time Liverpool had extended their unbeaten run in the First Division to ten matches from the beginning of the season, winning nine of them. They had already scored an impressive 29 goals, far more than anyone else including leaders Arsenal whose strike total was six fewer despite playing three games more thanks to the Kop sewer saga. The BBC build-up to the League match was predictable, with much talk of blood, guts and magnificent manhood. 'Not a place for anyone with a faint heart or nervous disposition,' grinned the programme presenter, Jimmy Hill. 'The atmosphere is electric as always,' confirmed easy-going summarizer Trevor Brooking. The cameras panned around the stadium as Barry Davies, with Bobby Charlton as expert sidekick, intoned for a bit about 'the pride and passion of those Merseyside streets focused again on Anfield'. There was a brief shot of Barnes stretching a thigh muscle near the halfway line as the teams lined up for the kick-off. Interference on screen caused the director to switch swiftly to another camera. It was the sole reference, vocal or visual, to the player who had suffered the unacceptable face of that 'electric atmosphere', the previous Wednesday night.

Everton kicked off. The early scurries ensued. McMahon steam-rolled into Everton's left-back Pat Van Den Hauwe, retribution for an off-the-ball incident with right-winger Craig Johnston in the previous match. The fans screamed at each other. Johnston broke down the right touchline and caught the Everton captain Kevin Ratcliffe cold, right in front of a bank of his own supporters. He crossed to the far post. Barnes, with two defenders turning towards him, tried to kill the waist-high pass with his left foot and failed. The ball ran out for a goal-kick. The opposing fans broke into song: 'Hello! Hello! Everton are white, Everton are white!' Liverpool attacked down the left through Barnes again. Everton defenders streamed across to contain him, full-back Stevens plus Reid, plus Trevor Steven, plus Ratcliffe. The ball cannoned chaotically between Barnes and a succession of his own team-mates. Everton fans booed manically with every one-touch pass he made, digging in with the abuse as fast as the Everton players made their tackles. 'It really has its own atmosphere, the city of Liverpool derby,' remarked Davies. 'It's as sharp as the wit of Merseyside.' The camera cut to show a seated area where fans of both teams sat together sporting their favoured colours. A tribute, thought Barry, to the good spirit that prevailed beneath the fervour, both on and off the field. Barnes got the ball near the touchline. Reid took it off him. The Everton fans rubbed it in with another tirade of boos. An Evertonian went down injured and the trainer came on to the field. The camera closed in on a knot of Liverpool fans near the Everton end as the two exchanged malicious gestures and chants. 'Well, the crowd have always got something to sing about,' said Barry in the heat of the moment. 'Niggerpool, Niggerpool, Niggerpool!' howled the Everton contingent.

All this occurred in the first quarter hour of the BBC's live coverage. Twenty minutes later, Beardsley scrambled the ball away from Snodin on the right. It fell into centre-field, thirty yards from goal. Barnes had strayed in from the touchline and the ball bounced into his path. Caught sideways on, with the goal to his left, he had a precious split second to spare. In that fragment of time he nudged the ball forwards with his right foot, then jabbed the outside of his left smartly through, to execute a cushioned chip into a chink of daylight, floating it with exquisite control into the path of McMahon's forward spirit. McMahon coaxed the ball forward, saw the formidable Neville Southall hurtling from his line and lofted the ball directly into the furthest corner of the goal. Priceless seconds. Suddenly, all the tumblers had clicked sweetly into place and Everton's safe was cracked. It was blood and it was guts but most of all it was poetry. Suddenly you understood what people used to say about the truly great players – that if they only contrived one magic moment in the course of the afternoon it was still worth the entrance fee.

The goal gave Davies and Charlton their cue to get stuck into a serious bout of purring. But the main emphasis of the various pundits throughout the broadcast was to highlight the predominantly combative character of the match as illustrating all the best things about the English game. Charlton, ever the model prole patriot, kept using the words 'commitment' and 'competitive'. At half time, Jimmy Hill told us that 'you have to admire the physical efficiency' of the players. Down with Bob Wilson outside the dressing-rooms, former Liverpool goalkeeper Ray Clemence made mention of the 'good-natured banter between the two sets of fans.'

The action resumed. Halfway through the second half, Barnes, his back to the goal, guided the ball with his left heel inside Stevens for McMahon to run on to. McMahon crossed low towards Aldridge, the ball popped up and Beardsley smashed it just under the Everton cross bar: 2–nil. The racist chanting petered out with the optimism of the Everton fans. Barnes's two moments of inspiration had built a stockade around him – at least, till the next game. In football, a point is sometimes all you can make.

The BBC's presentation of the match was an object lesson in the way television's production values effectively sanitize football and largely exclude reflection on the social issues connected with it. Discussion of the game rarely strays beyond a narrow definition of 'entertainment'. The obsession with 'personalities', with extracting banal quotes from star managers and players, brings TV journalists into a relationship with the football industry which is inconsistent with the demands of objective, critical reporting. The game is never debated in its wider context as an important part of the national culture. Instead, TV constructs football as a commodity, one whose unsavoury characteristics are dealt with by being either marginalized, dismissed with platitudes, or, better still, completely ignored. Fans are reduced to providers of 'atmosphere', a production resource, no more. The result was that an entire, central element of a major footballing occasion – the violently racist behaviour of Everton fans – went utterly unremarked.

But no one could quite keep the lid on Pandora's box. Barnes's brilliant form had already put him in demand as a media interviewee, but the crowd scenes of the Everton games made him a fascinating subject for sections of the media *outside* the insular world of sports journalism. Barnes found himself a focal figure in discussions about the whole question of football racism. Interviewers with a more detached perspective on the game questioned him about his reaction to what the Everton supporters had done. His response was the conventional one, pleading indifference, the black footballers' only practical course. He had experienced worse with Watford at Chelsea and West Ham. It was water off a duck's back. It never affected his game. Football officialdom followed its own predictable course. Barnes's response was taken up and used to lend authority to their preferred explanations of the problem. Phillip Carter, quoted in the *Daily Mirror* before the second derby game, set down his diagnosis alongside his condemnation. Enter the 'lunatic fringe' theory. 'They are a few maniacs on the fringe who are doing the club and Merseyside a terrible disservice ... How a few hundred senseless people can spoil the enjoyment of thousands is absolutely appalling.' At Liverpool Peter Robinson subscribed to a similar viewpoint. 'There was a small section. John Barnes had been very successful here, Everton hadn't got a coloured player and, you know, a few lunatics showed what they felt in that way. But again, I have a feeling that he's done so much here, John Barnes, that genuine supporters of both clubs are very attracted to his playing.'

Carter and Robinson implicitly propose a distinction between an anti-social minority and a silent majority, the 'lunatic fringe' and the 'genuine supporters' – and, of course, themselves as representatives of the clubs. It is a good example of the way in which football administrators habitually seek to distance themselves from the uglier aspects of the spectator sport which they are responsible for running.

Interesting too is the way their indignation is focused not on the broad issue of racism but on the effect it might have on the individual player's efficiency: 'Thank goodness it didn't seem to upset Barnes,' said Carter, 'because he was always in the game.' Similarly, Denis Law, having voiced his disapproval live on Radio 2, went on to reassure us that the only reason it was happening was that Barnes 'is such a good player', and, what's more, he was sure Barnes did not let these things affect him. The messages in these explanations are clear: they are only doing it because they fear his talents as a player; don't worry, Barnes himself won't let it put him off. It is still a marvellous occasion. Do Not Be Alarmed.

There was another line of apologism too, a kind of Scouse Nationalist position that sought to defuse the racial offence by lumping it into the category of rough diamond Mersey wit. It goes a bit like this: the rivalry – the *friendly* rivalry, remember – between Liverpool and Everton supporters is so intense, that *any* player who, by his habit or his appearance, stands out, might be made the target for a spot of Merseyside mockery. Evidence of such activities, rich in the flavour of Scallywag folklore, abound among Liverpudlian football supporters. Sammy Lee, a short man and rather squat, would be punished for being 'fat'. Mick Lyons, an Everton captain and centre-back of the late seventies and early eighties, scored a stunning own-goal in a derby match and was made to suffer for it for the rest of his career. Goalkeepers traditionally enjoy a special status among Kop loyalists. It is an attractive feature of the Kop ritual that a warm welcome is routinely extended. There was, though, one Everton incumbent who was the subject of particular attention. His name was Gordon West and there were rumours that he didn't go out with girls. (Surely apocryphal – footballers fear homosexuality worse than death.) This theory stemmed from the day West ran out for a derby match carrying his 'keeping accessories' in a dainty little bag hanging on a strap. Subsequent fixtures were marked by minor pitch invasions shortly before the kick-off. A scurrying delegation of Liverpool supporters would vault the perimeter fence, make their way over to West and present him with a bright red handbag.

The Goodison faithful could have similar proclivities. Bruce Grobbelaar, so critical of the way Howard Gayle resented his brand of racial 'joke', recalls in his autobiography his chagrin at the stick Evertonians dished out inspired by his nickname 'The Clown'. It was Grobbelaar's first derby and it took place at Goodison Park: 'Shortly before kick-off two Everton supporters dressed as court jesters ran onto the pitch and presented me with a cardboard cut-out of a clown before running back into the Gladys Road End. I laughed and made a joke of it but inside I was furious . . .' Taking the piss and learning to take it. That, the Mersey romance tells us, is what every Liverpudlian expects. Bald, red-headed, anything you like, it all gets the treatment. One year, Ian StJohn was presented with a bunch of bananas – they thought he looked like a ape. And so, runs the apologists' reasoning, blackness inevitably enjoys the same attention. Come on, lads – it's only a joke.

Well, maybe it was a particularly corrosive sense of comedy that lay in the hearts and minds of at least some of Barnes's tormentors. Maybe it explains, too, the actions of those who burned a cross one year at Goodison Park when Alex Williams was Manchester City's visiting goalie. And maybe the Liver birds can fly. But humour is a serious business. The question that matters is not whether they thought they were joking or not, but how come a vast body of football opinion, from terrace chanters to company executives to men behind typewriters, are unable to divine the qualitative gulf that lies between teasing a guy who is losing his hair and howling in uninhibited unison the word 'nigger' for all the nation to hear? It is not the words that matter, or the physical differences that inspire them, it is what those words *mean*. Racial abuse, at this point in British history and especially in this British town, amounts to much, much more than pulling someone's leg. Lynch mobs in the

American south did not string you up from poplar trees for being fat; a receding hairline does not diminish your chances of obtaining already scarce employment in the city of Liverpool or make your family four times less likely to be allocated a council house than your white counterparts; even the deadly combination of a beer pot and a pate as polished as the Pope's does not prompt unknown assassins to come in the night and firebomb your home as happened to an Asian family one night in 1988 in the heart of the white-dominated district of Anfield, Liverpool 4.

To call someone a 'black bastard' is to do more than object to the colour of their skin. 'Baldy' says that a man is losing his hair. It attacks his personal vanity. 'Black bastard' strips a man or woman of their identity, goads their exclusion from the right to equal treatment, their right to be an individual, their right to dignity. It attacks that man or woman's status as a human being, and nowhere in England is that more true than in Liverpool, once the slave trade capital of Europe, the city where 6 per cent are black but are almost never to be seen in the shopping precincts or the football grounds. And that is why throwing a banana at a black footballer's feet is not really such a good joke after all.

Liverpool people have this way of making all the best things you ever heard about them come true. It would be a cold-hearted person indeed who could visit this town and fail to find the people generous. Only the terminally frigid could fail to feel their warmth. Those things are real. Reach out and they are there to be enjoyed. John Barnes enjoyed them too. From supporters of Liverpool Football Club his welcome was as near total as to reduce doubters to fearful silence. It was as if, after years of living up to a reputation for the most merciless mickery-taking, the most acerbic self-promotion, they seized all the more gladly the chance to welcome another kind of underdog. He was, after all, wearing a red shirt and delivering priceless goods. If the significance of that acceptance evaded the Anfield crowd then the Evertonian chanters brought it home with a shuddering crunch. The Kop's response was to embrace their hero tighter still.

'For the Liverpool crowd, and I think for a lot of Liverpool people, it solidified Barnes in their affection,' says Kop regular Rogan Taylor, 'because somebody they had taken to their hearts was being treated in the way they'd treated black players for years. I'm quite sure that if Everton had bought Barnes the situation would have been mirrored because the potential for that behaviour existed at both clubs. So Barnes has certainly had a tremendous impact, not just in terms of what he does on the pitch, but in making people realize that once you've accepted a black player you *can't* go hooting another one. It's been interesting watching the Kop go through the transformation, realizing that it's impolite to John to boo someone *else* who's black.'

The sudden saintliness of the Anfield thousands was so complete as to be almost comical. 'I remember the reaction of those people around me,' says Stephen Kelly, a season-ticket holder in the Main Stand. 'It was so funny. In the previous season they were all talking about "black bastards". Then as soon as the Everton supporters start screaming this kind of filth, everyone's going on about what a shower of scum they are over there ... short memories.' Koppite self-consciousness about the derby disgrace soon manifested itself. A few weeks later, just before Christmas, Liverpool played Sheffield Wednesday at home. Towards the end of the match, Wednesday made a double substitution, sending on Colin West and Larry May, the first white, the second black. Club public policy being by now well established – that the best way to deal with questions of race was to pretend they didn't exist – the stadium announcer named the twin replacements and, as an aid to identification, said: 'Larry May is the one with the bandage on his wrist.' The place erupted in mirth.

There were other kinds of fall-out from the two derby encounters. There were button badges saying 'Everton Are White – Defend The Race'. It emerged that before the second game Everton supporters had been stopped at a turnstile attempting to smuggle a live monkey into the ground. How funny was that? Mark Walters, a black winger from Aston Villa, almost signed with Everton, but chose Glasgow Rangers instead – perhaps the most onerous challenge of all. Then Everton and Liverpool were drawn against each other in the fifth round of the FA Cup, to be played at Goodison Park on 21 February, with the BBC again in attendance. This time the moral guardians of the game had learned their scripts in advance. For Phillip Carter the stakes were higher than ever. The derby was in his back yard and his customers would be in the majority. He went for a pre-emptive strike in the form of another public statement, threatening arrests if necessary. But once again the thrust of his remarks was to invoke the Merseyside legend and, by extension, defend the good name of his product rather than admit the possibility of negligence: 'It is a very small minority,' Carter insisted, 'but we on Merseyside have given a lead to the rest of the football world on how to behave and it would be a disaster if something happened that destroyed that special relationship.

Some 48,270 participants in that 'special relationship' crammed into Goodison Park to see the game. Another seven million glued square eyes to the corner of their living-rooms. The game kicked off, John Motson commentating. Barnes had come on to the pitch with a freshly shaven head, a style greatly favoured by black boxers. Was the Jamaican gentleman trying to tell us – or specifically the Everton contingent – something? From the first minutes he received the familiar greeting from among the blue sections of the crowd. It continued unabated throughout the first hour and it was not until then that Motson felt moved to remark: 'A few boos being directed there at John Barnes. We could do without that.' And from then on, the matter was treated as closed.

Liverpool won the match by a single goal and again Barnes, though stifled for much of the afternoon, played a big part in the breakthrough, working a sweet one-two with Beardsley near the touchline, then centring for the unexpected figure of Ray Houghton, another new signing, to head the ball past Southall. It was not the end of the derby saga. The final instalment took place one month later when Goodison hosted the second of the season's two League games. Liverpool required a win or a draw to complete 30 unbeaten First Division matches from the start of their campaign, and so overhaul Leeds United's record set in 1973–74. In another pile-up of a contest, Everton's Wayne Clarke picked up the pieces after Grobbelaar dropped a cross. The goal came after fifteen minutes and that was the end of the scoring. A historic run was ended and the private Merseyside Test series ended in a draw, two wins-all.

By this time, the full force of the racist storm had diminished. Barnes, though never at his best in any of the games, had had a decisive impact on two of them and showed no signs of being got at. Patrick Barclay elaborates: 'It was a joke that became meaningless. Grobbelaar was called a clown and Everton made as much capital as they could out of that. That joke was used as long as he kept chucking goals away. But Barnes was not behaving like a savage. Barnes was the most civilized player on the field. The joke simply died the death. It was a nice piece of theatre while it was happening and a disturbing one. It wasn't a comedy. It was a short-running farce that didn't stay long in the West End.'

But what about that other, deeper Liverpool drama, the epic tragedy that just keeps rolling on? The impact of Barnes upon that extended script may have been vivid. To what extent, though, could it be said to have upset the course of the plot? In Liverpool 8 reactions to him were mixed, a combination of solidarity and cynicism: enthusiasm for the success of a black man in a place where none had succeeded before, but a pleasure tempered by realism. 'I know black people who go and watch Liverpool now,' said Steve Skeete, 'but just because John Barnes is playing for them. It's him they're interested in. Before, nine out of ten wouldn't bother.' Their renewed enthusiasm was for the player, not the team; the individual, not the institution. Barnes himself has come to be regarded in Liverpool 8 as a perfectly likeable guy. He was the star attraction at the opening of a barber's shop in Granby Street not long after joining his new team. He has returned there for haircuts ever since with no ceremony and no fuss.

At the same time, there is an acute awareness that Barnes knows nothing of the trials that assail them. In a way, 'colour' and a love of football are the only things he has in common with them. Even his experience of racism is not so total, not the same. 'Look at the background he's from,' says Almithak's Eugene Lam. 'You're talk-ing, like, upper class. No disrespect to him. I like the man and he's a good player. But he's well-spoken, well-educated. He's had the best and they can't really slag him down. You know, the press, like to go into people's past. But he's a really clean guy, isn't he? And on the pitch, I've never seen him retaliate and he's had some bad tackles. He's so gentlemanly, he's like the perfect player to have. So their attitude is, "We don't mind him. He's black, but he's a good black. We'll give *him* the job."'

There are white Liverpool fans who make the same type of distinction but offer quite different interpretations. 'I don't think before John Barnes there had been any coloured players who were good enough for Liverpool,' said one. 'Being quite honest, and not in a demeaning way, you look at a lot of West Indian culture and it is quite come-day-go-day. You know, they're up one minute, they're down the next. But John Barnes's greatest asset is his temperament. Nobody can rattle him. If he loses the ball, or even if he's fouled, he will brush himself off and get on with the game. You look at the players that Liverpool have had. Part of their trademark is to show that if they get into the team they can play consistently for up to 60 games a season. John Barnes is probably the first black player that fits into that category.'

It is an assessment which appropriates Barnes as an honorary Englishman, an honorary white man, even. Meanwhile, the football establishment can use him as a fig leaf to cover their shame, even as Barnes's very presence has exposed it. He has, unwittingly, no doubt, played a part in the process himself, effectively aligning himself with the general outlook of the club. The following remarks are attributed to Barnes in Viv Anderson's biography: 'What is strange in Liverpool is that none of the black people in Toxteth have any interest in football at all. The black population is quite big – but Merseyside has never had any black players so they don't identify with the game, whereas in London it's different.' Such is the received wisdom at the Anfield citadel.

In Liverpool 8, there is a different perspective: 'As far as they're concerned, he's just got a suntan.' It is a sardonic comment, but not without good reason. Listen to the Liverpool stories, the Liverpool jokes, harsh and nasty, but full of self-knowledge, the product of a city's persona that comes at you with laughing gas in one hand and a switchblade in the other. A man rushes into a pub and says to his mates: 'Guess what! I just saw John Barnes outside in a car with two niggers!'; Barnes is fouled near the touchline by an opposing black defender. A Liverpool fan screams, 'You black bastard'. Our hero says to the fan: 'So what about me, then?' 'Oh no John,' returns the fan. 'You're not black, you're as white as I am.' Liverpool loves John Barnes. Ask little boys on the backstreets why and they look at you with pity: 'He's sound, isn't he, John Barnes? He's the best in the world.' But ask Anfield partisans why his story has turned out to be a glorious one and many respond with a piece of football jargon delivered with a pile-driving irony that, for once, is wholly accidental: 'A lot of Liverpool supporters weren't too sure at the beginning. But since he's come here, he's been playing out of his skin.'

12

'Almost Real Madrid'

1987–88 was the season Vinny Jones was photographed giving Paul Gascoigne's testicles a squeeze. The scene was not a public convenience in Earls Court but a football field down Plough Lane, London SW19, with several thousand people looking on. The incident, and the media flurry that ensued, should not be underestimated. It confirmed Wimbledon, Jones's club, as the *Carry On* brutalists of the season in which Liverpool sailed away with the hearts of football's dreamers. A bunch of soccer navvies on £150 a week, Wimbledon embodied the kind of nightmarish vulgarity that all lovers of refinement pray will never burst, belching and blaspheming, through their patio doors. But suddenly, there they were, and nobody knew what to do. The unwritten rules of football etiquette were subjected to a liberal reinterpretation. Wimbledon drew up guidelines of their own, whereby their abject and obvious poverty – of art as well as finance and prestige – became their badge of pride. It is the oldest underdog trick in the book and Wimbledon made it work.

Liverpool went to Plough Lane one autumnal Wednesday night to play Wimbledon in the League. It was a bit like the Household Cavalry charging the local abattoir – it ought to be a rout, but look out for rotating knives. Wimbledon's is a tiny, tumbledown little stadium where greyhounds scamper round the circuit three nights a week and the 13,454 they got through the turnstiles that evening turned out to be their best gate of the season. It was beyond derision, really. Even the Liverpool contingent spared their humble hosts the humiliation they like to rub in to the other paupers they visit: 'Shitty ground, shitty ground, shitty ground.' There was lots of room on the away fans' terrace, so it was easy to take up a position from which the skills of Barnes could be viewed close up. In the first half, Liverpool attacked their own supporters' end. The line-up featured most of the prime personalities of a season in which Liverpool's dominance ensured wider public exposure than even they were used to and brought them not just admiration but acclaim.

In goal was the bizarre, gymnastic Grobbelaar. In front of him were aligned one of the most creative back-fours English football has ever seen: Steve Nicol, Gary Gillespie, Alan Hansen and Mark Lawrenson. It was Hansen who had come to epitomize the evolution among Liverpool's defensive players since the traditional stopper, Yeats. A slender, dark-haired figure who can look almost frail at a spectator's distance, he is a performer of finesse as well as physicality whose capacity for making ground out of defence with the ball at his feet has become a personal trademark. Down near the touchline at Plough Lane, the first forty-five minutes provided many examples of the delicious fluidity a football team can achieve when even its supposed artisans are artists. Building from this cultured backline, Liverpool poured down the left-hand flank, a red mist, all smooth movement and short, sweet passes, simultaneously machine-like and amorphous. Hansen, Lawrenson and Barnes combined with the central midfield components Whelan and the prodigal Liverpudlian son, McMahon, in a series of effortless exchanges, cultivating conditions under which the ball could be delivered into their opponents' goalmouth to maximum potential. The starting line-up was completed by Beardsley and Aldridge, who, inevitably, had suffered by comparison with the phenomenal Rush. But before this, Liverpool's twelfth League fixture, he was averaging a goal a game. The expensive Beardsley, meanwhile, had been, if not exactly struggling, then not quite shining as expected – he had been overshadowed by the drama of Barnes's entrance – though he was to come good later on.

Meanwhile, over on the right wing Craig Johnston was about to become a figure of unsung pathos. After several years as the man most likely to be dropped, the South African-born Australian expatriate had been invited by England manager Robson to join his squad for a European Championship qualifying game against Yugoslavia. And yet, after one hour of the Wimbledon game he was withdrawn by Dalglish and replaced by his latest signing, like

Aldridge from Oxford United, Ray Houghton, whose ability to run with the ball, pass it and harass the opposition would give him the nod over Johnston from this game onwards. Of the twelve men who took the field for Liverpool that night, only three would find the coming months a disappointment. Two – Whelan and Lawrenson – would have their season curtailed by injury. Johnston would declare himself completely disillusioned with the game. The rest would probably come to regard this Plough Lane line-up and its variants as the most satisfying they had ever played in.

As the red mist rolled forward, it looked set to smother shabby Wimbledon. The only problem was, Liverpool couldn't score. Wimbledon's defenders scratched about like chickens awaiting slaughter, but somehow they made it to half-time with their heads still screwed on straight. It was an omen, but one so nondescript that few would have identified it. Perhaps if Jones had been playing onlookers might have extracted a bit more meaning from the entrails of the game. The fragrant Vincent had earned his tabloid headlines after the sides' meeting the previous season at Anfield. Passing under the Liverpool crest that hangs over the players' tunnel exit, Wimbledon's ignoble warriors had covered the imperious inscription 'This Is Anfield' with a fountains of phlegm. They then proceeded to complete an unlikely double over England's most illustrious team. Dalglish had played in that game and after one sharp engagement with Jones had been advised by the Wimbledon man of his intention to 'cut off your ear and spit in the hole.' Now Jones – 'Psycho' as he had been fondly dubbed – was absent from the Wimbledon team on this drab London night, suspended for disciplinary reasons, and Dalglish was on the visitors' bench. But the spirit of their encounter lingered on. Not the violence of it – by the standards of much modern football it was a peaceable game – but the sense of unreconstructed oiks sinking their teeth into the backsides of royalty . . . and hanging on to the bitter end.

So who were these suburban mutations? John Fashanu, we'd heard of him, the bearer of another archetypal Wimbledon nickname: 'Fash the Bash'. Grrr! Then there was the goalkeeper, Dave Beasant – 'Lurch' to his friends – a curly-haired giant with a Texas

Homecare accent whose claim to fame was the impeccably wide-boy ploy of dribbling the ball out of his penalty area before sending the thing bombing forward, as far into enemy territory as possible, for 'Fash' and the lads to head, kick, barge, elbow or employ any way possible to hound the ball, cowering, into the net as if to save itself from further punishment. This process of forward propulsion had been dubbed by the Wimbledon men 'putting it in the mixer', a building-site term which illustrates their positive embrace of manual labour aesthetics. As for the rest, well, Terry Gibson, freakishly minute alongside the hulking Fashanu, had played for Spurs and Manchester United. Apart from that, Wimbledon had not the merest whiff of even second-hand glamour among them. They looked, and played, like men pouring out of the trenches. Wimbledon offered, in short, a distilled and overpowering essence of English football and felt no compunction whatsoever about sticking it right up everybody's nose. After all, how else were they meant to survive?

When Houghton came on he immediately struck a blow for the ruling class. Scurrying forward, he willed the ball through a string of ricochets before lifting it over Beasant's sprawl. Then Beardsley hit a post and the visiting supporters strained forward for a better sight of the massacre that would surely, belatedly, come. But the hod-carriers humped on. After seventy-eight minutes full-back Ryan took a hoof at goal from twenty yards. Fairweather prodded instinctively at it *en route* to the corner flag and the ball squirted past Grobbelaar for a perfectly artless equalizer. Liverpool were held for only the second time in a dozen games. That, of course, was just the start of their problems with Wimbledon.

How many ways can Liverpool versus Wimbledon be characterized? Rich versus poor, beauty versus beast, brain versus brawn? All are valid, up to a point. But guardians of the wellbeing of the game should not be too glib in contrasting the values of the South London mob and those embodied by the great and good northerners in red. Wimbledon may be a mutation, but they are not an aberration. Rather, their football enshrines the logical conclusion of what the ugly, brutish and poor so often become if they are ever to compete with kings. Wimbledon's achievement has been to make virtues of their vices and the only reason they may be justified as virtues is because they, unarguably, enable Wimbledon to do what the mores of the 'profession' demands that footballers should do – win. Football is not ice-skating. You do not get points for artistic impression, just for beating the other team. Nor are Wimbledon's vices exclusive to them. They simply practise the same 'professional' unpleasantries as most professional footballers. The difference is that a flair for dubious practices is one of the few resources they have. Once Wimbledon decided not be to ashamed of themselves, having grappled their way from non-League football to the First Division in just eleven years, they simply built themselves up as champion sinners in a sport where sin is integral.

All professional footballers scream at each other, wind up and goad each other as part of building the chemistry of the team. Wimbledon's boys just do it better, each relentlessly bad-mouthing the rest into redoubling their commitment to the cause. Professional footballers have always tried to get at the other team, intimidating them physically, verbally, any way to secure that psychological edge, to implant doubt or fear or worry in the opposition's mind. Wimbledon just do it all the time.

Photographers who crouch on the goal line tell extraordinary stories of remarks made by Wimbledon men at corner kicks and other set-piece plays, as everybody elbows and jostles and shoves and trips and pulls the other guy's shirt, whatever bit of fiddling they can get away with where the referee can't see. Wimbledon men make remarks about the other team's looks, about what they heard is deficient in their manhood – just the sort of stuff tender male egos cannot stand. All professional footballers, especially midfield men, make it their business in the first few minutes to let their opposite numbers know that they're about. Crash, bang, pitch in, he who wins the first 50/50 ball is king for the afternoon. The only difference with Wimbledon is that when they run out on to the pitch, steamed up for combat, clenched fists dangling to their knees, they intend to keep those little dogfights going, grinding down the will of the opposition and keeping on grinding, even if they fall a goal behind or two goals behind. Because of that, it doesn't very often get as far as three. And all the time they're hoofing it up field, 'putting it in the mixer', like gamblers tossing the ball into the roulette wheel, knowing that some time or other they're going to hit the jackpot. A part of all professional football is war. Wimbledon is the cannon-fodder that refuses to lie down and die.

Liverpool, on the other hand, and John Barnes in particular, orchestrated their gilded operations with priorities that were saintly by comparison. Some of them don't mind giving referees a piece of their mind, but they collected less than a dozen bookings in the course of the season with no sendings-off. On the other hand, Wimbledon's disciplinary record was so bad they were hauled up before the FA to explain themselves. Liverpool do their bit of shirt-pulling, elbowing, verbalizing, pushing and shoving, but in the end they – unlike Wimbledon – know they have more chance of scoring a goal by trying to run past the other man than by calling him a nasty name. McMahon is tough and puts it about, but he does not favour a hard-man image because there is more to him than that. Nicol is stern in the tackle, but he is no mere destroyer. He comes forward, passes well, scores goals. He is Liverpool's renaissance man. By the time they met Wimbledon for the first time that season, Dalglish's new side had shown the public of five major cities and millions of television viewers that they were different from the Liverpool teams they'd seen before: free-flowing, free-scoring, paragons of grace and elegance as well as awesomely implemented power.

A visit from Liverpool always ensured the home side one of its biggest audiences. Only local derbies and Manchester United rivalled them as the number one draw. But as the 1987–88 season moved into its second quarter, Dalglish's new Liverpool became the undisputed number one box-office treat. Barnes was the brightest star in a glittering firmament.

Following the drama of the new stars' home débuts against Oxford, Liverpool won an Anfield cliff-hanger against Charlton Athletic by 3 goals to 2. The big scores mounted up. Liverpool went to Newcastle where 24,141 spectators and, for the first time that season, a live TV audience, saw them obliterate United 4–1. In their next League game, a midweek match at Anfield, they thumped

Derby County 4–nil, then repeated the score-line, again at home, against Portsmouth four days later. After the first of these two fixtures Bobby Robson likened Barnes's performance to those of George Best, and he was not the last to make the comparison. In the second, Portsmouth attempted to combat Barnes by setting the abrasive Barry Horne to mark him man-for-man. The ploy was half successful. Barnes had a quiet game, shackled by Horne and supporting cast. This, though, only liberated the other ten Liverpool players. They duly ran riot.

The theory that Barnes was not the right style of player for Liverpool had been comprehensively disproved. What the Liverpool system had done was compensate for Barnes's weaknesses by playing to his strengths. Dalglish's belief was that Barnes was a player whose potential could be liberated and whose talent could be improved. While he could not be relied upon to dictate the proceedings, given the right service he could dominate them. He needed the ball at his feet. Liverpool were the team to put it there for him. Ability, timing and instinct would do the rest.

Being part of the Liverpool team resolved the contradiction in Barnes's play, the gifted individualist who seemed to lack initiative, the disciplined team man whose contributions could be fickle. Liverpool gave Barnes a team pattern to conform to, but one which was geared to unleashing his most impressive and distinctive traits. He was at once part of a collective consciousness and a free man. His individual indulgences occurred under controlled circumstances rather than on a whim, and they served the best interests of the team.

Dalglish has described him as the best crosser of a ball in the English game. It is not hard to agree. With his left foot, Barnes can deliver the ball with startling accuracy, swirling it towards onrushing colleagues in great, looping parabolas. He has, too, the capacity to provide such a service when apparently hopelessly corralled, able to exploit even a fractional imbalance in his challengers to thread the ball between them and into the danger zone. It was from those wide forward positions that he most often expressed himself, beating one man, two men, sometimes three, still having the ball . . . and then crossing it for Aldridge, Johnston, Whelan, Houghton, Nicol,

Gillespie, Beardsley. Goals were coming from everywhere. Barnes let his talents explode into the role, not only of solo star, but also of dazzling provider.

When Queens Park Rangers visited a delirious Anfield, Barnes exhibited his full repertoire. Despite Liverpool's record, the home games they had missed at the start of the season meant that Rangers were top of the League. But not for long. For most of the first half, the Londoners, using an unusual formation for English football, with a sweeper at the back, held Liverpool at bay and played some very tidy football. Johnston had a goal disallowed and it seemed as if the Reds had a struggle on their hands. But four minutes before half-time, the ball came to Barnes on the left-hand side of the Rangers penalty area. He pushed it towards the dead-ball line, shielding it from full-back Warren Neil. What followed was a cameo of the sort of thing he did all season. The ball seemed sure to run out of play. Then, suddenly, it was back at Barnes's toe inches from touch. He shaped and squeezed it back at an angle of 45 degrees, all along the ground, between the gasping Rangers defenders and into the path of Johnston. A goal in the wink of an eye. In the second half Barnes took a free-kick near the left-hand corner flag. He prepared himself, bent forward, hands on hips, elbows jutting high, then looped the ball into the Rangers goal mouth. A hand went up which wasn't the goalkeeper's. Aldridge converted the penalty.

Rangers began making mistakes. Byrne, their talented forward, lost the ball in front of his own defence. It came to Whelan, who played it to Barnes in a central position. He skipped a step forward, shunted it to Aldridge and rushed towards the penalty spot. Aldridge's first-time return fell sweetly back into Barnes's path and he struck the ball low and directly into the corner of the goal. Receiving the acclaim of his team-mates, he turned to the Kop crowd and punched the air in triumph: even then, the diplomat's son. Then came the grand finale. With Rangers run ragged, Barnes won the ball off Brock in the centre circle. He ran on to the rebound at speed and ate up the open ground that lay between him and the opponent's penalty area with three touches of the ball and a punishing stride. As he surged towards the Kop end, the murmur of the crowd rose to a crescendo of anticipation. Barnes beat one man, then two men and he still had the ball. Barely needing to steady himself, he struck it with his right foot, channelling it to the left of goalkeeper David Seaman and into the corner of the net. Priceless.

Before John Barnes, the Liverpool of the eighties would not have been able to score a goal of that type. It created pandemonium among the home supporters, a moment for the memory banks. And it is worth considering the quality of that goal, the wonderful eloquence of it. When the crowd rose, revelling, to its feet, it was not simply to goad the visiting supporters in their despair, but to hail a piece of magnificence, a crowning illustration of the many things which set Barnes, the footballer, apart: pace, power, balance of a special order; all of that. But the point about such sporting moments is that their effect is somehow more universal than merely an achievement in the service of a team. Barnes's goal was lovely for itself, giving us a clue as to why it is that while the Liverpool teams since Shankly have always been admired outside the ranks of their own partisans, they have not always been loved. That accolade belongs elsewhere, along the East Lancashire Road in Manchester, where, more than twenty years ago, Bobby Charlton, Denis Law, and the ineffable George Best captured the imagination, not just of Old Trafford and a rapturous Stretford End, but people the length and breadth of Britain and all over the world. For all the grudging parochialism enshrined in English football culture, Manchester United were adored.

Since 1968, when they became the first English team to win the European Cup, Manchester United have not enjoyed consistent success. They have won the FA Cup three times, but the League Championship has eluded them. Yet it took all that time before little boys up and down the land wanted replica Liverpool T-shirts for Christmas instead because John Barnes is their favourite player. Dalglish's new Liverpool gave birth, at last, to that overdue generation. Once upon a time, Liverpool were just winning. Now they were winning *gloriously*. They were the nearest thing the English public has had to a love affair with a football team for as long as it could remember. It was not just a matter of winning, but a matter of style. Rogan Taylor offered a perspective: 'When I watch

Liverpool now, I know I'm not watching the kind of side I watched for a decade, right through the seventies. I think we were beaten fourteen times in ten years at home in the League. It was a team nobody could bloody beat, virtually, but I spent a lot of time yawning me head off. Whereas now I'm not looking at a side which is unbeatable, but which could almost be that great Real Madrid side. They weren't unbeatable, with DiStefano and Puskas and those guys. But you felt as though you were in a cathedral when they were doing it.'

At Anfield, tickets for every home game were at a premium. Public attention became focused on the team's epic deeds. The chronic nostalgia of football writers began to take on a rosy tint instead of a scent of bitterness. Matt Busby's Manchester United were the last gasp of an English football culture that dated from before the *business* of football, the obsessional personality cultism of mass media sport, the dawning of prodigious turnovers, the onset of 'professional' insularity, the post-war pressures for the national game to shackle itself to a bogus national machismo. Manchester United were loved by the people, because they were a side that the people might have dreamed up for themselves: quicksilver, per-sonalized, swashbuckling, *glorious*. When they won, it was a win worth having. Now Liverpool were offering just a whisper of a reprise. Their achievement was all the more refreshing for being led by a black man, who exemplified a lost age of sporting style, flourishing in the face of all the most barbarous characteristics of English sporting life.

13

'Theirs or Ours?'

Moving among the Liverpool fans throughout that vintage season was an education. On Saturdays, they seemed to be everywhere. Even when the team was playing at Anfield, they would be queuing on the platform at London's Euston station for the Saturday morning train. Some were lads who had moved down south for work, returning at weekends to see football and family. Others had first learned to love the team from watching them on TV. At away games, the travelling loyalists, many, as ever, next to naked in the winter winds, always managed to provided a little of what tradition demanded. 'Cheerio, cheerio, cheerio!' they chorused happily when nearby Tottenham fans rose from their seats, fleeing the scene as Johnston completed the scoring on a 2–nil win. It was the Londoners' first game under returning hero Terry 'El Tel' Venables. Midfielder Steve Hodge had been sent off in the first half and Liverpool's cool execution of the ten men in white was greeted in the visitors' enclosure with glee.

At Watford, the travelling Kop choir composed a special little piece of abuse for the host club's famous chairman, recently the subject of what turned out to be spurious front page scandal treatment in the *Sun*. 'He's bald,' they sang, 'he's bent, his ass is up for rent, Elton John! Elton John!' demonstrating one more time the homophobia that is an integral prejudice in football culture. Then they extracted a response from Dalglish on the touchline bench ('Kenny, Kenny, give us a wave') and by the end of the game, exhausted of insults and asides, they went through a repertoire of Beatles songs. Barnes received a warm reception from his old home crowd, scoring a goal in an irresistible 4–1 win (the returning Blissett retrieved Watford's pride), with Beardsley outstanding in the Vicarage Road mudbath. Barnes was substituted near the end to save his legs for a midweek England game, and was cheered as he left the field, responding with a wave. As the substitute came on, a little knot of travelling Koppites saw the joke. Sides splitting with the mischief of it, they erupted into a cover version of an Everton original: 'Liverpool are white! Liverpool are white!' The refrain tailed off into giggles. A crack that flirts with tastelessness, it none the less betrays a caustic self-awareness that proves its authors are not as stupid as some people think. It is a pity they do not get more credit for it. For years, fans have accepted the squalor and discomfort and the dismissive outlook of the institutions they sustain. The ordeals of those who pass through the turnstiles invite a cynical interpretation of the mutual need supporters and players express for each other. It is hard to resist the feeling that those relationships are being exposed for what they are: fleeting meeting points between star producers on the one hand and, on the other, mere consumers, for the poorest of whom – the caged humanity who stand and sway in the wind and rain – the biggest price is paid not in cash but in loss of dignity.

Yet John Aldridge – the striker who stood on the Kop in his youth and dreamed of turning out for 'my beloved Liverpool' – is only the most obvious example of how the lads on the field and the lads on the terraces start life as mirror images of each other. There is a sense in which the shared exhilaration when a goal is scored symbolically affirms those common roots. The roar of the crowd speaks of an empathy running deeper than anything the boardroom wheeler-dealers could ever hope to understand. The audience explodes, the players embrace and, like the seamen who stepped off the boats and on to the Mersey docks, the moment of fulfilment is seized, every drop of pleasure squeezed from it while it lasts. Even in the midst of joy, players and spectators alike are gathering themselves for a resumption of effort, an investment of labour for uncertain reward. The ball goes back to the centre spot and we all begin again. Football grounds are not supermarkets and fans do not go there just to make a purchase – they go to *participate*.

When the final whistle is blown, though, a gulf opens up. The Koppites filter out through the litter and the puddles of piss. They head for the bus stop or a pub in the town. The players take their showers, are praised or chastised by the manager. They blow-dry their hair, smear themselves in lotion, try to slip past the journalists shuffling outside, then set off in their sponsored cars to flash homes in the Wirral or Southport-on-Sea. For them, the game is the weekend showcase for the work they do all week. It is work which offers the potential for catharsis, prestige and material reward.

For the people who pay their wages, though – the fans – the chance to share in the emotions invested in those exploits is more transient still. It is not something that most who stand on the Kop find in their own daily lives. Unemployment is always there, a reality or a threat. Those in work are being de-skilled, disenfranchised, demoralized. It is an insecurity that the players would recognize themselves, the fear of being suspended, injured or dropped, a fear whose motivating power the manager perceives only too well. But there are compensations. It is these that bring the players and spectators close in spirit again: the anxiety, the passion and heroism of the game is the one chance all week to feel a part of something epic, to feel alive, to witness a display of splendour from their fellow human beings . . . and they are required to suffer before savouring even that.

Between September 1987 and May 1988, John Barnes provided more of those opportunities to participate in splendour than any other player in the Football League. There were many times when his feats were of an order which was clearly beyond the capacity of his peers to emulate. In moments his inspiration was almost inexplicable. The footwork which enabled him to dismiss the challenges of QPR's defenders was one example. The swathe he cut through Oxford United's defence was another. In the season's fourth and final Merseyside derby, he sent a shudder through the Goodison crowd when, in the opening minutes, he received the ball on the left-hand touchline, halfway inside his own half. Facing the crowd, with opponents closing in, he materialized through a gap between Stevens and Reid that did not seem to exist. It was a trick that almost confounded logic, the sort of manoeuvre which leaves fans gasping, delighted, enthralled. Without the crowd, the players' heroics become, if not meaningless, then massively diminished. Players need crowds, and crowds adore players like Barnes.

And yet while the success of such a player revives and embodies the finest ideals of the game, it also throws into sharper relief the barbarities that also attend it. It is ironic that Dalglish's new Liverpool was filling the gap in little boys' hearts that used to belong to Manchester United. Contests between the two teams had become marked by acrimony between players and between fans. Liverpool supporters know all about the enduring Manchester United charm and the power of a glamour that cannot be measured in points and silverware alone. That magic from the past contrasted vividly with the cultured executioners of Don Revie's Leeds and lasted even through Liverpool's phase of European domination. A rancorous rivalry took root between the two sets of supporters and a frenzied desire in each for their team to master the other. Partisanship went beyond pride and plumbed the pits of depravity. The first side that Matt Busby built, the famous 'Busby Babes', had been all but destroyed in a plane crash. One year, a banner in the Liverpool crowd crowed about it: 'Munich '58'. When Bill Shankly died, Manchester fans retaliated: 'Shankly '81'. In 1982, Liverpool fans even launched a gas attack on United players as they stepped off the team coach. Grown men spat on Sir Matt Busby, by then an old man, long retired. There are no words to describe the blight that afflicts some people's minds. But this is a part of what football has become.

At Old Trafford on 15 November 1987, Liverpool ran out before 47,106 people to meet their aristocratic foe once again. It was probably the first time Liverpool had entered the fray on equal aesthetic terms in the popular imagination, carrying with them the potential to overrun any team in the land. Barnes was a symbol of both that equality and that promise. His presence inspired United's frontline fans to a special level of loathing. They abandoned the abstinence usually observed by racist supporters with blacks in their own team – Viv Anderson was actually marking Barnes at right-back – and booed Liverpool's number ten anyway, throughout a gruelling 1–all draw.

It is a testament to the bigotry that resides behind the goals in English football that after the Everton games, booing John Barnes became a convention at away grounds. Where millions were excited by the verve of Barnes and his team, thousands could only feel resentment. It was as if in the eyes of the nation's most vocal working-class racists, he had somehow become *extra* black, the target of all targets. His qualities as a player and a gentleman made a vivid contrast with the violence around him. Barnes became a figurehead for people's noblest hopes for the game and a target for all its nastiest distortions. With every match he played, football's civilized followers urged him to silence its most vile with some flash of unanswerable skill.

As for 'Kenny's army', they provided a non-stop diet of food for thought. Up and down the British Rail network they rode, jumping buses, trudging through back streets, getting from game to game. Occasionally you could spot a black face among them, usually in the segregated visiting fans' compartment at away games. Just ones and twos, but feeling, mostly for the first time, that Liverpool was a safe and appropriate team to follow. They were there because of Barnes – he was the best and his presence was their protection. From other Liverpool fans, the mad, bad, Scallywag hardcore, evidence emerged that scousers are capable of sustaining just as deep a schizophrenia as any other football supporters. The best Kop story comes from the home game against Charlton. They were the first team since Barnes's arrival to visit Anfield with a black player in their line-up. Garth Crooks was in his usual striker's role and his early goal alarmed Anfield. The next time he got the ball, a cry went up from an isolated voice: 'Get that black bastard!' Seconds passed. Then someone replied: 'Which one? Theirs or ours?' Straight to the heart of a hurtful truth in the space of five words. The Kop was working through a double standard – which way would it fall?

It was a rejoinder which stayed in the mind throughout the season. In April, a midweek away game against Norwich City provided Liverpool with the opportunity finally to clinch their runaway Championship victory. Barnes had been injured at the Mercentile Credit Centenary Festival (the Football League's débâcle of a celebration to mark their hundredth year), and was known not to be playing. The Norwich team came out to warm up before the kick off. Ruel Fox, their black winger, was among them. The Liverpool fans proferred a hostile greeting. Even now that 'Barnesie' was their hero, the old, atavistic urge had to be indulged. It was a display of double standards, which shows that the Barnes effect was at once profound and superficial. If he's in 'our' shirt, he's one of us. If he isn't, he's just another 'black bastard'. The embrace of black players as one-off exceptions when they pull on the right colour football shirt is a metaphor *in excelsis* for the history of black people in British life. The white world might want your labour – but how much does it want *you*? Had Barnes been accepted as being black, or just forgiven for it?

The Norwich match was a dull, disjointed, goalless draw. Beardsley battled, but with no Barnes there was a missing dimension. The result required Liverpool to, as the press put it, leave the champagne on ice for Anfield the following weekend when the champions-elect were due to meet Spurs.

On the late train back to London, a motley handful of Liverpool supporters shared the same carriage. A middle-aged white woman sat chatting to a young black girl, a sturdy kid in her teens, with short hair and wearing a silver Liverpool official tracksuit replica. She was at home games, too, later in the season, trudging down Oakfield Road, dressed exactly the same. 'They love John Barnes now, don't they,' remarked the white woman. 'But they didn't want him at first.' The pair were joined by another Liverpool supporter, this one more typical. A white lad, around 18, good-looking and not too proud to talk to a couple of females. He and his mates had done well, he explained. They'd ducked out of the police escort back to the station and grabbed a quick drink in town. They talked about the Norwich match, the Tottenham game to come, how the Catholics are supposed to support Everton, so they'd heard. The women got off at some suburban backwood and he went back to his mates. They spent the rest of the journey swopping stories about fights: how they'd jumped a couple of 'Mancs' leaning against a wall outside Anfield a few weeks before ('I said, "We gorra 'ave these"'); how one of his pals had been jumped by a couple of Mancs at the away game in November and this lad got out a Stanley knife and held it to his mate's throat and said, 'I don't ever want to see you at Old Trafford or at Maine Road ever again.' He and his travelling partner reckoned that any time you saw a black supporter at a Liverpool–United match, it had to be a United fan. We all got off at

Euston and the affable Liverpool lad, who'd chatted to the ladies and battered the bewildered Mancunians, marched off to who knows where in the mild North London night.

Beneath the adoration lavished on Barnes, there is a lurking ambivalence. He is accepted for producing the goods on the park. He is accepted for being ready to take a dressing-room joke. He is accepted for being a polite, modest young man, which is not always the way black sportsmen are perceived, the slightest delight in triumph being condemned as conceit. He is only being himself, but he is regarded as an exception. It is an ambiguous and insecure position, however much the crowd sing 'Johnny Barnes, Johnny Barnes'. In a town where the game enjoys unique status, but where racism is ingrained, Barnes needs to move with care. One bad game too many, a few indiscreet remarks, and suddenly the walls of his palace could all come tumbling down. He is lucky that humility comes naturally.

'I don't think John even really thinks of himself as doing well,' says the Liverpool insider. 'He's just there and does what he does. He was shocked when he came to Liverpool at the extent of the football mania here. He and Peter [Beardsley] couldn't believe that they were getting mobbed and needed a police escort to get to their cars after the game. They weren't expecting to be super-heroes and I don't think John wants to be a super-hero. He just happens to be a very nice guy that gets on well with people. He's not big-headed or egotistical in any way, so they've adapted to him. It could have been very different. If it changes him it could be very difficult for him, particularly because he's black. They'd have something to have a go at, the fans and the players. I don't think he'd be able to stay.'

But Barnes is not likely to let that happen. He is a very level-headed young man. Interviewed in *Liverpool* magazine, he was asked if he ever felt like storming out of the ground in response to racial abuse. 'No, I never get like that,' he replied. 'I have to say that I'm not really a very emotional person. I'm not an angry person, a violent person . . . At school I remember having a fight. That is the sum total of my aggression . . . but what can you do? You either put up with it or you don't play.'

Off the field and on, Barnes projects a sensibility that tells us he relates to the idea of a distinctive black culture that is aspiring, respectable, affluent rather than fired by rage. He dresses well, sharp but not too flash. Barnes likes black music and he spent much of his English adolescence moving to the dance groove in glitzy West End clubs. One night his father, the Colonel, was roused from sleep by one of his daughters, saying John was at the door with two policemen. He had been walking home from Oxford Street's voguish Studio 21, when a couple of men from the Met stopped him, searched him and demanded to know where he was going. When the teenage Barnes said his home was a mews residence near Harley Street, the police did not believe him. When he put his key in the lock he discovered the front door was latched on the inside. His sister let him in and by the time the Colonel arrived on the scene, the policemen were taking their leave.

The Colonel was astonished: 'I said to Johnny, "What's the matter?" He said, "Oh, nothing." I said, "But why did they stop you?" He said, "I suppose they were just suspicious. What are you making such a fuss about? I get stopped every Friday night coming home. It's no big thing." But he'd never mentioned it, and it never struck me before. He certainly never expressed any bitterness about it. Now some people would say that's racism. But with him it didn't seem to have the slightest effect. I suppose he takes these things in his stride.'

Barnes's image was so amenable he was even considered fit for exposure to readers of the *Daily Express*. Leading feature writer Philippa Kennedy wrote a three-part profile that made him sound like he had stepped out of a Malibu commercial, a carefree, wholesome Caribbean beach boy. He was quoted saying amazingly stupid things, like 'everyone had servants in Jamaica', and posed for pictures waving a bottle of champagne, a cartoon image of conservative black success. With this clean-cut public profile went a sense of civic responsibility. He made himself available for visits to schools organized by Brian Thompson. He agreed to lend his presence to local fundraising functions, and, as at Watford, he did it all for free, causing his team-mates to complain that he was undercutting the market and queering their pitch. He gave his endorsement to campaigns to improve standards of nutrition and promote the responsible use of alcohol – good, wholesome causes for a responsible professional athlete. Nothing controversial, nothing too closely aligned with difficult issues like 'race'.

For a man in the spotlight, Barnes kept a low profile. At the end of the season, both Beardsley and Aldridge had lightning bi-ographies lined up, and Grobbelaar was due to work on a wacky, wisecracks-and-picture book. Barnes's agent says his client received offers 'in the high five figures' to commit his life-story to print, but declined them all. 'Too modest', insists Mr Still. When Barnes did succumb to demands for exposure, he was always at pains to explain that he was not a celebrity or a star, just one component in a larger unit, conforming to the demands of the team. He emphasized it in an interview with *New Musical Express*, when the Liverpool squad released their Cup Final single 'The Anfield Rap'. The song itself reflected the chemistry of the dressing room: 'When I get the ball, the crowd goes bananas,' sang Barnes. His desire to make comedy out of racism in the company of his team mates went further still. He turned up at the players' Christmas fancy dress party as a member of the Ku Klux Klan. The news was received in Liverpool 8 with sharp intakes of breath. Other black professionals admit they could not have brought themselves to do it. But at the party it went down a treat – for 'Barnesie', it seemed, this was an acceptable part of the repertoire of being one of the lads.

The fans responded in a similar spirit. The humour reflected both a need to acknowledge him as black and yet laugh the ramifica-tions away. A joke can crystallize an issue and enable its maker to wriggle out of the repercussions at the same time. Some smartass dubbed Barnes 'Tarmac' – the black Heighway, geddit? By referring to a past player of comparable style the moniker confirms Barnes's place in the Anfield pantheon, but at the same time acknowledges that his blackness sets him apart. It is a tribute to the generosity with which Liverpool loyalists had taken Barnes to their hearts, but also to an undertow of tradition which one man cannot eradicate alone. Anfield's embrace of Barnes is a reminder of a potential for generosity and a history of bigotry, both of which Merseyside can pursue with a most Liverpudlian vigour.

As championship victory came closer and the prospect of the Double loomed, the full gamut of Anfield passions rose to a fever pitch. The Easter programme pitted Liverpool against Manchester United at home. It was their third match after Everton had ended their unbeaten First Division run. They had won the first, slightly unsteadily, at home to the unsettling Wimbledon, by two goals to one. They lost the next game by the same score away to Nottingham Forest, making two League defeats out of the previous three. Was there a short-circuit in the Reds' psyche? Would their second deadliest rivals make them crack? Liverpool had failed to defeat United at home for seven consecutive seasons. A ferocious encounter saw the lead change hands twice and Liverpool surrender a two-goal margin despite United having defender Colin Gibson sent off. The game ended in a bloody 3-all draw. Dalglish and United manager Alex Ferguson squabbled over the refereeing live on Radio 2. Dalglish, clutching a new baby daughter, suggested the interviewer would get more sense out of her. The Kop was a ferment of frustration.

It was not, however, an extended agony. On 23 April Tottenham Hotspur and their fans came to Anfield to play the role of ritual sacrifice as the Championship was clinched. In a scruffy, half-baked match, they declined to roll over and offer their throats. But Peter Beardsley's artful goal was enough to complete an Anfield occasion, as instructive for what happened off the pitch as on it.

The day's best entertainment came in the train on the way up from London. Rival hooligans have no problem recognizing one another and any Anfield hardcase on the hunt would have spotted the young Tottenham contingent a mile off. Half a dozen sat prattling in a bunch, suburban to the stitching on their socks. Their hair was perfectly parted, disciplined with handfuls of gel. Their trainers were clean and chunky. Their ski-ing sweaters were chic. Peering at the small print of the previous night's *Evening Standard*, they checked their Tottenham share prices with innocent delight. When the train pulled in at Stafford, they took to daring each other to wave a tenner at the people on the platform. As they entered the outskirts of Liverpool, they gawped in amazement at the sight of back-to-back terraces: 'Strewf! They ain't got no front garden!' Then they passed a piece of graffiti, sprayed on a railside wall several seasons back. 'Cockneys Die', it said. 'Oh, that's nice, innit,' said the Tottenham lads, cut to the quick.

They were having an easier time of it than the Koppites, though. A line of fans already stretched right up round the corner before 11.00 a.m. No one was there to supervise the queue, no stewards, no police, no one. Only the wan, wiry young men, digging in for the long, long wait. By half-past one, two things had happened to the queue: it had condensed, as everyone shuffled forward, magnetized by the promise of the turnstile shutters being, at long last, removed; and it had swelled sideways as fans came out of the pubs and latched on to the edge of the line, as casual as you like.

Just before half-past one, the mounted police showed up. They swaggered and scowled and barked orders at what, by this time, were thousands of irritable people squashed together, sardines in a purgatory sauce, impatient but somehow horribly resigned. A ragged-arsed scouser with a moustache and a belly full of beer decided to tell us a 'nigger' joke. Everybody laughed that sulphurous Liverpool laugh. There was a screech and then a shout from the road to our right. A body lay crumpled in front of a now stationary car. A policeman went over to look. 'Go on, ya bastard,' goaded the scallywag comic, 'ger 'is fuckin' ticket!' And with that, after four hours of boredom, exhaustion and impotent rage, we squeezed towards the slit in the wall, arms pinned to our sides, pursued by threats from the Merseyside police.

Liverpool completed their victory and did a lap of honour. A limping Barnes, still recovering from his Centenary groin strain, joined the posse on the pitch. The crowd chanted his name. Barnes waved and clapped. The Tottenham fans waited in their enclosure until the police escort was ready to take them to their transport home. Later that evening, waiting in the station, the occupants of a quiet railway carriage on the last train back to London pricked up their ears in alarm. From somewhere in the distance came the slurry tones of alcoholic euphoria. 'We're on the march with Kenny's army. We're all going to Wem-bel-ee!' They were on the platform now, and then they were on the train. Closer and closer came the beery incantation, up the passageways, one carriage at a time. The victory anthem rattled the window panes and everyone held their breath.

Then the door burst open. Through it, red-faced and resplendent, fell a young man and woman fresh from a wedding reception – their own. They were pursued by a carousing conga-line of lads in red scarves, carrying the newly-weds' luggage on their heads. 'Will this do for you?' asked one, shoving a suitcase on to an overhead rack as the astonished couple slipped obediently into their seats. Clutching his ring-pull can, the volunteer porter stood and made a short announcement in thick, quizzical scouse: 'I know it's against me principles, being a socialist, and that. But shouldn't we have a whip-round so's these can travel first class?' Nobody knew what to say. So he shrugged, stumbled into a pew next to his mates, and proceeded to talk football, loudly and without respite for the entire journey to Euston. They had been among the crushed congregation outside an unwelcoming Anfield, waiting to take their hard-won place with Kenny's army on the Kop. For them, and many others, it was a way of life. One year later, at Hillsborough, it would become a way of death.

14

'My Stomach Turned Over'

The only team to threaten Liverpool's virtual monopoly on the higher forms of football were Nottingham Forest. Their victory over the champions-elect at their home City Ground was one of two defeats Liverpool sustained in the League all season and the only match they lost in any competition where it might be claimed that their opponents produced the sweeter football. Brian Clough, the marvellous, monstrous Nottingham manager, had fashioned a side which, by general consent, were the second most attractive in the First Division that year. With an average age of twenty-three, the Forest team too possessed enormous finesse and no player epitomized it more than Clough's son Nigel, a forward-lying fulcrum on which Forest's attacks were balanced. Their encounters with the Merseyside heavyweights provided memorable meetings of competing football minds and some of the most sumptuous goalscoring action of the year.

The fascination of the Forest–Liverpool contests was given an extra twist when, through a quirk of fate and fixture arrangements, the two teams met three times in the space of eleven days: first at Nottingham, third at Anfield and, in between the two, in an FA Cup semi-final at Sheffield Wednesday's Hillsborough ground. The tactical battle was joined by Dalglish on Clough's home patch in typically unorthodox style. Throwing pundits into a most satisfying confusion, he named Beardsley and Houghton as substitutes and employed a formation that was almost unheard of in the English game. Molby was promoted into a five-man midfield for his first full game of the season. The unhappy Johnston returned to fill a wide, right-hand side position with Barnes a deep-lying complement on the left. Aldridge was the lone striker. In terms of getting a result, the ploy did not work. Gary Crosby, a flyweight outside-right who had come straight into Forest's team from non-League

Grantham Town, gave Liverpool's raw left back Gary Ablett, a local lad who had come up through the ranks, a miserable afternoon. Forest took the lead when a cross was deflected by Hansen into his own goal. Then Clough, who had a penalty saved by Grobbelaar straight after half-time, scored a second from Crosby's pass. A foul on Barnes gave Aldridge the chance to reduce the deficit from the penalty spot, but that was all the headway Liverpool could make.

The brusqueness which sends shivers of anxiety through the spines of football journalists was more than evident in Dalglish's response to enquiries about this, apparently disastrous, tactical change. Poker faced, he parroted the party line: 'It is not my policy to discuss the reasons for my team selection in public . . .' And so on. But there was a silver lining – the element of surprise was intact for the forthcoming Cup semi-final.

The match was anticipated as a potential classic. In the event, it did not yield John Barnes's most magical performance, but it did provide the stage for one of his most complete. Once again, the contrast between watching the actual football and getting to the ground in the first place was depressing, sad and sobering. Shepherded off the platform at Sheffield, it was clear that the only way to make it to the ground was to take one of the special buses provided. A policeman, with an alsation straining at his side, muscled a pair of recalcitrant Forest fans into the waiting crush. On the bus, dozens of sweatily oblivious youths jumped and shouted and babbled on. The vacuum door closed and a bunch of them spotted an Asian family on the pavement outside. The Forest fans pounded on the window: 'Black bastard, black bastard, black bastard.' A tiny, shabby little black kid found that he was no longer one of the lads: 'Let's not have any of that,' he quipped, meekly. Did any of them know what they were saying? Had anyone ever explained? The coach set off. The two Forest hard nuts at whom the police dog had snarled found their straining bladders could stand no more. Leaning sideways in practised fashion, they pissed blithely down the sides of the wooden pews. The warm, yellow stream slopped up and down the length of the upper tier as the bus juddered, crawled and cranked through the gears. Feet were duly raised to rest on the bench in front. No one batted an eyelid.

The press facilities comprised a single room with a makeshift bar and a TV set mounted on the wall. The smoke hung thick in the air, an inert, carcinogenic mist. Inside every camel sports coat there stood the shell of what once might have been a man. But the view from the complimentary seats . . . now that was worth all the bronchial disorders in Fleet Street. On one side, a great bank of silver and red. On the other, an edifice of brick red and white. Between them a lush expanse of grass, centrepiece of one of the finest football stadia in the land. It was a vista filled with promise. That's how it seemed at the time. A year's hindsight provokes shudders at so fulsome a description. But the memory is worth clinging to, as a reminder that football, terrace crowds and all, *can* be a beautiful game.

After thirteen minutes, Barnes cruised on to a pass that put the full-back Steve Chettle out of contention. But the Forest youngster did not admit defeat. As Barnes advanced into the penalty area and eyed up his options for administering the *coup de grâce*, Chettle's desperate recovery tackle brought him down. Aldridge scored from the spot in the teeth of the Forest support.

Seated in the press enclosure, with the whole field in view, it was possible to appreciate the full and lucid co-ordination of the Liverpool team. Dalglish had reverted to what, by this stage of the season, was his strongest available line-up. Lawrenson had retired and gone on to manage Oxford United. Whelan was still not back from injury. Houghton had established himself over Johnston and the workmanlike Nigel Spackman had stepped up as an effective foil for the swashbuckling McMahon. The team sheet read: Grobbelaar; Nicol, Gillespie, Hansen, Ablett; Houghton, Spackman, McMahon, Barnes; Beardsley, Aldridge. Together, they offered an education in interpersonal chemistry. Never did the ball stand idle for long, nor was it put to aimless use. The confidence of each player in the others seemed close to total, with passes tumbling together in neat combinations, holding possession, creating options, until a flurry of swift exchanges sent a spare man racing clear. Liverpool's sophistication glowed. It was an exercise in instant geometry, the human instincts not subordinated but honed to fit a greater collective sensibility in which all the components might flourish. Liverpool Football Club might have been founded by a Conservative businessman, but there is a certain poetic aptness in his team's first-choice strip being red.

Forest had their moments of epiphany too. Clough junior's touch was sweet, and with Crosby in possession there were always possibilities. But it was here too that Barnes played his part. With Ablett's anxiety obvious, it was part of Barnes's job to help do to Crosby what other teams had spent most of the season trying to do to him. The crowding operation was a success without diminishing Barnes as an attacking force. In the second half, a wall-pass with Beardsley, who had drifted to the touchline, sent him once more motoring into the inside-left position *en route* to the penalty area. It was a combination which had bamboozled both Manchester City and Everton in previous rounds leading to goals from Aldridge and Houghton. Now it was Forest's turn. The ball was still bouncing as Barnes bore down on it, with Aldridge the sole Liverpool attacker in an advanced position. A Forest defender chased back beside him, obstructing a direct pass. The television replay showed Barnes glance upwards and sweep the bouncing ball on the half-volley across the face of the goal in a deft curve, past the groping centre-back at the perfect pace and height to intersect Aldridge's path. The native Liverpudlian crashed the ball directly into the goal. After that, not even the younger Clough's scrambled consolation could threaten the Merseysiders' ride to a place in the Final of the Cup.

Downstairs, the gentlemen of the press encountered the exultant players in a dark ante-room next to the changing area. Scrubbed, lacquered and immaculate in their double-breasted suits, the Liverpool men emerged to be surrounded by huddles of grovelling hacks. Hansen, the captain, fiercer in his civvies than in his jersey and shorts, had his lines polished in advance. Yes, he had heard that at White Hart Lane Luton had lost to Wimbledon in the other semi-final. 'A lot of people criticize Wimbledon,' he said, 'but we don't. They play within the rules, and how they do it is up to them.' Gillespie, McMahon and Nicol edged towards the coach. Houghton made a few bright noises. Aldridge, bubbling like a schoolboy, made some more. Then out came Barnes. The newshounds snuffled round. Barnes made a little joke, manifestly more at ease stringing quotable quips together than most of his team-mates. Everybody laughed. What a nice lad he is.

Dalglish came last of all, ages after everybody else, hands planted warmly on the shoulders of his son, Paul. This time the pressmen did not snuffle . . . they *sidled*. Every question was preceded by a string of apologies: 'Look, I know you don't like to single out individual players, but would you say, do you think, that John Barnes has fulfilled all the hopes you had when he signed for you?' Dalglish said he was very pleased with Barnes. Also, he was pleased with the way Mike Hooper played in goal in the fourth round game against Stoke when Grobbelaar was injured. Let's not forget him. 'Yes, Kenny,' said everyone, and if they'd had tails they'd have wagged them. Anyone who holds the popular press in such contempt as Dalglish cannot be all bad.

When Forest came to Liverpool the following Wednesday night to complete the three-game sequence, the Merseysiders demolished them. Tom Finney's comment afterwards, that the 5–nil triumph was the finest single performance he had ever seen, was widely reported.

Forest were tired, demoralized and carrying injuries. But, for all that, Liverpool's form was majestic. Elderly gentlemen in the main stand could not find the words to describe their delight. They just made noises instead: 'Awwwww!; 'Ahhhhh!' 'Uh, ho, ho!' They gasped and sighed and slapped each other on the back as Barnes nutmegged a defender on the far touchline, swept like an arrow past another to the byline, then turned the ball back low for Beardsley to wallop it past goalkeeper Sutton. Rogan Taylor, watching from the Kop, cites that goal as the perfect example of what Barnes had brought to Liverpool that wasn't there before: 'Heighway was a super winger and Thompson even more so. But I've seen Barnes doing things that have been really spectacular this season.'

Taylor is a doctor of psychology and religion as well as being national secretary of the Football Supporters' Association. His interests in ritual, magic and popular culture are the natural intel-lectual territory for a devoted Koppite. His response to Barnes's performance that night prompted intriguing parallels. 'One of the things that I wrote about was Houdini. I was very interested in reading crowd reactions to him and the physical effect of watching somebody do something that your eyes tell you they can't do. Your stomach starts doing peculiar things. I've had that at Anfield for the first time ever, where my stomach has turned over, thinking, "My God, he's not gonna make that" – but he *does* make it. In that match against Nottingham Forest, he went from a standing start and he nutmegged the first guy. The ball appeared to drift away. There was a second guy lined up and I said, "He's not gonna get that." And there was this physical thing of his legs actually appearing to lengthen and you go, "Oh, what?!"' And suddenly, there it was, and Liverpool had scored again, their fourth in a 5–nil carnival.

In his book, *Inside Anfield*, Aldridge conveys a genuine sense of delight in the side's showing: 'This was the greatest team performance I have ever experienced. It was exhilarating, pulsating football at its best. If the crowd at Anfield and the millions who experienced the highlights enjoyed it, just imagine what it was like to play in this match.' Most people who have played any kind of sport have a day like that once in their lives, when it really does feel as though you have taken on some inexplicable extra gift of timing and perception and you find yourself operating on a plateau way above even what you would normally think of as good. It was a sensation which seemed to ooze through the entire Liverpool team that night.

If only the same memories applied to the Cup Final. The showpiece that football's idealists hoped would yield a Liverpool triumph and a moral for our times just didn't work out that way. Pessimists now console themselves by saying it was bound to happen. There was a whole month to go between the Forest annihilation and the big Wembley occasion. Liverpool had gone on to hammer Sheffield Wednesday 5–1 away from home, but since then, with the championship well won, they had negotiated three slightly haphazard 1–1 draws. In the last, at home to Luton, Spackman and Gillespie suffered a mid-air collision and both required stitches. The pair were doubtful starters throughout the Final build-up and eventually took to the field heavily bandaged. By the time Liverpool were ready to face the Wimbledon grapplers again, this time at Wembley, they had acquired a taste for perfection but their battery had gone flat.

The Cup Final scene was both depressing and bizarre. Of the

92,000 present, only a small platoon were conspicuously and devoutly Wimbledon fans. Touts had a field day with Wimbledon's ticket allocation which massively outweighed demand, and the huge preponderance of red that lined Wembley's interior was ample evidence of the number that had found their way up the M6 to Merseyside. The journey to Wembley was the usual grim adventure, despite the big match atmosphere, this time given a strange twist by the glaring discrepancy in support for the two sides. Wimbledon's supporters took after their team in glorying in their underdog image. At Anfield a few weeks earlier they had delightedly indulged their self-mocking humour, affectionately putting themselves and their own players down. They had a little tune for their marauding centre-forward that was as uncomplicated and as effective as its subject: 'He's big, he's black, he leads the Dons' attack, Fashanu, Fashanu.' A tiny minority squeezed in among Liverpudlian interlopers unable to get seats anywhere else, they hissed impertinent insults at Beardsley every time he ventured near their goal: 'Ug-leee! Ug-leee!' To Barnes they sang: 'Hello, Hello, Watford reject!' A gallows mentality and not to be underestimated. At Wembley, the Wimbledon players brought it to bear on Liverpool and sent the banks of Merseyside supporters into seizures as the imperious League champions fizzled, floundered and faded away.

There is a loose consensus among more thoughtful football observers as to why it was that Wimbledon prevailed. Some of it is obvious enough. It was the biggest day in their players' football lives, one which they might never experience again. They were bits and pieces players for the most part, some picked up from lower divisions and honed to fit the Wimbledon mould. Others, though respected, were little more than spirited artisans if assessed individually. But Wimbledon were in their meanest, nastiest frame of mind ... and how they wanted to win. Their desire could not be doubted. Their bloody-minded doggedness never had been. Psychologically, that adds up to a pretty disturbing prospect for any team to face. Liverpool, on the other hand, were expected to do much more than just win the game. Though some casual sentiment was with the underdogs, Liverpool were now loved for their style. Connoisseurs wanted them to give Wimbledon a lesson, to vaporize them and all they stood for. Liverpool's professional pride insisted that it should be that way as well. The demand was for champagne all the way.

It is known that Wimbledon players' efforts to intimidate Liverpool began in the tunnel even as they readied themselves to say 'hi' to Princess Di. McMahon, Liverpool's most abrasive midfield player, was the target for much of it and also for early punishment from a psyched-up Vinny Jones once the game was under way. Beardsley, in his biography, confirms that 'The Wimbledon team were shouting things in the tunnel before the game,' and you could hear them at it as the TV cameras pried into the darkness. As Barnes walked from the tunnel, you could see him grin uncomfortably as Jones pushed his mug into his face.

Beardsley denies that Wimbledon's verbalizing upset Liverpool's concentration. 'We're experienced enough to cope with that and laugh it off.' He also makes light of the backchat on the field. But if Liverpool were not spooked by Wimbledon's snarls, they played as if they were. And when the run of the ball seemed to go against them, they suddenly ran out of ideas. Beardsley was denied a charming goal thanks to a famous misjudgement of the advantage law by referee Brian Hill. Though he was fouled by full-back Phelan, Beardsley still got through and chipped the ball past Beasant. But the whistle had already gone. Liverpool had barely got over their consternation, when Wimbledon were back down the field. From set pieces they are aggressive, well drilled and blessed with plenty of brawn. Wise, their most subtle performer, chipped in an angled free-kick and Lawrie Sanchez popped an innocuous glancing header into the far corner of the net.

From then on, Wimbledon were in their element. Having tweaked the nose of the aristocracy they were not about to touch their forelocks. They did what they are best at – digging in. Liverpool muddled on, struggling to find a route through a wary, retreating defence which refused to unbutton itself. It was a flawless defensive operation. As Liverpool pushed forward, Wimbledon gave ground just enough to take their momentum away. Attack after attack petered out around the penalty box.

Kenny's massive army fell into an eloquent silence as the time slipped away. In goal, Beasant surpassed himself, rising to the occasion the few times Liverpool breached Wimbledon's stout resistance. When Aldridge was awarded a debatable penalty kick, it seemed that the tide must turn. But the man who had seemed infallible from the spot failed to convert. Lurch lunged to his left, saved the kick and lifted the Cup. 'The crazy gang have beaten the culture club,' thrilled John Motson on the BBC.

But there was not much romance in this underdog victory, no matter that TV priorities demanded that some be found. A match-day official who was down on the pitch listened to Wimbledon celebrate: 'We got the bastards. We did them.' As the droves of Liverpool fans slouched, numbly, back down Wembley Way, everybody tried to figure out what went wrong.

It was a result that begged many questions. Tommy Smith says that if anyone had tried winding up the Liverpool teams he was in, there would have been a fight in the tunnel. Others maintain that if it had been Shankly's Liverpool out there, Jones, and one or two others, would have watched the second half from a hospital bed. But, notwithstanding Wimbledon's likely willingness to walk it as nasty as they talked it, it seems glib if not unjust to attribute Liverpool's misfire to fear. Luck played its part. The penalty aside, Liverpool had precious little of it. They had two men short of fitness. Beardsley looked tired and tried too hard. The midfield was battened down and Aldridge walked alone. Barnes, mean-while, was totally neutralized by a man who looked as if he had baled out of a Sopwith Camel in 1914 and only just found his way home. Clive Goodyear was the full-back detailed to mark the double Footballer of the Year and, with a posse of helpers to hand, he soon began winning battles that more illustrious contem-poraries had been losing all year.

Dalglish appeared to try no radical tactical change. It was as if Liverpool, held hostage by their own high expectations, did not believe an entire match could pass without them slipping into gear. They died quietly in the end, with no single player doing himself justice. Barnes's weak showing was grist to the mill of those who insist that truly great players always find a way to impose their will on a game. It didn't happen with Barnes. With the Liverpool system disrupted he didn't know where to plug himself in. As for Wimbledon, they did what they went out there to do. They did what football demands. They won.

15

'Nothing to do with Football'

Not all the England fans who went to the 1988 European Football Championships are card-carrying Hitler freaks. But plenty of those who weren't think the National Front lads have got the right idea. They were on the march with Bobby's army. All foreigners are beneath contempt. A foreigner is anyone who isn't of the true blue English master race. The words 'wog', 'coon' and 'nigger' were blithely and violently employed. These were joined by the word 'cunt', and you could measure the mentality by the malice in their mouths – xenophobia and misogyny twisted together to define the ultimate in Englishness. As the likelihood grew that England would make a miserable, early exit from the competition, there were England football supporters who reached for the unspeakable to describe John Barnes – 'that nigger', 'that cunt'.

England's fans had mixed feelings about their celebrated 'Invasion of Germany, 1988', to quote the slogan on the notorious T-shirts. The aggravation had been fun, but on the pitch it had hardly been a glorious campaign. First stop Stuttgart: lost to the Republic of Ireland, 1–nil. Second stop: Düsseldorf: lost to Holland, 3–1. Defeat stiffened the loathing of Bobby's Barmy Army. Plenty of fighting, plenty of drinking, plenty of hard-pressed police. Only the Frankfurt fixture remained and England's faint mathematical chance of reaching the semi-finals depended on defeating the Soviet Union, while hoping the Irish would lose decisively to the Dutch. With half-time approaching, even that slender lifeline had dissolved. The England team were two goals down and in danger of falling apart. The England fans were looking for a scapegoat. It was no surprise they chose the man in the number eleven shirt. 'Fuck off, Barnes,' they crowed, almost eerie in an otherwise silent stadium. 'Fuck off, Barnes.'

It was not a universal chorus, but the substantial minority who delivered it sang with all their hearts and with no fear of censure from those around them. In those moments, finally, the English hooligan beast articulated its true nature before a watching world. Not that the British authorities took this latest sledgehammer hint. As the Union Jack brigade belched and bruised its way across the Federal Republic, turning railway stations into garrisons and streets into battle grounds, Colin Moynihan MP, the excitable Minister for Sport, had made the usual irrelevant noises for the benefit of British TV. 'We are dealing with hard core criminals,' chirruped Margaret's man. 'We must make sure that we take a very tough line.' And so on and on, the familiar refrain.

Is Mr Moynihan really stupid, or does he just think the rest of us are? His shrill PR performance, as ever, completely missed the point. England's top boy-thugs did not congregate at the centre of the Stuttgart Schlossplatz shopping precinct and chant 'Sieg Heil' just to spite the local constabulary. It was not by chance that straight-arm salutes accompanied the close of their rendition of 'God Save The Queen', the banner of the nihilist Blood and Honour sect unfurled and to the fore. Nor was it coincidence that the first of the bottles was thrown when a solitary black teenager with eyeliner and a quiff happened to wander through a bemused, onlooking crowd. The kid's name was Rodney, an American bohemian naïf. They chased him across the paving slabs amid cascades of breaking glass until the snatch squads steamed in and hustled the ringleaders away.

It was a blood-curdling scene, a performance as depressing as the platitudes uttered in its aftermath. English neo-Nazis and inebriated kindred spirits launch an assault on a foreign land. The British government responds by spouting about the sanctity of the Law. Yet the truth could not be more stark: what spurs English travelling hooligans to do their barbarous deeds is not merely a criminal mentality, but a *fascist* one. Football's witless role is to provide it with a platform.

The 1988 European Football Championships exposed, in all its complacency, the true nature of English soccer's soul. The cry that politics should be kept out of the sport is never far from its mealy spokesmen's lips, be they broadcasters, columnists, managers, chairmen or Home Office marionettes. Yet it wallows, so very smug, in its own philosophical torpor, in its implicit politics of insularity and indifference. As the game shrinks resentfully from all external criticism, its role as an arena where bigots preach their creed is reconfirmed. Just as the national team is meant to represent the essence of the national game, so its most ardent, devoted followers exhibit the vilest instincts of its terraces. And no one seems to mind. 'Nationalism? That's what international sport is all about,' remarked one football writer, cheerfully, as England's sole black player was singled out for abuse from his own fans. Two behind and struggling, Barnes went down under a fair but heavy challenge inside his own half. Numbed, he received treatment from the trainer before rising, uncomplaining, to his feet. A true-grit recovery, more English than the English. But the England contingent booed. 'It's understandable really,' reasoned the English journalist. So fascist thugs have feelings too, right? 'Oh, they're just a bunch of nutters, aren't they? Nothing to do with football.' And nothing, needless to say, to do with him.

These are the symptoms of a demoralized sporting culture, unwilling and unable to diagnose the sickness that assails it, a disorder which manifests itself throughout 'the game', from board-room to bad lads on the rampage. Scratch the surface of the men in the directors' boxes and find much the same mentality as behind the goals, the same attitudes to women, to foreigners, the same stolid stereotypes about what it is to be a man. Often the only difference between the chairman and the thug is that the thug knows more about the team. The 'hooligan minority', glibly dismissed as an unfortunate aberration, is really just the most garish symptom of a malaise that thrives in the bones of the national game. Lining up for the anthems, Bobby's barmy army hymned their favourites: 'Oh, Gary, Gary . . . ' and Lineker turned to acknowledge the call. What was passing through his mind? 'There's only one Peter Beardsley', the Union Jack gang carolled at Lineker's striking partner, and the Liverpool man offered a wave. It was too far away to see if he had his fingers crossed.

As the England team kicked-in, the strictly segregated areas allocated to its followers were festooned in Union Jacks. By this, the third England match, they had become a familiar sight. Draped across the perimeter fence, or spread out on the pitch's apron, each bore the name tag of the team or town of its bearer: Chelsea, Walthamstow, Blackburn. The sun beat down on pink, bulbous bodies and a thousand crude tattoos: 'You'll never take the English,' they announced.

The authorities were well prepared, their strategy built upon a blend of behaviourism and the threat of force. The public address system churned out a hopeful stream of soothing schlock: 'Imagine there's no heaven,' sang a tinny John Lennon, 'It's easy if you try.' Well, he had a point there. A column of police strolled briskly out to a curve of bench seats, facing the caged, potential threat. Placing their helmets at their sides, they checked their holsters, stroked their truncheons and pondered the cruel twist of fate that had given them seats so tantalizingly close to the action, but facing the wrong way.

It was hard to decide which was the most depressing sight – the England fans or the England back four. Stevens, Adams, Butcher and Sansom swiftly plunged into a state of ludicrous disorganiz-ation. Shuttling up and down in increasingly futile attempts to work the offside trap, they looked like a bunch of trainee Territorials abandoned by their sergeant. They were leaner and mostly fitter than the flag-wavers behind the wire, but their haircuts were the same. So too their attempts to assert a guileless muscularity which the nimble Soviet forwards matched physically and outmanoeuvred intellectually. Barnes, meanwhile, confounded his reputation for inconsistency – his performance against the Soviets was his third woeful showing in a row.

The England campaign began with riots in the streets already making the headlines. 'No surrender to the IRA', they sang. The Irish Republic's team were the tournament's outsiders, but they had many talented players, Liverpool's Whelan, Houghton and Aldridge among them. It was Houghton who scored a headed goal in the eighth minute, following a catalogue of defensive embarrassments. Against this, England created a clutch of goalscoring chances which even Lineker, initially the most feared striker in the championship, was unable to convert into goals. Half-time came and went.

England became frustrated, then demoralized, then inept. Barnes was first neutralized, then marooned. Jack Charlton had clearly instructed his team to crowd out the Liverpool forward, cut off his supply lines and starve him out of the action.

It worked. Chris Morris, a flame-haired right-back from Glasgow Celtic, did the best part of the shepherding, policing Barnes down on the touchline, never committing himself to tackles he could not be sure to win, standing back to minimize the chance of being burned-up on the outside, coaxing him on to his less lethal right foot. With the defence squeezing forward and the long ball method central to their attack, the Irish midfield was free to concentrate on a destructive role. So Houghton helped to closely mark his Liverpool team-mate, hounding him out of the game. Barnes and Morris entered into an off-the-ball barging match. Sharp words, no doubt, were exchanged. It might be argued that the wealth of opportunities Lineker enjoyed owed something to this extra deployment of resources on one of his team-mates. But the most obvious effect was to underline how one-dimensional Barnes can become when handled appropriately. With defenders refusing to panic, Barnes did not know how to induce it. With no momentum to take him forward, he stood on the ball and passed it back. With no fluid midfield passes honed to his forward stride, he did not know where to put himself. With less licence for self-expression he became an ordinary player. With half an hour of the contest gone, Barnes had already disappeared. He stayed that way as the rest of the afternoon trickled slowly by and the essence of English malevolence simmered nastily on the terraces.

The Düsseldorf encounter with Holland had long been anticipated as the championship's hooligan high spot. The Dutch had visited Wembley for a friendly international earlier in the year. A last-minute police decision to annex segments of seating in the interests of segregation left hundreds of supporters besieging a makeshift office in vain attempts to collect their re-allocated standing tickets. Most got nowhere near. Meanwhile, thousands were arriving at the stadium late, thanks to traffic congestion and England fans pulling the emergency handles on the tube lines serving the stadium. With the Kings Cross disaster fresh in the memory, they gathered in sullen groups near motionless escalators, smoking, drinking, scowling, looking for something to do. Inside the ground, England hung on against the fluent Dutch team, featuring AC Milan's Ruud Gullit, a tall, fast, athletic and wonderfully skilful player of Senegalese extraction with a head of handsome dreadlocks who names his heroes as Diego Maradona and Nelson Mandela. He was met with a chorus of boos every time he touched the ball. 'Gullit getting some good-natured barracking when he gets in possession,' piped John Motson, blandly, on the BBC TV highlights. England managed a 2-all draw.

In Germany, the Dutch team had started badly, losing against the Soviets. Against England they were fortunate not to concede a couple of goals in the first half. Lineker struck the post from a tight angle when he might have expected to score. Then Hoddle hit the same post with a superb, swerving free-kick. But it was Gullit, roaming around the pitch, probing for space, who provided the crucial break just two minutes from half-time. He made a fool of Gary Stevens just inside the England half, arrowed down the wing and poked a low cross towards striker Marco Van Basten. Flummoxing Adams with the sweetest of turns, Van Basten beat Shilton at the far post. English hopes rose in the second half, when team captain Bryan Robson scored after a characteristic, surging run from midfield. But Gullit and Van Basten combined again seventeen minutes from the end. Pouncing on the ball just outside England's penalty box, Gullit trapped it, rolled it back and pushed it to his AC Milan partner in one fluid movement. Van Basten finished flawlessly and scored a third, close in, two minutes later. 'Cheerio, cheerio, cheerio', as they say.

The England fans, meanwhile, had behaved as charmingly as ever. Their Dutch counterparts had poured across the border in great waves of orange, caked in face paint, wearing giant animal masks and sporting jockey caps with fake woolly dreadlocks in honour of their black football icon. Dominating the handsome Rheinstadion, they unleashed huge Mexican waves which rippled right round the stadium until they reached the England contingent, who remained surly and stationary. Gullit continued to profit down the left-hand flank, floating into wide positions whenever Stevens least expected it. Down near the corner flag, in the shadow of the Union display, he tormented the England defence, while the England supporters poured down a resentful frenzy of boos and jungle chants.

At the other end of the pitch, John Barnes laboured in vain. After a few bright moments in the first forty-five minutes, he had become bogged down. Possibly instructed to change places with Beardsley, he spent much of the third quarter operating down the middle, but to little effect. Unable to unravel the Dutch defence, his passing became hurried and anxiety seemed to seize him whenever he received the ball. The harder he strove to make his luck turn, the more his confidence seemed to evaporate. The rapport he had enjoyed with Beardsley as a Liverpool team-mate might never have existed. The England team lost shape in the midfield and, in stark contrast to the cultured Dutch, had little creative impetus from the back, no fluidity, no verve. England crashed out of the tournament and the city of Düsseldorf braced itself for another night of beery English machismo on the rampage.

It is possible to make a case that the England team were not as appalling as a hectoring popular press campaign made out. Against Ireland, they created far more chances and might legitimately explain their failure to take them as a freak. Equally, they could easily have led against the Dutch, who eventually won the tournament, defeating the Soviet Union 2–nil in the Final in Munich. England, then, were beaten by the two eventual finalists.

Put this way, their defeats look much more honourable. Yet there was something in their style which could only invite despair. If the pre-war English football heroes expressed an imaginative industrial working-class sensibility, then this cream of the late eighties spoke of spiritual stagnation and a crisis of imagination. On paper, you might have argued that six members of the England squad were capable of special things: Shilton; Robson; Lineker; Hoddle; Beardsley; Barnes. In the event, only Robson distinguished himself, while the team as a whole had an air of dull predictability and brittle self-belief. They had nothing to compete with the sparkling chemistry of Van Basten and Gullit.

Meanwhile, the backdrop of the team's performances was grimmer still. The barbarity of England's supporters was only a part of it. There was something perversely comical about the contortions of the various interested parties when Bobby's unwanted Barmy Army made more headlines than the team. Fuming with indignation, full of tough talk and laments for the good old days, the game's authorities, the government and the press alike came more and more to resemble those whose destructiveness they so plainly could not understand as being a mutated reflection of themselves. All the sub-divisions of the football world are characterized by remarkably similar parochial and ritual modes of behaviour, and adherence to them is essential to remaining part of the scene. Among the hard nuts on the terraces, dress sense, drinking and commitment to the team are paramount. The same goes for the board-room, except the handshakes are funnier. Like the police, with whom they have so much in common, football establishment dignitaries like to hold forth about disrespect for authority and the decline of traditional values; yet you will find few more traditional Englishmen than those who fought pitched battles with German policemen in the summer of 1988. And on top of everything else, they have an overwhelming tendency to be very, very white. The football culture perpetuates an idea of Englishness which militates against all the valuable things that football is supposed to represent.

When it is viewed in such a light, the progress of black footballers in this country is truly and remarkably heroic. Assailed by prejudice at all levels, excluded from the status of Englishmen, even as they grace the national team, they have asserted themselves on the field of play against enormous odds, refusing to be denied access to a milieu whose chronic introversion is driving it towards self-destruction.

In such a context it is ironic that John Barnes, of Liverpool and England, has come to symbolize the struggle to rid football of its debilitating conservatism – the Colonel's son is not the revolutionary type. But his place in the hearts of British citizens the length and breadth of his adopted nation says much for the existence of a football community that is more fair-minded, more gracious and more appreciative of the true glory of the game than that sorry set of spivs and jingoists which currently hogs the foreground. Football has become a microcosm for the country at large. But, when Barnes gets the ball at his feet, takes it, Jamaica-style, past one man, two men, three men, and bears down on the goal, he does more than merely threaten to score – he carries with him the hope of not just a better game, but a better nation too.

Postscript

4th June 1989

One year after the League Championship triumph, the Cup Final catastrophe and the European Championship ignominy, John Barnes, Liverpool Football Club and the whole of English soccer are once more at the centre of the nation's attention. The Hillsborough disaster inquiry is under way. The agonized deaths of ninety-five people at the FA Cup semi-final, a repeat of last year's corresponding fixture, is now to be officially explained.

Lord Justice Taylor's investigation takes place in the wake of a nightmare that was horribly real, one whose immediate aftermath saw a degree of dignity finally asserted only after a display of indecent haste to lay the blame. Propriety was finally provided by the club's supporters, the people of the city of Liverpool and the men who play for the team and their wives. It was an alliance of compassion whose components were symbolic. As the stars filed into pews at the funerals of ordinary folk, they found themselves standing shoulder to shoulder with the only other people who really matter in this blighted, marvellous, stupid sport. The *business* of football may fall apart tomorrow, but the game will survive. In the end, all it requires is a flat piece of land, a ball and a community of people who care who kicks it, how and where. The Hillsborough deaths imposed an equality without which no true respect can ever exist. For all the media flannel about Liverpool the 'family club', the compassion was real because, for once in modern football, no one was trying to sell anything to anybody else.

John Barnes's role in the affair was remarkable. Unlike the ex-soldier Grobbelaar it had not previously been his fate to watch people meet their deaths. Unlike Dalglish, the devoted family man whose look of joy when receiving the acclaim of a crowd has never been matched, he had no special responsibilities of leadership. Unlike McMahon, Gary Ablett or Aldridge he was not Liverpool-born and bred and unlike Aldridge in particular he had never enjoyed the other side of the Anfield experience, the sense of participating, of *belonging*, in the massive, swaying communion of the Kop.

But Barnes felt a sense of duty to those bereaved which transcended everything else. Bobby Robson's England might not be his favourite team to play in, but his decision to opt out of a World Cup qualifying match and attend funerals instead suggested the very same sense of priorities which has exasperated managers and fellow players in the past. In other circumstances, this would have been a professional heresy. Effectively, Barnes was saying 'football isn't everything'. But, at the same time, his actions made us realize why it is that football matters at all – that without the people who come to watch, it means next to nothing anyway.

Paradox had already attended Barnes's rise to the status of idol of the Kop. His acceptance as a black man in a white man's domain had depended most of all on balls in the back of the net. Now, it was his readiness to set football aside which earned him a deeper gratitude from thousands of Liverpool people. This time it was an affection based on his *humanity*, rather than simply the ability to do the business out on the park. It is an important distinction – it marks the difference between being afforded the status of celebrity and that of a fellow citizen.

By the time Barnes and the rest of his team-mates finally pulled on the red shirts again, the big wheels of bitter-sweet Mersey melodrama were already rolling. Goodison Park was the scene of their comeback to League action, a match preceded by the first of a string of one-minute silences, each impossibly affecting both for the losses they marked and for the tension they imposed. Would the stillness be respected? Could peace prevail for that long, at least? At Goodison it did, and Dalglish's team began a rough rehabilitation as another Merseyside derby clattered its way to an exhausting goal-less draw.

In terms of results, this sharing of the points interrupted a run of Liverpool victories characterized, belatedly, by the charismatic football they had displayed the previous season. It had been a long while coming. Injuries had disrupted the team chemistry in the first half of the 1988–89 campaign, notably those to central defenders Gillespie and Hansen. Ian Rush, bought back, sensationally, from Juventus for nearly £3 million, had been on and off the treatment table and never found his form. Liverpool started well enough with a healing victory over Wimbledon in the Charity Shield curtain-raiser, and with an imperious away defeat of Charlton in the opening League game. But progress soon became a struggle. Their home form was distinctly patchy. After a Littlewoods Cup epic against Arsenal, finally won in style in the second replay, they capitulated spectacularly to West Ham in the following round, conceding 4 goals. A 3–1 collapse at Old Trafford in the League was the lowest point of all. Further thoughts of Bob Paisley, still a club director, appeared in the *Daily Mirror*, putting the team down, an episode that led finally to a dressing-room apology.

But it was not until the side came close to resembling the previous season's line-ups that Liverpool looked peerless once again. Barnes, himself an injury casualty, suddenly clicked into gear. Aldridge was still scoring goals; in fact he had never stopped. McMahon was stoked up to full boilerhouse power. By the eve of the Cup semi-final Liverpool was suddenly once more in conten-tion to become the first club in history to win the Double twice – and in irresistible style. Red Merseyside prepared for another bout of chest-beating, another ritual display of self-esteem.

But it took those broken bodies spilling on to Hillsborough's grass for football, fleetingly, to be glimpsed as something other than just a sport: something in itself trivial, but also emblematic of an English way of life. As a fumbling Football Association allowed Liverpool to postpone fixtures and contend with the trauma, the shabby, insular world of the football culture was briefly opened up to the kinds of debate it should have had a quarter of a century ago. What do football fans want? Are football's authorities fit for office? Where do hooligans come from? Has the authoritarian response to them really helped? Rogan Taylor, National Secretary of the Foot-ball Supporters' Association, made more sane, insightful and plain honourable observations on national radio and television than all the other pundits put together. The city of Liverpool closed ranks around its dead and turned the Kop end of Anfield into an unforgettable shrine, giving the lie to the club hierarchy's apparent conviction that they are only providing a product. Even the Liverpool police criticized spokesmen for their West Yorkshire colleagues as the latter rushed to cover their force's behinds.

It was, though, a transient silver lining to football's darkest cloud. The Government's glib adherence to its Football Supporters Bill was hardened by predictable pitch invasions at the end of the League season. With perimeter fences around the country torn down in a rush of guilt, the recalcitrant took the chance to overrun the playing fields of England and make them, briefly, their own. The incidents prompted a shift in the positions of those disputing the issue of identity cards. The League and FA had always been opposed to the Government's 'enabling' legislation on financial and organizational grounds. But, for all their feuding, the opposing factions ultimately have more in common than divides them. Authoritarians all, they cling to the blinkered belief that the impulses behind football violence can be policed out of existence. A gutless compromise on the identity card issue is in the air.

But the punitive model is already a lamentable failure. What is required, and desperately, is the courage to face up to the fact that England has brought upon itself the football culture it deserves. The lessons of the John Barnes phenomenon are among those that must be learned if that culture is to change, because racism is intimately linked with it; an inherent part, a logical product of a theory of Englishness acted out behind the goal, which is just the crudest manifestation of the Bulldog mentality routinely invoked in the name of national pride. Police, authorities and fans all play their part in screwing up this brutalism to a feverish tension on Saturday afternoons. At Hillsborough, the spiral spun out of control. It is no coincidence that none of those who died were black. John Barnes's presence notwithstanding, this was a white Liverpudlian occasion and a white English catastrophe. No solution to English football's crisis will be found until its white supremacy is purged.

The prospects are not good. The 1988–89 season saw some positive fallout from the previous twelve months, but it was limited to the point of lip-service. Barnes was still booed by the fans of opposing teams. The BBC's TV commentators were sometimes moved to remark upon it, but when Millwall's meat-head hard core – who also laughed during the post-Hillsborough minute's silence at the Den – persecuted him throughout a fifth round Cup tie, Barry Davies did not talk about *racism* in his passing condemnation, just a rather ambiguous 'treatment of Barnes'. Even the rehabilitation derby was marked by Everton fans hurling their now traditional bitter fruit. Even the most emotive Cup Final occasion ever, a thrilling finale, won 3–2 by Liverpool after extra time, was not free of jungle chants. One week earlier, Steve Skeete and Almithak won the FA Sunday Cup Final 3–1 after extra time, but black people still do not go to Anfield or Goodison Park, or populate the ranks of the youth teams in noticeable numbers. They know the chances are that if and (more likely) when Barnes takes off again, to Italy or France, the old habits will return, and the Kop, now to be lined with plastic seats, will chant 'kill the nigger' once again.

The way Liverpool was denied the League and Cup double at the last gasp yet again was heart-rending (as was Howard Gayle's latest hair's breadth failure to win promotion with Blackburn Rovers), but not without its moral vindication. Arsenal, who finished at the top of Division One, is another of the gluttonous big five clubs, but its manager George Graham built a large part of the team from local London lads. Their style is not the ecstatic blend of desire and poetry that Dalglish has nurtured, but they have something which football's received wisdom once insisted could never be – a primarily black midfield. The elegant Paul Davies did not play at Anfield the night Arsenal stole the League, but the fast, industrious David Rocastle did, and it was Michael Thomas, the scrapper, tackler and piston-engine of the team, who steamed into the penalty box, lungs screaming, to score the decisive second goal in the final minute of the game. No bottle shortage there, my son.

Seconds earlier, Barnes had gone bearing down on the Arsenal goal, swerving past Adams and into the penalty box, looking to equalize Alan Smith's opening goal. A 1–nil defeat would have been enough for Liverpool. Other players, perhaps wiser, perhaps more cynical, would have stood on the ball, taken it down to the corner flag to kill a few more seconds, or just hoofed it into the crowd. Barnes, though, wanted to score in front of the Kop. He lost possession. The ball was returned to Arsenal's keeper and three passes later, Thomas's dream came true. But, even as Barnes sat, slumped on the Anfield turf while the Arsenal players soaked up the plaudits of the Kop at its most generous, his contribution to a very English saga remained undiminished. The day white England embraces him and all black England as its own is the day that England may begin to save its soul.

Bibliography

Aldridge, John: *Inside Anfield*, Mainstream Publishing, 1988

Beardsley, Peter: *Beardsley – An Autobiography*, Stanley Paul, 1988

Cashmore, Ernest: *Black Sportsmen*, Routledge and Kegan Paul, 1982

Dalglish, Kenny: *The Liverpool Year*, Collins Willow, 1988

Davies, Hunter: *The Glory Game – A Year In The Life Of Tottenham Hotspur*, Mainstream Publishing, 1972

Dunphy, Eamon: *Only A Game? – The Diary Of A Professional Footballer*, Penguin, 1976.

Fishwick, Nicholas: *English Football And Society 1910–1950*, Manchester University Press, 1989

Fryer, Peter: *Staying Power – The History Of Black People In Britain*, Pluto Press, 1984

Graham, Matthew: *Liverpool*, Hamlyn, 1984

Grobbelaar, Bruce: *An Autobiography*, Coronet, 1986

Hamilton, Al: *Black Pearls Of Soccer*, Harrap, 1982

Hargreaves, John: *Sport, Power And Culture*, Polity Press, 1986

Irwin, Michael: *Striker*, André Deutsch, 1985

Kelly, Stephen F.: *You'll Never Walk Alone – The Official Illustrated History Of Liverpool FC*, Queen Anne Press, 1988

Lane, Tony: *Liverpool – Gateway Of Empire*, Lawrence & Wishart, 1987

Liverpool Black Caucus: *The Racial Politics Of Militant In Liverpool*, Runnymede Trust, 1986

Longmore, Andrew: *Viv Anderson*, Heinemann Kingswood, 1988

Mason, Tony: *Sport In Britain*, Faber and Faber, 1988

Merseyside Area Profile Group, *Racial Disadvantage In Liverpool – An Area Profile*, Liverpool University, 1980

Neal, Phil: *Life At The Kop*, Queen Anne Press, 1986

Radnedge, Keir (ed.): *World Club Football Directory*, Queen Anne Press, 1984

Rollin, Jack (ed.): *Rothmans Football Yearbook 1988–89*, Queen Anne Press, 1988

Wagg, Stephen: *The Football World – A Contemporary Social History*, Harvester Press, 1984

Williams, John, Dunning, Eric and Murphy, Patrick: *Hooligans Abroad –
   The Behaviour And Control Of English Fans In Continental Europe*,
   Routledge and Kegan Paul, 1984
Woolnough, Brian: *Black Magic – England's Black Footballers*, Pelham, 1983

Index